Also by Carole Radziwill

What Remains:
A Memoir of Fate, Friendship and Love

The
Widow's Guide
to Sex and Dating

The
Widow's Guide
to Sex and Dating

A NOVEL

Carole Radziwill

Henry Holt and Company
New York

Henry Holt and Company, LLC
Publishers since 1866
175 Fifth Avenue
New York, New York 10010
www.henryholt.com

Henry Holt® and ® are registered trademarks of
Henry Holt and Company, LLC.

Library of Congress Cataloging-in-Publication Data

Radziwill, Carole.
The widow's guide to sex and dating : a novel / Carole Radziwill.—First edition
pages cm.
ISBN 978-0-8050-9884-6 (hardback)
1. Widows—Fiction. 2. Manhattan (New York, N.Y.)—Fiction. I. Title.
PS3618.A3585W53 2013
813'.6—dc23   2013002412

Henry Holt books are available for special promotions and premiums.
For details contact: Director, Special Markets.

First Edition 2013

Designed by Meryl Sussman Levavi

Printed in the United States of America

1 3 5 7 9 10 8 6 4 2

"Love is like a brick. You can build a house or you can sink a dead body."

—LADY GAGA

The
Widow's Guide
to Sex and Dating

Charles Byrne, Sexologist and Writer, Dies at 54

by MARK IOCOLANO, *The New York Times*

Charles Byrne, renowned sexologist and author of the National Book Award–winning *Thinker's Hope*, as well as several pivotal studies on sexual norms and morality, died Monday from a head injury incurred at Madison Avenue near 61st Street, according to a statement issued by his longtime publisher, Knopf.

Charles Fisher Byrne grew up in Bristol, Connecticut, the only son of socialite Grace Thornton and the late Honorable Franz Byrne, chief justice of the Connecticut Supreme Court.

Charles Byrne attended Princeton for both his graduate and undergraduate studies, and held several honorary degrees. He published his first academic paper on sexual paraphilia, called "Erotic Variations on a Theme," his junior year. It contained the seeds of what was to become his most widely known theory, The Opposite of Sex, and launched the career of what is considered one of the preeminent voices in the field of contemporary sexology.

At 22, just out of college, Charlie, as he was known to his friends, was selected by Robert Rimmer to apprentice at the experimental sexuality retreat known as the Sandstone Institute, in Malibu. He remained close to Rimmer until his death and credits Rimmer's teachings on polyamory with influencing most of his own work and life. Mr. Byrne took Robert Rimmer's theories one step further and promoted promiscuity as an ideal state for fostering a stable, family-oriented culture. "Love and sex," he wrote, "make poor roommates. You may find one or the other in a companion, but never both." He believed that sexuality is the purest form of artistic expression, a theme that later proliferated in his first book, *Thinker's Hope*.

Byrne's career skyrocketed with the publication of *Thinker's Hope*. It won the National Book Award and sold over five million copies worldwide. It made Charles Byrne a household name. He followed it up the next year with *The Half-Life of Sex*, a commercial, if not critical, success.

In 1985, after a disappointing reception for *The Half-Life of*

Sex, Mr. Byrne wrote a series of critical essays on what he saw as the existential crisis of the penis, titled, appropriately, "The State of Erection." His theories of Love and Sex were, once again, a central theme.

Mr. Byrne went on to publish many books in the 1980s and '90s, including *Sperm and Whiskey*; *Sex, Sea Songs and Sartre*; and *Driving with Her Head in Your Lap.* He did not publish a book, however, after his collection of essays, *The State of Erection,* in 1999, choosing instead to focus on the lecture circuit and talk shows.

He counted among his friends a colorful variety of artists and intellectuals, from the controversial French *lettriste* Isadore Isou to the American comedian Paul Reubens.

Mr. Byrne is survived by his mother, Grace, and his wife, Claire Byrne.

PART I

A Man Falls Dead

1

THE UPSHOT OF THE STORY IS THIS: A MAN FALLS DEAD, the widow gets laid, love is a drag, the end. In the gaps, a woman finds meaning. The man fell dead on a Monday in New York; it was sunny, there was a breeze. Birds chirped in the suburbs, trains were on time, the postmen made their rounds. It was a mild day with a calm blue sky. Thoughts in offices around the city meandered from sex to lunch plans to the e-mail about smells in the break room. The day was ripe for calamity. It was the kind of day when the brakes fail on the tour bus, the leading man falls for a woman his own age, and the elderly pair in 4B shuffle out in handcuffs with the police. It was the kind of day when no one expects anything to happen, so it does. Blue skies can be misleading.

Claire Byrne was in Texas to see a man named Veejay Singh, a doctor, but not the medical kind. He taught sociology at the University of Texas at Austin, and he'd written a book titled *Why Breasts Don't Matter*. Dr. Singh was popular on campus, both for his friendly manner and for his notoriously easy grades. He was a minor celebrity, too, appearing on the *Today* show now and again to explain his evolutionary theories about mating. Claire was there to interview him. She was writing a profile piece for *Misconstrued*, the magazine "for women, like you, who defy definition!" She parked her rented car in the visitors' section by the admin building and began her stroll toward Singh's office at approximately ten after nine, weaving through oak trees and sun-dappled shade, her espadrilles marking lines across the dewy green quad. Claire's husband, Charlie, was at home in New York.

Well, he wasn't technically *home*.

RULE #1: Don't screw around on a Monday.

Claire had left the previous day, so Charlie spent the afternoon and night across town with the new publicist at Knopf. They'd spent their time in the girl's cramped studio apartment humping and screwing like dogs, but now he, too, traversed trees and dapples, crossing Central Park toward Madison to meet with his agent, Richard Ashe. Charlie had a book overdue by two years and Richard was anxious. He had a dwindling number of profitable writers and a heavily mortgaged co-op. Charlie didn't think much of deadlines.

Charles Byrne was the world's most famous sexologist—more mainstream than Kinsey or Masters ever were. As much sexual object as academic, he wrote on a subject that everyone likes to read about, and he looked like someone you could easily imagine in the act. At fifty-four, in fact, he bore a passing resemblance to Warren Beatty—in *Bugsy*, not *Reds*—and possessed a rough-edged but overpowering charm. He was crafty with words, engaging on many different levels, so that his appeal spread wide. When he wrote about the penis, he managed to be both educational and downbeat, couching bawdy locker-room humor in intellectual wit. When he wrote about vaginas, he wrote with the appreciative and admiring eye of a collector. His writing made even coarse men think of symphonic productions as they bedded their irritable wives. It made sophisticated men think fondly of their wives as they bedded their steamy lovers.

Charlie was thinking fondly of his own young wife as he interrupted his walk for coffee at a diner on Madison, and this is a good place to play *what if.* You know—*what if* he hadn't stopped, or not stopped for so long, or *what if* he'd been distracted by some small thing that slowed his pace.

In the diner, Charlie skimmed the sports page and phoned Richard to say he'd be late. He ordered a second coffee to go (*what if* he hadn't?), put four dollar bills on the counter (*what if* he'd fumbled and only put three?), then left to resume his walk.

While Charlie was perusing pitching stats—Wang and Hughes out of the Yankees rotation, Pettitte in—Claire was taking in cowboy-booted coeds in sundresses, thinking how she'd describe the scene back to him. (Russ Meyer directing a commercial for the Gap? No, more like a Playboy production of *Oklahoma.*) She'd been tempted to buy him one of those T-shirts in the airport: a buxom cowgirl riding a cactus, below the slogan EVERYTHING'S BIGGER IN TEXAS. It was the sort of thing Charlie might wear under his suit coat to the theater just for laughs.

Charlie enjoyed causing a scandal; he relished the attention. Claire, on the other hand, preferred anonymity. She was a petite woman, size 4, not tall—in heels she reached Charlie's shoulder. She had dark hair that she wore long and loose, youthful skin, pale brown eyes, and what Charlie called complicated lips—they could be plump and sensual one day, and the next day nondescript. She was attractive, yes, but she wasn't fooling anyone. She wasn't a girl who lounged around uninhibitedly, slugging whiskey from the bottle. She wasn't like the women Charlie wrote about. She didn't know how to produce cigarettes for randy men to light; she wasn't boozy or dramatic, her necklines didn't plunge. She was ordered and neat, in contrast to Charlie's flair. She was the ingenue to his rogue. Charlie was the main act. Sasha, Claire's closest friend since college, called Charlie "Sundance," to Claire's Butch Cassidy. "He cheats at poker and shoots up the room," Sasha liked to say, "while you collect the chips and tidy up." Charlie cast a long shadow. Claire had learned early on with him that one of her better qualities was knowing where to stand in it.

CLAIRE'S ASSIGNMENT IN Texas that day was dull, but drama was waiting in the wings. By the time she reached Singh's office with its view of the tree-lined South Mall, her husband was dead. A Giacometti—a large and very expensive piece of bronze—had dropped on top of him, in an unlucky twist of fate.

Days later, looking back, it seemed inevitable. Claire couldn't imagine it playing out any other way. One minute Charlie was strolling down Madison working out sound bites in his head for the Nobel speech he was sure he'd eventually have to give. The next minute—poof—he was dead. One minute off to a postcoital meeting with Richard, the next instant, gone. Life changes in less time than it takes to say, "Fuck."

He'd been preoccupied. He didn't see the thing drop from the sky. How could he? There was no warning, no fear, no panic or pain; for Charlie, it was over quickly. Elsewhere, though, there were ripples. There were witnesses, for instance, like Mona Glisan, who were affected. Reporters converged, then multiplied like flies, mining stunned tourists for sound bites. There was a noise, "a loud crack," was how Mona described it. The bronze had been hanging from a crane and the cable holding it snapped, and she described it like that—a *crack!*—followed by a hollow-sounding jingle like an enormous key dropping to the ground. It made Mona's ears ring. She put her hands over them reflexively while she described it.

The sculpture that dropped was over six feet tall. It weighed three hundred pounds and fell from twenty stories up. It had cost Walter White—his is another story altogether, we'll come back to it—millions of dollars and was supposed to be lowered onto his terrace. Instead, it dropped on Charlie's head.

Mona Glisan's account was the first of many. Steve Johnson saw it, too. He was an art major at Columbia, and he spoke about the motion of the object and the illusion of weightlessness. "The absence of nothing," he said, "is something in itself." No one knew what he meant, but he spoke very slowly, which gave people the impression that they should. He was too slow, however, for the sergeant taking statements, who quickly moved on, leaving the lingering crowd at Steve's mercy. "The serene elegance and grace," he continued, "of this exquisite piece of art, floating on air . . ."

Alberto Giacometti, who'd made the bronze, was dead, too. A large and brooding man, he'd been known for colossal bouts of depression. He would disappear into his studio for months at a time, whittling obsessively and shunning visitors, until he emerged with clay prototypes of the unwieldy, thin, and rutted works that made his name. Charlie's piece was called *Man Walking*: a tall, skinny man formed into a walking motion with his head down, absorbed in thought the way Charlie had been until the two collided in mutual distraction. The sexologist and the statue were an unusual pairing, to say the least. Their introduction was made possible by Evelyn White, Walter's wife. Her cursory pretentions in art, coupled with the discovery of her husband's affair, had set the whole thing in motion. But we'll come back to that, too.

Among the others who saw the collision was a woman from Ohio visiting New York with her church group on a theater package—one of those six-shows-in-three-days kinds of things that never include first runs. She saw *Mamma Mia!* and *The Lion King*, and was viewing the Simon Doonan window displays at Barneys when she saw Charlie die. She offered herself to Channel 6. "It was horrible," she said in a shaky voice as she wiped away tears. Then she lowered her voice an octave and addressed the camera directly. "The Lord works in mysterious ways."

Another witness, a man from Brooklyn, performed for reporters as if he had a scene-stealing bit in a mob film—"Dere was dis *huge* (he pronounced it "yooj") fuckin' thing. Comes outta noweh— Bam! Poor fuckin' guy." The network channels didn't air his remarks, but two days later *The Howard Stern Show* did; Stern's producers had him reenact the scene between strippers in a tribute of sorts to Charlie. Howard had been a big fan.

But it was Paul Bowman, an ad exec, whose account got the most play. He seemed to capture the spirit of the incident. "It was, for lack of a more original word," he said, "surreal."

"What went through your mind?" asked the reporter from ABC News. "Well, I think the stillness," Paul said. "It was abnormally quiet. I felt it, that stillness. That's what made me look up. It was like an Ingrid Bergman, or Bergmar, film, you know, that French guy. It was like everything, just briefly, paused."

Paul's were the words that somehow hit the mark. They played on WFAN, they ran in the *New York Times*, and after the Associated Press picked up his version it spent two days on Yahoo!

News—Most Viewed. His estranged wife, Amy Strauss-Bowman, a film studies professor at Rutgers and the reason Paul Bowman even knew the name Bergman/Bergmar, sneered when she read his account and its gratuitous but bungled display of cineaste. Amy knew that Paul's greatest art form thus far was to belch out the fight song during televised football games. She also knew that, obviously, a rare Giacometti fluttering down the side of a forty-three-story building against a bright blue backdrop of sky was vintage Kenneth Anger, or maybe Fassbinder, but certainly not Bergman.

The sun, after Charlie's death, remained out. The day ticked on unmoved, though a large bronze sculpture and a man both lay still on the sidewalk. Charlie was clearly dead, but there was concern about the bronze. Walter White had been called, and Walter White summoned lawyers. A lot of money lay on the ground tended by the unappreciative eye of the NYPD. Then, too, there was concern with liability.

Sidewalk traffic bunched. Taxi drivers honked at stopped police cars. Men in suits hurried past, unimpressed. A family from Denver stood, mouths agape; the mother put a chubby hand in front of first one child's eyes, then the other's. Fire trucks closed in, sirens wailed.

Charlie's denim-clad legs, toned from years of tennis, were bent at unnatural angles; his arms were askew. He'd wound up ungainly. He would have been mortified.

Paramedics moved slowly about the body. The ambulance driver lit a cigarette and joined the firemen a few feet away. The men stood talking for a time; now and then, one would laugh. They argued over the Yankees and the Mets, and traded jokes about another stiff they'd picked up that week. Policemen continued to take statements from the witnesses, one at a time, writing in small notebooks with blue ballpoint pens. None of it came to much.

At some point midmorning the body was covered and Charlie's limbs were secured to a metal bed. One arm slipped from beneath his sheet and dangled, the way arms sometimes do in suspense films to reveal something—a birthmark or tattoo, some important clue that has been overlooked. But this was Charlie's right arm—no watch, no marks—and a paramedic replaced it beneath the sheet without incident.

Gawkers stayed stubbornly put. Finally, the medical examiner's van arrived and Charlie was removed from the scene—one hour and thirteen minutes after leaving his four-dollar tip at the diner.

Another team arrived to load the Giacometti into an evidence truck. Walter White stood nervously in his doorway, inquiring. *We're taking it to the Sixty-First Precinct, Mr. White. I can't tell you yet how long we'll need it. We have to file the usual reports.* At that moment, Walter was unaware of who the dead man was.

Cleanup, for the most part, was brisk.

Meanwhile, in Texas, Claire sat in an uncomfortable chair across from Veejay Singh and worked to establish rapport. Dr. Singh, like Charlie, moved easily between pop culture and more serious arenas. His subject specialty was the biology of attraction— the whys and hows of picking a mate. Men like long hair and big breasts, we assume. But is that really the case and, if so, why? Dr. Singh had a theory, and he'd spent five years measuring women to prove it. He circled their hips and their waists with tailor's tape and divided the second number by the first. He compared these ratios with estrogen levels and fertility data, and through his findings he promoted his idea that men are hardwired to seek a certain shape. More specifically, his research showed that women with a

.7 hip-to-waist ratio—wide hips and small waists—are good breeders. These women have the best odds of conceiving a baby, so men intuitively seek them out to reproduce. The famous hourglass figure, in other words, is not just a fashion trend but an important step in evolution.

Dr. Singh was tall, like Charlie, and lean. He dressed simply— dark slacks, V-neck sweater—but his clothing flattered him. He became animated when he spoke about his work, punctuating his sentences with wide sweeps of his arms, and short bursts of laughter that were intended, Claire thought, to disarm her. She wondered if he slept with his students.

Singh's book had debuted at #2 on the *New York Times* Best Sellers List. The book was why Claire was sitting here, why *Misconstrued* deemed his measurements worthy of print. Charlie, for his part, had snorted when she'd told him about the assignment—as if only a hack would write a bestseller about breasts instead of balls. That Claire was writing pop stories for glossy female magazines at all had everything to do with Charlie. He had discouraged her own literary ambition. For a few years after they married she had been content looking after Charlie's needs and writing an occasional piece freelance. Then the temporary adjustment in her focus became what she did permanently. Charlie worked, and Claire found things to do.

They were just starting, Claire and Singh; they'd finished shifting in chairs and clearing their throats and were on Claire's second question.

"Is there any evidence, then, that the size of the *penis* matters, reproductively speaking?" Just as a hint of a smile crossed her face, Claire's cell phone began to buzz. She had set it to "vibrate." It lurched noisily across the desk.

"I'm sorry, please ignore it," she said, and made a gesture with her hand to mean "go on."

"Before we get too far," said Singh, "let's do this." He was holding a measuring tape. He jumped up, then motioned for Claire to stand so he might measure and calculate her own ratio, her own potential for reproduction.

"I've studied every *Playboy* centerfold since 1954," he said, with his arms around Claire's waist. While Claire held her arms up and out of the way, Singh dipped his head down, beneath her breasts, to read the thin tape he'd pressed against her. His hands felt warm through her blouse. He had a tantalizing mess of dark, thick hair; a heady shot of cologne hit her nose. Claire couldn't remember the last time a man's hands had circled her waist. Somewhere along her nine years with Charlie, certain interest had, well . . . waned. Singh mumbled a number and jotted it on his notepad. "And though the bunnies have gotten thinner"—he paused as if about to reveal a great secret—"their hip-to-waist ratios have remained the same!"

A stack of transparencies lay on his desk—anatomically correct line drawings of well-ratioed women: Eva Mendes, Marilyn Monroe, Raquel Welch. He showed Claire, laying the drawings one over the other, how the shapes were different but the ratios stayed in line.

"Watch this," he said, putting a transparency of Kate Moss over Scarlett Johansson. "Hmm? Surprised?"

"Well, Kate's skinnier, and her breasts . . ."

"But that's it!" Singh shrieked, delighted. "It's not the breasts!" He lowered his voice and leaned toward her. "It is strictly the proportion of the hip to the waist. It signals health and fertility. This is the true essence of desire."

Claire looked down at her own small breasts. She wanted to

believe him. She wondered if there was a Mrs. Singh and, if so, what size her breasts were. He jotted her measurements on a notepad and did the math. "Ha! Point seven five," he said, appraising Claire's reproductive area and nodding in approval. "Almost perfect!"

The buzzing persisted. Claire's phone lurched forward, then stopped, then lurched again. Dr. Singh took in the spectacle.

"We should take a short break," he said.

Claire agreed, and while Singh ruffled papers she punched in the number for voice mail and pressed "1" to play her messages. There were four: The first was a policeman in a somber tone: "Mrs. Byrne, this is Officer Callan from the Nineteenth Precinct. I need you to contact me immediately, your husband . . . there's been an accident." The second was Richard, who also asked her to call back and spoke in a suspiciously measured tone. The third was Ethan, Claire's close friend and Charlie's longtime assistant, who just said, "Honey. I'm sorry. Oh fuck."

Sasha was fourth. She was sobbing and Claire could hear ice hitting glass. "Jesus, Claire, why aren't you answering your phone? They dropped a Giacometti on Charlie. Turn the TV on! I can't believe he's dead. God . . . Richard said he didn't suffer."

Claire set her phone on the desk and looked at Singh shuffling paper stacks. She ran a couple of versions through her head, then settled on this: "My husband, I think, is dead." She looked toward the window and her gaze fell on an oak tree. Dr. Singh took a step toward her then stopped. He lifted his arms up and dropped them. There were an awkward few moments of silence. "My God," he finally said.

* * *

CLAIRE WAS MARRIED—seconds, minutes, hours ago?—and now she was not. A recent image of Charlie flashed before her. Last week, high off a tennis win and flush from gossip and scotch, he'd come home and whisked Claire off to the Circle Line tourist boat. For three hours he charmed and regaled her beneath the stars. It had been years since he'd been flirtatiously impulsive this way, with her. Had it been a sign?

Saturday, five days from now, they were expected at Charlie's mother's. He'd promised to make his veal fettuccine, Claire's favorite dish. Only last week they'd been planning their summer rental with Sasha and Thom on the Vineyard. Charlie was here, moments ago, just yesterday in all of his celebrated charm, and now he was gone. Claire was looking at breasts, less than a minute ago, and now she was not. The rate of change in her life, the death-to-change ratio, if you will, had peaked.

The sky in Austin, too, was blue.

2

THERE ARE MANY THINGS THAT FALL FROM THE SKY, IT turns out. There are statistics about this; it's not like Charlie's thin man was the first.

On the day the Giacometti fell on Charlie, a peregrine falcon crashed through the plate glass window in Margaret Grabel's Austin kitchen. Right there on Round Rock Circle, *smash* onto her floor. The falcon fall happened in the morning, and by the time Claire got to the airport for her flight back to New York, it was the hottest story in town. She watched it three times on the local news, three different channels on the television bank, while she waited to be called for standby. Peregrine falcons, like Giacomettis, are rare, especially in Texas. Claire learned this from the story. She learned, too, that they can dive very fast, up to two hundred miles per hour. There were three distinct visuals that each of the local news teams focused on: the falcon, the flustered Margaret, and the mottled-green geometric design of her linoleum floor.

The story was gripping, and Claire let herself get caught up in it. A dead bird somehow made sense to her right now. The idea that her husband was in the same condition did not.

IT CERTAINLY WASN'T Margaret Grabel's intent to kill the bird, yet Claire couldn't help but feel scorn. If Margaret had had a normal-size kitchen window, maybe a small one over the sink, it wouldn't have caused such confusion. But she had an unreasonably large window, plate glass. She probably cleaned it twice a day with Windex; she probably kept it unnaturally streak-free.

Tragedy never comes in the form we anticipate, Claire thought, watching the screen.

A man wearing bright plaid golf pants crossed in front of Claire. He looked young, in his thirties, but had a gray beard that reached his chest. The first year they were married, Claire had flown to Chicago without Charlie—a wedding, distant cousin; he'd begged off. In the airport, she'd spotted a middle-aged woman in pink leather leggings and jacquard top who somehow pulled it off. Claire had snapped a photo of the woman with her phone and sent it to her new husband and this launched a little tradition of theirs—to collect characters when they traveled, whether together or apart. There was Neon Tube Dress, Atlanta. Feather Hat, Portland. Then, like most things with Charlie, it became serious. Last year, MoMA had run a showing of the Byrnes' collection— *Character Sketches*—alongside Bob Dylan's abstract silk screens. There was no use, of course, in taking this man's photo now.

CLAIRE TURNED HER attention back to the televisions. Because the dead bird was in no shape for viewing, the television producers showed, instead, a colorful picture of a healthy one with small black eyes. Claire couldn't help wondering why they were showing another bird, not the bird who had died, but a completely different one, a bird who had nothing at all to do with the dead one, nothing.

She wondered if in New York they were running Charlie's story on the news (they were), and if they'd put a picture on the screen of a different man to represent him (they hadn't). She'd understood from the vague details she'd gathered on the phone that Charlie was in no shape for viewing either.

He would have been horrified to find her riveted like this. Charlie considered the news a pedestrian form of entertainment. He wasn't one to sit quietly in the open seating of an airport, in any case. He would have been in full swing at the bar. Charlie's airport routine was simple. He wore a uniform of jeans, blazer, and button-down shirt. He gathered his reading materials at Hudson's News— gossip magazines like *People* and *Star* that didn't come to the house. And then he prowled. In the beginning, Claire had often traveled with him to his conferences and lectures. He always seemed bigger to her in airports, where everything else looked so small. And he was always recognized. It was here where he collected people, here where he found his "vox populi." Airports are the great leveler, he said. He coaxed out the secrets and stories of people from Kentucky to Juneau. Charlie got them to talk.

On the airport television screens, Margaret was animated. Her eyes darted left to right as she spoke; her face was flushed. Her hand gestures were sudden and jerky. She bore a strong resemblance—in her movements, the roundness of her eyes, the angular limbs—to Charlie's mother. Oh God, Charlie's mother. Who had called?

* * *

SHE'D BEEN "STARTLED," Margaret said, her right hand flying to her breast. She'd heard a "god-awful sound"—she waved her arm toward a location off camera. She'd rushed in when she'd heard the crash—a finger on her right hand jabbed toward a room down the hall—then she'd screamed loudly enough that Abby had heard from next door. Abby Price ran from her yard, clutching a fistful of forget-me-nots, right into Margaret's house. She hadn't bothered even to knock first. It was that kind of scream. Both women were breathless—clearly shocked, still—in the recounting.

Claire couldn't help noticing, though, the measured excitement in Margaret's voice as she pointed to where the bird had landed, as she re-created the crash, as she detailed the gruesome scene. There was a marked sexual repression in her diction. Charlie had taught Claire what to look for: breathlessness, excitable language, dramatic dips and changes of tenor in the voice. There was a lingering close-up to show glass shards, feathers, and a tiny red streak on the floor. (Claire might have imagined it. The bird was dead from a broken neck; there would have been little, if any, blood.)

After her third time watching the story, it was fixed in Claire's head—the characters, the plot, the metaphor. After years of living behind him, she'd come to imagine scenes through Charlie's eyes. There were many different ways, many different words to describe this one: Margaret's red-checkered shirtdress, her cloth-flecked sewing room, the last attempts by the bird to right himself, the pitcher of iced tea on the counter that Claire hadn't seen, but imagined, next to a ceramic bowl of wooden fruit. It all played through her head like a slide show on an endless loop; a virtual tour of Margaret's shattered home.

Claire began to cry. She looked around to see who might have spotted it—Charlie despised public displays of emotion. But this was too much. She grieved for the falcon and she grieved for the man from Fish and Wildlife who'd had to drive out and retrieve it. She grieved for Margaret, who looked too ripe for the moment, like she'd been waiting in her sewing room thirty years to hear glass shatter, to cover her mouth, to have Abby burst through her front door. Thirty years was a long time to wait to have KVUE 2 News standing in her house, for all of Austin to see. Thirty years to tell a ninety-second story on television.

Now what? CLAIRE looked at the phone in her lap. She had nine messages and thirty-three texts. She turned off the phone. She couldn't quite grasp the situation regarding her husband. She hadn't seen a body or feathers, or anyone visibly shaken by whatever it was that had occurred. It seemed improbable that Charlie was dead, yet the callers and texters were adamant. Richard—usually cool as steel—had faltered when she'd called back, his voice had cracked.

After his initial shock, Dr. Singh had offered water and apologies. He'd patted her awkwardly on the head while standing above her. He'd thought it disrespectful to sit down in his comfortable chair. He would suffer, too. Claire sipped the water, and they stayed that way for a time in silence. She was sure he had appointments or faculty meetings, yet there she was in his office, her husband dead.

"Things happen," Dr. Singh said finally, looking for closure, "for a reason."

He sent her off with the measuring tape and, for some reason, a packet of cheese. He insisted she keep the transparency of Marilyn Monroe. This was Claire Byrne's inauspicious induction to widowhood: an hourglass waist, a bronze statue, a dead bird. Her life, the one she'd grown used to, had come abruptly to an end. In the morning, she'd been a wife, the sun had been out, it had been ordinary. In the afternoon, alone in the airport, watching footage of swooping birds, with Marilyn Monroe on her lap, Claire wished that breasts mattered. She wished Charlie had known she had an almost perfect waist-to-hip ratio. She wished she'd bought the no-pulp orange juice that week, the kind he preferred. She wished that she smoked.

IT'S HARD TO get from Austin to New York, even on a good day. So when Claire finally got onto an overnight Delta flight with two connections, she splurged on an upgrade to first class. She ordered a red wine, then regretted it. She'd never cared much for wine. It was a source of friction with Charlie (*had been* a source of friction with Charlie), an accomplished gourmand—fricasseeing and braising and sautéing seasonal grass-fed this and that, all of which called for big bold reds, the kind you swirled around in large glassware and sniffed at like a hound.

"It's Gallo," said the man across the aisle, crisp suit, smooth jaw. Charlie had always worn stubble.

The man nodded at her drink. "First class, but they serve shitty wine." He chuckled. "British Air has good wines, anywhere else I stick to gin." On his tray was a plastic tumbler with a lime wedge and ice cubes, and a clear bubbly drink. He held it up to her, as if to toast.

"Gin," Claire said when the flight attendant came back around. She'd never been the sort to order gin, but she choked the first one down, then ordered another. The man, still watching her, smiled. "My husband is dead," Claire said to him, and opened her packet of peanuts.

3

IN CHARLIE'S FIRST HOURS POSTMORTEM, CLAIRE FLEW from Texas to North Carolina, to Washington, D.C., and then to New York while Ethan worried over what to wear to pick her up, and Richard just paced. Dead. Dead. *Dead.* Claire chanted it to herself as her plane touched down at Kennedy; that Charlie was, in fact, dead was not getting through.

Ethan greeted her in thin cashmere, but he was uncharacteristically unkempt. She spotted concealer hiding the redness around his eyes.

"Clarabelle," he said somberly, opening his arms. As she stepped into them, he put his hand up. "Wait." He produced a small white pill, broke it in two, and fished a bottle of Evian from his bag. He held a half pill in front of her. "Open, sweetie. Good. Now swallow."

In baggage claim, she leaned on his shoulder while they waited for her suitcase to come around. Her dreams on the plane had been frenzied; she felt like she'd been gone for weeks.

"Ethan? Why was he uptown? Where was he going so early?" she asked.

Ethan put an arm around her and squeezed. "He was meeting Richard. He never made it."

Ethan knew as well as Claire did that Charlie was a slave to routine. He woke at seven every morning, made coffee, read the papers, and checked his e-mail. If he went uptown to see Richard he took the subway to Forty-Second Street, walked a block north to Forty-Third, then west to Fifth Avenue. There was no reason to be *above* Forty-Third Street at that time of the morning.

"Okay, but why would he be walking *down* Madison?" She knew why, of course, she just didn't know who. *Dead*, she silently repeated to herself. *Dead, dead, dead.*

Ethan dodged the question. Her suitcase appeared. He set it beside her. It seemed a ridiculous thing to care about—a few books, an outfit change and pajamas. She looked at it and sighed. "What do I do now?" she asked.

"Well, first, the hospital. Richard's waiting there for us."

"No, not *now*, I mean *next*. What do I do with my life?"

Ethan straightened the suitcase handle and took her hand. "Remember *Night on Earth*?" Yes, she did. They'd all watched it together, the previous summer at Bryant Park. The director and Charlie had met at a party when Charlie was at Princeton. She nodded yes and Ethan smiled. "Exactly. We'll figure everything out in the cab."

The ride to Lenox Hill Hospital was slow, through traffic on the Grand Central Parkway and across the Triborough Bridge. Claire stared out the window, not sure if she felt blurry from the Xanax or from watching the raindrops smear the glass. Ethan stabbed at his phone distractedly, checking e-mail, Twitter, the news.

They were going to see Charlie for the last time, a few short blocks from where he died. When they pulled up, there was Richard on his phone, pacing back and forth between ambulances. He snapped it shut when he saw them and gave Claire a long hug.

"They're waiting on you honey, so they can take him to the funeral home."

"Okay."

She put her hand out toward Ethan, and he deposited the other half of her pill. Then the three of them walked through the automatic doors like odd links in a chain: the motley shades of Charlie. The new widow, rumpled from flight, flanked by his agent and his assistant. She looked tiny alongside Ethan, clutching his hand. The two of them moored by Richard's calm authority and cool gait. *Daddy's got this.*

"How was the flight?" Richard asked. "You can't get a good connection out of Austin."

"I drank gin," Claire said. "Not too much, though." An ill-timed hiccup escaped her but it went unremarked. Reaching Charlie meant a long, windy walk through a trauma unit, past the blood donor center to the elevator, then two floors down to the morgue. The hospital chaplain met them at the door. He looked familiar.

"I'm sorry for your loss, Mrs.—" He coughed suddenly, hard. "I'm—excuse me." He coughed again. He put his hand out, then withdrew it. It was going to be a long day.

It was his nose, Claire decided, and thick brow—he bore an uncanny resemblance to Jimmy Cagney. She imagined herself with guns, in a doorway, calling someone a dirty rat. She imagined souped-up cars and getaways.

"Would you like to say a prayer?" he asked. Dead or alive, there were rules.

"Yes, of course," she said.

The chaplain led them to a gurney, where a body—Charlie's, they had to assume—was covered with a sheet. The chaplain cleared his throat. Ethan fidgeted. Richard's eyebrow shot up. Claire reached for the sheet, but Richard gently grabbed her hand. There was a tag hanging out from the end, where Charlie's feet were. His name and statistics, just like in the movies. Charlie had perfectly manicured toes. Claire had an odd urge to see them.

The chaplain read a psalm, paused at the end, then patted Claire's shoulder and left the room.

Richard ran a hand across his forehead. "Okay. Let's get you home, honey. Listen, I don't want you to worry about anything." The certainty of his tone almost made her cry. "Wanamaker and Sons is going to handle the service. You're going to go home, take a nap, and then, when you're ready, you'll go meet them. You'll sign some paperwork, choose a casket, that's it."

Choose a casket. That's it. Sure. No big deal.

There was another long taxi ride downtown. Sasha called and offered to come over, but Claire wanted to be alone. She dug her keys from her purse, unlocked the building door, and took the elevator up like it was any other day. She set her suitcase in the entryway and walked through the apartment. Hanging on the bedroom door was the brown cashmere robe she'd given Charlie for Christmas the previous year.

On the small table where they took breakfast was the faded Sunday *Times*, folded over to Charlie's unfinished crossword, and a brown bag with several prescription bottles inside from Zitomer's— Charlie's mother. There was a note attached: YOU MIGHT NEED THIS, DEAR. GRACE. *Amen to that,* Claire thought.

She changed out of her clothes and climbed into bed. The

sheets still conformed to Charlie's weight; they fell into wrinkles on his side. Her body, small and alone, stirred up nothing. It was as if Charlie were out and might walk through the door any minute. Nothing had changed.

PER RICHARD'S INSTRUCTIONS, Claire dressed in black and headed back uptown to pick a casket. She dipped into Grace's gift basket before she left. By the time she arrived at the mortuary, a tickly little cloud had scooped her up. She felt light—too light— like an actress auditioning for a role in an ironic comic film. The funeral home was a nondescript brownstone on Lexington. Claire had passed by here many times without knowing it. Inside, the showroom's floor-to-ceiling drapes and brass chandelier were intended, she assumed, to create a sense of sophistication for the bereaved. Instead, she found the decor theatrical and macabre, as if a ghoulish performance of *The Phantom of the Opera* were about to break out. Charlie, Carter the funeral director informed her, was in the basement.

Carter Hinckley of Wanamaker and Sons wore a lightweight gray suit and carried a black leather binder. He had a strong nose and confident stance; he was conventionally handsome. "My con-dolences, Mrs. Byrne," he said, and held out his hand. His hair was slicked back; he sounded older than he looked.

Claire wondered if Carter Hinckley knew her husband, if he'd read any of Charlie's books. She knew that people thought of her husband's work when they met her. Upon introduction, men and women alike reflexively visualized what they imagined must be a tunnel of gold beneath her skirt, to have snared such a discriminat-ing connoisseur as Charles Byrne. The men were typically intrigued, the women bemused; it showed in their eyes.

Claire watched Carter Hinckley's dark eyes and found herself hostage to lewd thoughts. Here she was, barely into her second day widowed, wondering how a young funeral director was picturing her cunt.

"I know this is hard," Carter said. *Hard.* Charlie had instilled in Claire a sophomoric obsession with sex; she was drawn to Carter's crotch as if he'd pointed.

She'd never thought herself the sort of girl who'd seduce her husband's mortician. *I know this is hard, said the swarthy undertaker. It doesn't have to be, Claire replied, unbuckling his belt.*

It's the pills, Claire thought. Carter held the Wanamaker and Sons brochure between a thumb and two fingers. His wrist was bent back at an angle to keep it from flopping, to keep the brochure, as it were, erect. He pointed it straight out at Claire, and Claire relieved him of it. She was impressed by Carter's comportment; she adjusted her posture.

"I'm going to cremate him," she said. "That is what he wished." *What he wished?*

She went on. "So I don't need a coffin."

There was an awkward pause and then Carter cleared his throat.

"You will still need a *casket*, actually." Carter stressed the word *casket.* He couldn't help himself. Coffins were for vampires, no one ever got it right. "Even in the case of . . . I'm sorry, excuse me." He reached for a cloth in his pocket, and as he turned away from her, his eyes seized up tight, his mouth stretched open, and his features became abstract, like Munch's *The Scream.* He paused, held the pose, then captured the explosion, quick and neat, in a light-colored cloth, which he wielded expertly with his right hand.

When had she last seen a handkerchief? Claire couldn't imagine Charlie with a handkerchief. She couldn't picture Charlie in a sneeze.

"Although you've chosen to cremate the remains of your husband—"

"I'm sorry," Claire interrupted. She wanted desperately to regain ground. "I know you told me it, your name."

"My name is Carter, Mrs. Byrne." The "Mrs." wedged twenty years between them. Was she even, technically, still a Mrs.? She could insist he call her Claire, but that might be awkward. *Call me Claire.* She didn't know how to behave with the "Mrs."; Carter wouldn't know how to act without it.

"As I said, although you're cremating Mr. Byrne, we do still arrange the body. He will go through his stages in a *casket.*" He spoke the words with dramatic flair, as though he were reciting a poem.

"Well, then, I suppose I should take the cheapest one."

She and Charlie had never worried for money; his royalties were steady and would, likely, see an uptick from his death. Still, that was no reason to be fleeced. He would have appreciated her pragmatism.

"I'm sorry?"

"The cheapest coffin. Is there something on sale?"

"It's a casket, Mrs. Byrne. And we don't typically run sales, no." Carter was flustered.

"Then I'd like the cheapest casket." They were burning it, after all.

"We have this." Carter took a single-sheet flyer out of his binder. The picture was of a light brown box. It looked like cardboard.

"Well," she reconsidered, "maybe the second cheapest."

As he replaced the flyer and opened the binder to another page, she followed his squared-off fingers to the girth of his wrist, the rakish charm of his platinum watch. Farther up, she could see a muscular definition in his chest and arms that was not well hidden beneath his suit. He had very defined elbows, too, like Charlie's. Claire could see it in the way he carried them; they refused to be overlooked. The first sex she'd had with Charlie, his left elbow had lodged in her rib for the entire twenty minutes. So as not to dwell on it, Claire had made herself count. First in French to *soixante-dix*, and then in Italian, backward from *ottanta*, and in this way she'd gotten through. Now here were Charlie's dead elbows, resurrected in Carter's suit.

"Mrs. Byrne? Are you all right?"

"Yes." Claire realized she'd been moving her lips, she'd been counting. She wondered how funeral directors were taught to handle an inappropriate advance. "Yes," she said. "How long have you been doing this?"

"This?" Carter asked.

"This," Claire said, gesturing across the room. "Arranging dead people."

He stood perfectly straight. No slouch, no swagger—grief was serious work.

"I've been working in the end-of-life industry for six years."

"I never see women in a funeral home. Are there women?" she said.

Carter stiffened, if that were possible.

"The conferences must be dull," Claire added.

He took a somber look at her. Claire looked somberly back. He cleared his throat. "I know this is hard," he said "Would you like to sit down?"

There was a small, green-patterned sofa behind them, a pattern remarkably similar, Claire thought, to Margaret Grabel's kitchen floor. It was positioned in front of a low table. A Bible—King

James—rested on the tabletop. Carter motioned her toward the furniture with his whole arm, a gentle but solid suggestion: *There. Or how about over there.* No question marks. It reassured her. That was something she had liked about her marriage, the assurance. Everything was always taken care of.

Charlie had screwed around from the beginning; he considered it research. Though he was discreet, for her benefit—he didn't bring his work home, for instance—it was hardly a secret. And after a time, it hardly mattered. Claire felt loyalty and fondness for her husband, but she wouldn't exactly call it love. Whatever she once might have felt for him had dulled. She had made a botched adulterous attempt of her own some time back, with one of the waiters from Zinc, their neighborhood restaurant. Armando. God, if Charlie had known. Armando was a kid, just twenty-four, and a painter—Italian, of course. Although sex hadn't technically occurred, she counted it because she'd planned for it to. She'd had the intention of sex.

She wanted Armando in her story. She wanted her lipstick smeared, her hair disarrayed, her countenance wanton in the middle of afternoons. She wanted to feel passion. So she'd gone to his apartment-slash-studio one day, because he'd asked. But when Armando set down his brush on the stained and spattered easel— the colors of women who'd posed here before, Claire thought— she saw him moving in. She stayed for one fumbled kiss, then apologized, politely, and left.

Her husband, throughout both his career and their marriage, had insisted that there could be love or sex between people, but never both. Whether she agreed or not, it was apparent to Claire Byrne, wife of adulterous Charlie, that she was not the sort of married woman who screwed Italian painter-waiters in afternoons. However badly she might have wanted to be.

Sitting with Carter, their knees almost touching, in the small space between couch and table, Claire's thoughts continued to wander. She found it difficult to stay on task.

"I think plain is best," she said. "A plain—" Claire stopped and straightened her posture. "A plain casket."

Slowly, Carter opened his brochure.

Everything in the hours since Charlie died had been maddeningly slow. The flight from Austin had been slow, Claire's reactions were slow, this thirty minutes with Carter felt excruciatingly slow. "There are a number of dignified choices for your husband, Mrs. Byrne. This one, for example."

"Well," she said, and wished she hadn't. It gave the impression she had a plan. She felt the Xanax wearing off. Funeral. Husband. Dead. Fuck. The week was going to be long.

"Mr. Byrne disliked adornment," she heard herself saying. "Do you have something more . . . classic?" Charlie's ghost was laughing at her from somewhere right now. *Charles Byrne was the sort of man who hates embellishment. Charles Byrne was of simple taste.* Charlie Byrne loved nothing more, in fact, than pomp and embellishment and being the center of attention.

"I'm not sure what you mean."

"Well, you know, straight lines. Plain, but not too plain. Nothing too showy, either."

Carter turned his brochure over to the back. "Maybe you'd like an Eco-casket." He tapped his finger on a photo. It was a rectangle with rope handles. "They are relatively inexpensive and are sourced from sustainable forests."

"Oh God, no!"

Claire looked up, and there, without warning, was Sasha, shattering their awkward stillness. She burst in huffily, trailing drama behind her like a wedding train. "Claire, sweetie, you're not burying Charlie in a biodegradable box." She kissed Claire on both cheeks. "I was worried when you weren't at home. Then Ethan said you'd be here." She squared herself up to Carter, who looked unprepared for the steep thrust of Sasha's cleavage above the plunge of her patterned wrap dress. "Hello, I'm Sasha." She put out her hand to Carter, palm down, and he took it, relieved to have somewhere else to look.

All of the first act, the slow steam Claire and Carter had built up—the pauses and gazes and looks—Sasha had smashed in one motion, like a bird crashed through a window.

"So listen, Carter, Mrs. Byrne should take the Marquis casket, don't you think?" Claire stared at the brochure. The Marquis was solid bronze with a velvet interior. It had a twin-lid design with hermetic sealing, an amber and sable finish, swing handles, and, of course, an adjustable bed.

"Do you like it, sweetie?"

"It's nice," Claire said.

"Margorie Dermott had it for her husband. Did you know he finally died? Jesus, ninety years old. Enough. He keeled over in his scotch after dinner. Margorie was so shocked, she threw the rest of the bottle out and it was twenty-five-year-old Chivas. Did you do that funeral, Carter?"

"Well, I can't—"

"Never mind. We'll take the Marquis, and the bronze Chalice urn with the etchings around the lid."

Claire suddenly started spinning, or the room did, she couldn't tell. "I'm not feeling well," she said. "I need to go."

4

FOR ALL THE DECORUM, DISPOSAL WAS SWIFT.

Richard took care of everything. Sasha drank, Ethan hid out, and Charlie's mother, Grace, handled theatrics. The casket had been Claire's only task. She wore a chic and mournful black dress to the funeral. She had her hair done. She tried to focus on other things beforehand, like the headlines in the morning *Times*. The Rangers had signed a goalie; the Dow was up; Evelyn White, of the dropped Giacometti, was on the *Today* show.

The ceremony kicked off with a gospel choir—Grace Byrne had insisted. There were also a priest and a rabbi, at Grace's request, like a bad joke. Charlie would have wanted neither. At least the glossy casket was closed.

Richard gave the tribute, of course. He was impeccably calm. He stood at the front of the church and spoke as if it were a pitch meeting.

"This is like a careless first draft," he began, pausing to scan the three hundred–odd guests, stopping short, Claire saw, on the book critic Ben Hawthorne, who sat alone in the third row wearing a wrinkled jacket and rumpled hair. The rift between Charlie and Ben—from his unforgiveable panning in the *Atlantic Monthly* of *Thinker's Hope*—was well-known in this room. Had there been more chance meetings between the two men, their discord might have rivaled Norman Mailer's with Gore Vidal; someone might have thrown a punch. Ben Hawthorne should not have been here. Ben Hawthorne with a ticket to Charles Byrne's funeral was an unfortunate oversight.

Richard went on. "I imagine him bringing it to me in manuscript—the dynamic, vital protagonist killed off in the second chapter—and me handing it right back to him. 'No, Charlie. I've never heard of such a thing. It won't sell.'" There was quiet but genuine laughter at this. Richard was famous in the industry for his wide-eyed appeals of ignorance—*I've never heard of such a thing. It just isn't done.* It was his parlor trick—the spider dressed up as the fly. He pulled off the shrewdest deals in town.

Claire's thoughts drifted, watching Richard. She saw Charlie's death, sudden and absurd as it was, like a sac of helium floating up and away from her. She tried futilely to snatch it back. She felt like an uninvited guest here, a voyeur, a stranger. Her mother-in-law sat beside her almost unnaturally erect, draped in black silk. Grace's hands were properly crossed, her lips were bright red—the widows Byrne.

There were velvet bows on the pews, as if they were presents. There was a long runner on the floor of the aisle down to the front. There were thoughtful arrangements of flowers, and smartly dressed people in grim and proper poses. Sasha wore a cream-colored dress in the sea of black and twirled her fingers absent-mindedly through her husband, Thom's, hair. Thom West was an unassuming man who was ruthless in boardrooms and quietly amassing a fortune. Charlie never liked him, but Claire always had. Behind Sasha was Bridget, Richard's girlfriend. She was grinning; she seldom didn't. She was sitting next to Claire's mother and father, Betty and Roger Jenks, who'd flown in from Illinois. Claire's brother, Howard, had offered to come, too, but he was on the West Coast and had children. There'd been an expectation of arrangements and Claire didn't see the point. She didn't care to entertain anyone after this performance, or stay up late with open liquor bottles, conjuring memories.

Betty wore a tasteful gray suit—she'd splurged. She wasn't about to come to New York and have someone peg her as Midwestern, credit card bills be damned. She snapped her handbag open and shut while Claire's father studied the program. She could have worn Armani, Claire thought, it wouldn't have mattered. Roger, in his serviceable slacks and ten-dollar barbershop cut, would always give her away. Ethan sat in the pew opposite Claire, with a houndstooth suit and a new boyfriend. He caught her eye and made a hand gesture she recognized. *Steady. It will all be okay.* Anna Bowers—the PR maven who ran New York's social life and who was the one loud nod here to Charlie's fame—sat fifth-row center in a wide-brimmed black organza hat. She was quietly taking phone calls. The rest of the room had filled with a mix of industry peers—writers and sycophants—and the odd city notable. The mayor, for instance, tastefully trim in Paul Stuart, was flanked by aides near the back. Tom Wolfe looked predictably dapper in his signature white suit.

Richard read from James Joyce—the quote Charlie had used to open *Thinker's Hope*: " 'The artist, like the God of the creation, remains within or behind or beyond or above his handiwork, invisible, refined out of existence, indifferent, paring his finger-nails.' "

Richard pulled his head up slowly, removed his glasses with his left hand, rubbed his eyes with the right. He was in full sales mode. Here was his chance to make Charlie epic and create a run on the books. Here was Richard making friends and influencing people and getting the good Glengarry leads all at once. He would call Sonny at Knopf tomorrow morning and talk about the electricity in the room; surely Sonny had felt it, too. He'd get them to go to press, to get *Thinker's Hope* back on the bill at their Monday-morning sales meeting.

There were a number of particulars about Charlie that Richard dutifully ticked off—the countless awards, the honorary doctorates.

When the formal piece concluded, everyone lined up to pay respects to Claire. Richard took charge of Grace, and Grace was pleased with that. They both came from, as Grace liked to say, good stock.

The mourners, weeping and patting, offered soft hugs and double kisses. Claire was embraced by a small, bony woman. She recognized her immediately but had forgotten her name. She remembered only that Charlie had ended an affair with her years ago, abruptly, and it had gotten nasty for a bit. Like Ben Hawthorne, this woman was someone Richard surely had not put on the list. Or had he? Claire didn't know what to think.

The whole thing felt off. Charlie would have laughed. Claire felt misled, she felt a fraud, she didn't feel sufficiently sad at all.

Kathryn Muller came forward with her husband, Kick, one of the pallbearers. Kick was a television writer. He and Charlie had gone to school together, and their friendship had revolved around intellectual one-upmanship; they'd go on and on about Jacques Derrida or Michel Foucault and quote different obscure passages, trying to top each other. Then one would jump suddenly to baseball.

"I keep expecting a fight to break out," Kick said, after kissing her cheek. At her startled look, he added, "I mean, I could see Charlie coming in here and throwing a punch to shake things up. He would have wanted a little more action."

"Kick," his wife said, putting a hand on his arm.

Claire laughed and felt solid again for a moment. "No, you're right. He wouldn't have suffered this sort of thing."

By 9:30 that night, Charlie was back to dust, Sasha was numb on brandy, Claire's parents were on a plane, and Claire was in her apartment swallowing sleeping pills and Diet Coke. Ethan called on the landline; she let it go to Charlie's voice on the machine. "Love you, darling," he said after the beep. "Kisses and dreams." She fell asleep to an old Dick Cavett show and slept for sixteen hours straight.

5

THE BYRNES WERE AN ODD MATCH, EVEN BEYOND THE age gap. You're not the first to think so.

They'd been married for nine years. Charlie had been married briefly, once before; he didn't put much stock in it. But Claire enjoyed being a wife, for the most part. Being married to Charlie Byrne was interesting. There were staggers and starts and extremes of all kinds. She'd watched most of their life curiously, from offstage. They went to films and the theater, and dinners—an endless stream of them—honoring Charlie or featuring Charlie or supporting something artistic of this or that. They spent late talk-filled nights with friends. He gave her entrée into the elite upper reaches of words and the people who traded in them; she gave him a wide berth.

Claire had once hoped to be a great writer, too, and to be vaunted like Charlie. She liked the rhythm of language—the cadences and the silent counts, the melody lines and the minor notes. She liked how a nondescript man in brown trousers could, with the fall of a shadow or twitch of a jaw, be turned into a lover, a dreamer, or a hard, cold psychopath. She liked how an omission or a reveal in a story could move the heart to great heights or drastic falls. She liked words at loose ends, and in books and songs and poems. She liked them in crossword puzzles, an obsession she and Charlie shared, and for which they'd found it necessary to maintain two separate subscriptions to the *Times*. Claire's major at New York University had been literary studies, with a focus in Victorian realism; she had set herself up to fail at everything else. Her senior year she entered a short-story contest in a prestigious literary journal called *Zoetrope: All-Story*. She was shy with her work, but paid the ten-dollar reading fee, sent off three thousand double-spaced words, and then got a call. She was a finalist—*a finalist*! There had been more than eight thousand entries, and the judges were big guns. Ann Patchett and Peter Pringle were two of them. The third was Charles Byrne.

Later, there was a feature in *New York* magazine, spotlighting the winner, Anna Kuznetsov, and runners-up. "Young Pens," it was called, a silly headline, Claire thought. Each of them had a pull quote next to their photo. Claire's was this: "I believe in the redemptive power of a good blow job." It was a cheeky nod to her story, "Hustling Woody." In it, the protagonist—a hard-luck prostitute—lost her finger but found her soul by performing a sex act on Woody Allen. (Claire sent a copy of the magazine to her mother. Betty, who was uncomfortable with blow jobs— much less ones written by her daughter in a magazine for all the world to see—stashed it at the bottom of a tall stack of papers in the study.)

The Young Pens were promised agents; they had big hopes. For a brief amount of time, in certain circles, Claire was a star. At this point in the game, she had plans, too. Such as: Paris with Sasha, who was her roommate at the time. They'd planned it for months. They fought over Parisian identities—both wanted Kay Boyle, but Sasha agreed, in the end, to Mina Loy. They dreamed up French lovers and smoky Montparnasse cafés where Claire would write her novel while Sasha undressed for art students. They went so far as to secure a sublet in the Left Bank for the year.

But what happened instead of Paris was that after reading "Hustling Woody" and seeing Claire's photo, with her symmetrical features and complicated lips, the great Charlie Byrne wrote her a letter. He'd gotten her address from an editor friend at *New York*, then stamped and posted his letter—the old-fashioned way. He'd flattered her tone and her style; his great triumph, she eventually understood, was his ability to effect a better version of himself in words, a man who was sincere, who had the capacity to love outside of the id. *Do you think I could buy you a drink*, he'd written, *in spite of my toxic eligibility?*

He was funny, he was charming, and for his books about cocks he was an intellectual star. Crowded rooms fell to a hush as he stepped in (they didn't actually, she realized later; it was an impression he'd successfully cultivated in her).

Claire was twenty-two; Charlie had just turned forty-five. In retrospect, she thought he must have seen a reflection of his own youthful success in her; men always seemed to want to recapture their early glories, even when they'd gone on to be far more successful since. She couldn't imagine, at twenty-two, in a cab on her way to meet him, how she could possibly hold this man's interest for any length of time, God forbid the hour it might take them to have a drink.

"You have sexy goddamn eyes," he said to her in the first five minutes. "They're like hot breath on the neck of my soul." This from a frat boy and Claire would have spit out her drink. From Charles Byrne, it sounded poetic.

Claire Jenks, suburban girl from Illinois, handpicked by Charles Byrne. Charles Byrne! She was flattered. She was confused. His attentions had come out of nowhere. There was no appropriate way to decline. She moved into his apartment within the month, and in less than a year they were married. Claire Jenks—*snap, poof!*—Byrne. Sasha had gone to Paris anyway; a family friend there had later fixed her up with Thom, so in the end it had worked out for both of them.

Once, after they married, Claire had submitted a short story to the *New Yorker.* She'd been politely rejected, but it incensed Charlie when he found out—not only had she submitted without his input, but it became clear, early on, that in their two-bedroom Village town house, there was room for one man and one writer, and Charlie was both. So Claire put her creative writing on hold. Richard, Charlie, and everyone else seemed to assume she was satisfied, and Claire assumed that if there was a difference between happiness and contentment, then content was what she was.

Then, this strange twist of fate. What had seemed a plain kind of happiness, her life with Charlie, her marriage, had been crushed by a large chunk of bronze.

The art that killed Charlie had a name—*Man Walking*—and a story. I told you we'd come back to it. The piece was one of a series, and Walter White bought it at auction for an unconfirmed sum (the rumor was thirty million). He bought it to make up to his wife after what you might call a fight. He'd been screwing her yoga instructor, literally right beneath her nose. You see, Walter liked risk. In sexual terms, it was his paraphilia, an area that Charlie specialized in—atypical, often harmful ways of going about sex.

The riskier the act, the more Walter reveled in it. He liked to almost get caught, so he and the yogi had done it in the closet below Evelyn White's reading room while she was at home and reading. They had done it on the dining-room table while she walked the pug, and knowing she was having a dinner that very night. They unsuccessfully attempted to do it in her bathroom when she was sprawled on her bed in what turned out to be a very light sleep. But it wasn't getting caught *en flagrante* that undid them, it was the yogi's big mouth. She'd whispered enough about their affair to enough of the right people that word of their unconventional ménage à trois got around.

White was the sort of carelessly rich, inelegant man that Charlie despised. The sort who bought sports teams, then hosted hot-dog-and-potato-chip receptions in his stadium suite to be ironic. The Giacometti had been procured because he'd been inexcusably sloppy. Once rumors of a "tummy bump" became a Blind Item on Page Six of the *Post* (*Which billionaire real estate tycoon planted his tenant in his wife's yoga instructor's womb?*), Evelyn came undone and White sought out the most pretentious piece of art available on short notice. It was cheaper than a divorce.

On the other side of town, a generous delivery from Cartier went to a certain fourth-floor walk-up. It couldn't be said that Walter White was unfair.

The sculpture had been a nuisance long before it landed on Charlie. There was the auction at Christie's where Courtney Love, of all people, scabbed but lucid, had scandalously bid up the piece, infuriating White. The attention the spiteful bidding war caused had dredged up the entire affair again in the tabloids, undermining the gesture and, furthermore, linking Evelyn—whose family had made their money at the turn of the century in proper, discriminate ways—with a former heroin addict from Washington State, a place Evelyn couldn't, with any sort of imagination, picture as more than a muddy swamp with trees.

Then, there was the problem of how to get the statue into the Whites' apartment. The bronze was an awkward, unreasonable shape; tall with dramatic angles. It wouldn't fit in the building's elevator, much less through the Whites' narrow front door.

By the time *Man Walking* was on a crane headed up to the Whites' penthouse balcony, it's very possible Walter hoped it would fall and shatter to pieces, smash to ruin, and allay the bitterness he felt at the entire episode—the overall sense that he'd been had. The bronze was already psychically precarious when the cable snapped on the crane and sent it tumbling from the sky like a three-hundred-pound bird.

It was said—sotto voce, of course, not seeming a very proper thing to point out—that Charlie had saved the Giacometti from ruin, breaking its fall the way he had. Without Charlie as buffer, the unforgiving stone of the sidewalk might have left the great work misshaped.

The yogi heard the story on the news, alone, from her treadmill, and Evelyn White heard about it at her pinochle game. That damned Strickland Nash, newly rich from pedicure socks, never let her phone sit more than inches away. She got a news alert while Evelyn beat her two tricks.

"Evvy, do you know that writer, the sex guy Charlie Byrne?" she asked.

Evelyn paused, feigned an effort of concentration, and shook her head. "I don't know. Yes. Vaguely." She bit her lip. With Strickland, you never knew what was coming next.

"Weren't you supposed to get your Giacometti today?"

Evelyn felt cornered; leading questions irritate everyone. "Yes?"
"Well, I think it killed someone. I think it fell on Charles Byrne."
Evelyn White was a cool customer. She took her tricks without
flinching and calmly drank her gimlet. Thank God, she thought,
for booze. Then she made a neat exit and waited for her husband at
home, where there was no new priceless art. He had some explain-
ing to do.

Alberto Giacometti had, ironically, made an appearance in
Thinker's Hope. It was the name that Schopenhauer had picked for
his goat. *My Gia-co-metti.* Charlie couldn't stand sculptors; it was
no accident he'd made him the goat. He thought sculptors coarse, as
artists went. Pretentious, melodramatic, overrated. Though, truth
be told, Charlie was bound to think this of anyone—writer, painter,
poet, chef—who'd had the fortune of stumbling upon critical praise,
himself excepted.

As fate had it, though, it was Charlie—not yet canonized—who
got the bit part in the bigger story. He became a footnote to Giacometti. A line about Charles Byrne was added to Alberto Giacometti's Wikipedia entry less than fifteen minutes after his death, under
"Trivia."

The first days postmortem are a grab bag of surprises. Stories
swirl. They ravel and unravel all around us, mostly beyond our
control, and often at a frightening pace.

6

CLAIRE WOKE UP THE NEXT AFTERNOON OUT OF SORTS, feeling like she'd slept through something important. Ten years of her life felt like one long Freudian dream, for which she lacked interpretation.

> RULE #2: You can fake an orgasm,
> but you can't fake a Giacometti.

There was a voice mail from Sasha.

"Honey?" Pause. "Did you see the *Post*?"

The Giacometti, it turned out, was a fake.

A fake! It had come from a father-and-son con team who'd been running a scam for fifteen years. The father handled sales. The son, a talented artist, made the copies. They picked a different artist every year, reproduced the least known pieces, sold them, and skipped town. They'd gotten greedy, though, with *Man Walking*. It was one of the art world's most famous works. They were busted outside of Brussels.

"It was counterfeit. What does this mean?" Claire asked Lowenstein. Judith Lowenstein was Claire's shrink. It was their first session since Charlie's death. "If it's a fake, then was the whole death a fake? Is Charlie a fake, was our marriage a fake, is sex a fake, is love? Is this the world's least subtle metaphor?" Lowenstein scribbled down a number of things on her tablet, but by the end of the hour she still did not seem to have answers for Claire. Suddenly, the unexpected, surreal beauty of the particulars of Charlie's demise—the movement and swirling and *Man Walking* fluttering down from the blue sky like a wounded bird—felt like cheap vaudeville shtick. Charlie's grandeur, the extravagant service with tributes, Sasha's cream-colored dress, and the presence of Ben Hawthorne all seemed poorly contrived.

There was obvious distress at the White home at this news. Walter was out a lot of money, Evelyn was out reparation, and the yogi—we might as well name her at this point: Sande—was dealing with way too much shit. The scandal was costing her business. Evelyn White's pinochle group and extended friends were the yogi's steadiest source of income and they turned on her fast. Sande's classes were deserted. Paparazzi milled at the door of her building, her co-tenants scowled. What had begun as a harmless little venture for her—there'd been extravagant gifts, short luxury trips—had morphed into a New York City–style lynching. In Sande's mind, Walt had fallen far short. No dinners since the dropped bronze, no money, no jewelry after that initial Cartier box. She was behind on her rent and still had to keep up appearances for the photos that were running in all the papers. "This, Walter . . . all of . . . this," she said in one of many frustrated rants to his voice mail, "is fucking *bullshit*! I didn't sign up for *this*!"

The scandal cast a shameful pall on what began as at least an interesting sort of death. For the next couple of weeks, Claire lay low. Wadded up in bed, she kept the television on mute and the stereo on soft. She watched the same handful of DVDs over and over: *Now, Voyager*; *The Philadelphia Story*; *North by Northwest*. She watched *The Odd Couple Complete Series*. Jack Klugman's gravelly voice drifted in and out of her dreams. She relished Oscar Madison's encapsulated New York, a little dirtier, a little grittier than her own, and his petty anguish: the problem of deadlines, small gambling debts, and a roommate who made him pick up his socks. Her languor was cut short.

Sasha should have been on the Vineyard, it was well into June, but there she stood in Claire's doorway, unannounced, with a box of green garbage sacks and a thermos of Stoli for martinis.

"Don't get up, sweetie."

"Oh God," Claire groaned.

"Relax," Sasha said. "The sacks are for you, the vodka's is for me."

She took in Claire's mismatched pajamas at two fifteen in the afternoon. "Honey, look at you. You'll be crumpled up here for months if we don't keep you moving. You can't let this place turn into a museum." Sasha walked past Claire into the kitchen; she was making a point about being in action. She pulled a jar of olives from her handbag, dropped one into the bottom of a glass, and grabbed a jar of vermouth from the cabinet above her.

"Fine, but a little notice is nice," Claire said. "I mean . . . this?" Claire motioned to the bags.

"Forget it, honey, I'll do it. You get back to your malaise," Sasha said. She started pulling books off a shelf. "You don't need any of this cooking crap, that's for sure."

Claire surveyed the room. Sasha was right. Since Charlie had died she'd been treating the apartment like a crime scene, as if everything he'd ever touched was now evidence. She'd steered clear of the kitchen, clear of his Mauviel cookware and his Wusthof knives, and of the large wine rack of bottles she knew nothing about. Avoiding Charlie's things meant avoiding what he had done with them—and what she had done, all of their habits. She was avoiding the memory of his Sunday tennis game, of his homemade consommé, of the *chop chop chop* of his knife whittling onions and carrots into a studied mirepoix. She was avoiding any reference to his noises, his movements, his smells. Had you asked Claire, the week before Charlie died, she might have admitted she found some of their life dull—the problem is, though, she put a lot of stock in routine. Without it, she floundered.

Sasha, standing behind Claire suddenly, startled her. "Oh my God, don't do that. Make noise!" Sasha smiled and held out a bag. "Start with clothes, sweetie. They're easiest."

"What do you know about it?"

"Margorie Dermott. She threw Alfred's clothes out before the death certificate was even signed and she slept like a baby."

Walking from room to room, images skipped through Claire's head like a slide show. She and Charlie dancing at a wedding. Charlie making omelets. A close-up of both of them smiling, then Charlie kissing Claire's cheek. A candid glimpse at Sasha's for Christmas, everyone drinking pink champagne. In this one Charlie's feet are perched solidly on the ottoman and his free hand is circling the air. Then, unexpectedly, Walter White popped into her head—the photo from the papers. He was balding.

Charlie's toiletries cluttered the bathroom, a towel he'd used still hung wrinkled on a hook. Claire was no Margorie Dermott. She left the bathroom as it was, walked into their bedroom, and began filling a garbage bag with her husband's shoes and shirts. When the bag was full, she carried it out to a chute at the other end of her floor. Her singular small sounds overwhelmed the quiet hall. Claire's heavy apartment door creaked open, then closed, the latch clicked; her rubber soles narrated her march to the chute. When she heard the thump as each bag landed three floors down, she felt a surprising sense of relief.

Claire didn't dispose of everything. She saved Charlie's robe. She kept a carton of letters from strangers who liked his work and a box of notes he'd written to her the year she moved in. She kept his belts. She buckled them at the well-worn notches, conjuring up the exact circumference of Charlie's waist. A physical memory shivered through her; was there anything as intimate as unbuckling a man's belt? She left one coat to hang in the hall and one pair of tennis shoes beneath his side of the bed. There was unopened mail; mail had continued to arrive, and she left it stacked on his unused desk. Ethan could deal with that. She left Charlie's office untouched.

"That's better," Sasha said, scanning the apartment with approval. "But we're not done. We need food. I'm starved. And then, I hate to do this to you, honey, but photos. Let's walk through."

The high, narrow dresser in the bedroom housed a number of awkward decisions, which Sasha insisted they address. There was their wedding photo, for one, the picture Richard took just after they were pronounced Byrne and wife. Charlie looked uncomfortable;

the city hall ceremony had been rushed. It had been late August, unbearably hot, and the air-conditioning was out.

"Yes? No?" Sasha asked.

It was not a good picture. It didn't flatter Claire at all; the lighting was poor. Claire shook her head. Sasha put it in a drawer.

There was a double frame with a photo from a trip to Peru and an ill-lit pose in Paris. Sasha held them up one at a time.

Claire nodded yes to Peru, no to Paris. "I feel like I'm two different people," Claire said.

Sasha put three more frames in the drawer.

"I'm this new person I didn't ask to be, a widow with all the trappings, whether I want them or not. But then I'm this other thing, too—a hermit crab groping around, blind, for a new shell."

"That's lofty, honey. And melodramatic, don't you think?" Sasha grabbed her purse and pulled out a pack of cigarettes. "You're rich and gorgeous and you get to start over again, do whatever the hell you want. It's not like divorce, where you're fighting over sconces and he's screwing cocktail waitresses to be an ass."

"What are you doing?" Claire asked. "Since when do you smoke?"

Sasha shrugged. She was holding a burnished gold lighter and a long herringbone cigarette holder with the cigarette attached at the end. She struggled with the light.

"They're menthols," Sasha said by way of explanation, teeth clenched around the long stick. "I'm just saying. Embrace your life or you'll miss it."

"I didn't expect this life."

"Warren Beatty didn't expect to be a wealthy tycoon in *Heaven Can Wait*. He wanted to play football."

"And?"

"And . . . well, I guess he died, but you're missing the point. Don't you get it? Widows are the new virgins, Claire. Men are licking their chops for you right now. They're all going to want to pop your widow cherry. You have power, and no guilt. Enjoy it! And believe me, you'll want to keep that shell—or body, whatever—the one you've got."

Claire's phone rang. She didn't recognize the number. They both studied it and then Sasha picked it up. "Hello, this is Claire."

"Hello. Mrs. Byrne? This is Carter. Carter Hinckley, from Wanamaker and Sons. I hope I'm not bothering you."

Oh my God, Sasha whispered. *It's the funeral guy.*

"No, of course not, Carter. How are you?"

"This is just a courtesy call, Mrs. Byrne. I wanted to remind you we are still holding Mr. Byrne's remains, divided as you requested. If you're unable to collect them here, we can deliver them to you and to Grace Byrne, as it says in the instructions."

Sasha covered the phone and whispered to Claire, again. *You haven't picked up the ashes?*

"Yes, actually, Carter, that would be great. Please deliver them. To myself and to Mrs. Byrne as well. I'd appreciate it very much."

Sasha hung up the phone. "Honey, are you serious? Who would take care of these things if I didn't come around? You can't just abandon the *remains*. Jesus. Does Grace know they're sitting there in the morgue for all the world to see?"

"The whole world isn't seeing anything. And no, she doesn't. I was going to pick them up."

"And lug them downtown on the subway? No wonder you've been odd. That's karmic suicide, honey. Anyway, they're coming tomorrow."

Sasha poured the last of the vodka into two shot glasses. "Here," she said, handing one to Claire. "It's infused with bacon. It tastes like breakfast." Sasha poured herself a second as Claire struggled to choke down her first.

"Honey, don't get bogged down in this. You have a chance to do whatever you want now. Don't screw it up. You could have been in a sexless marriage for the next twenty years and wound up hating him. Charlie was a story in your life, but he's not the story. You've got a lot more to do."

RULE #3: Life is long. Pace yourself.

Sasha put her sunglasses on and gave Claire one last look. "You don't look so well, sweetie. You shouldn't drink on an empty stomach."

AFTER SASHA LEFT, Claire went for a walk. She zigzagged a familiar route and kept her earphones in for distraction. There were piles of newspapers on every corner—the *Post*, the *Daily News*, the *Times*. The circumstances of Charlie's death, even three weeks out, percolated through all of them. His death was still a mild sensation. Sande the yogi was very photogenic. Charlie's morning-of-death conquest had chosen to speak out, too. "I Was with Him Before He Died" was the headline that, unfortunately, caught Claire's eye. She stopped and picked up one of the papers. Below the headline, next to a photo of a twenty-ish blonde (well-endowed enough not to care about hips or waist), was the subhead "Paramour Reveals Details of Charles Byrne's New Book."

As far as Claire knew, Charlie hadn't written a word of a new book. For the first time, it crossed her mind that there was an advance she might have to pay back. The execution of Charlie's will had been delayed.

She returned the paper to the stack without buying it, dialed Richard and left a message at his office, then turned the corner and threw up her bacon-flavored vodka onto the curb.

7

"THIS IS SOME FUCKING SITUATION!" CLAIRE AND ETHAN were in her apartment. Richard was on the phone; they had him on speaker. It was rare to hear him curse. "I have to read about my client's book in the *Post*? Jesus, Ethan, you must have known what he was working on."

Ethan looked wounded.

"He was always working," he said. "As far as I know, he hadn't settled on a particular topic. Did you read the article? There was nothing specific. And she's a bottle blonde, obviously." He reached over and patted Claire's hand. Richard cleared his throat. "You have to admire her for sitting on it until the Giacometti died down—she got a Page Six scoop. I'd say it's a good career move, except that she just got herself fired." At that, he sounded a little happier.

"Don't think about this," Ethan said, after Richard hung up. "It seems like a lot of drama, but he's a writer, honey. No one will care for long."

"I think Richard cares."

"This is slapstick. A two-bit art scandal, slutty yoga instructor, and a perverted, rich fuck. We should be writing a sitcom." Ethan walked down the hallway toward the kitchen. "Need a drink?"

"Except it was my husband," Claire said, sinking into the couch. "It seems a little less funny."

"Well, it was an inconvenient death. He wouldn't have wanted all these loose ends."

"That's not true. He never liked a neat story. He would have loved this," Claire said.

Ethan handed Claire a soda. "Yeah, he would."

Ethan was tasked with sorting through Charlie's papers and computer files posthaste. He was to send Richard anything that looked like it might be part of a manuscript and organize the rest for the library at Princeton. Claire was relieved she had a reason to keep him employed.

Ethan had been Claire's first crush in college. They had lived in the same dorm freshman year and shared a loose set of friends, including Sasha. He had the kind of lopsided smile mothers warned their daughters about—except that they should have been warning their sons. Claire didn't understand it until a ski trip during winter break. They'd gone in a group that included Tyler Hayes, a scruffy jock from Hayden Hall. On their second night, in the great room of the huge cabin they'd rented, Claire saw the longing looks Ethan shot Tyler's way and it all became clear. While Claire led Ethan out from the closet that year, it was Sasha who nabbed Tyler Hayes. Ethan moved to Los Angeles after graduation and Claire, of course, met Charlie. They kept in touch, though, and when Ethan was ready to come back to New York, Charlie was looking for a new assistant. Fate? Chance? Well, it was something.

Ethan was perfect. Not only was he a fan, but thanks to his time in L.A., he knew his way around ego; he knew how to flatter his new boss—he caught on fast. He was the only person Claire knew who had read every single thing Charlie wrote; Richard always went to him for pull quotes. Ethan had a savant's grasp of the cumbersome Byrne opus.

When it came to dating, though, he was slightly less adept. He had a penchant for middle-aged men with stout portfolios. Ethan was trim and fashionable—he had no trouble attracting them—but he bored easily, he was erratic. He had difficulty holding on to any one man. His date at Charlie's funeral, for instance—an environmental lawyer from Virginia—bolted a week later.

Claire watched Ethan work. He was intent. And muscular and tall, and probably great in bed—

"Oh, God. Ethan?"

"What?" He looked up, startled.

"Never mind. I need some air."

"Okay, love. Good. I need caffeine."

On the walk to Starbucks Claire felt a familiar wooziness, like she'd had the day after Charlie's death, at the funeral home. But somehow between Bedford Street and Waverly she muscled through it. Inside, she stared at the chalkboard menu of swirly letters, overwhelmed.

Ethan ordered an Americano with cream and Claire panicked, like she'd stepped up to the dais in a crowded auditorium without her notes. "Cappuccino," she said, though not with conviction.

"Wet or dry?" asked the barista. Claire looked back at the chalkboard. Sizes and shots and flavors and fats. There were three different measures, four blonde roasts, eleven dark, and five kinds of milk. There were espressos, Americanos, macchiatos, and half-caff frappes, with foam and without.

She felt the impatience behind her—shifting feet and heavy sighs. Ethan shot her a nervous look. Her stomach began to hurt. She picked up a packet of trail mix and set it on the counter. The barista glared. Claire grabbed Ethan's arm.

"Hey, sweetie. It's okay." He took charge with the barista. "Dry, let's make it dry." His calm assurance, his lean body and long limbs, his very certain and solid presence tipped Claire over the edge.

"Why is coffee so fucking complicated?" The barista took a step back.

"It's okay, honey." Ethan put a five-dollar bill on the counter and led Claire out of the store. People parted on both sides of them, watching carefully, sensing that a woman might come unhinged right here in front of them, over whether to have wet or dry foam.

OUTSIDE, CLAIRE SHOOK loose and ran to the curb. She sat down. Immune to the dirty sidewalk and gutter litter, she buried her head in her hands and started to sob. It came out in high-pitched squeaks that she couldn't control. "Oh my God. Oh my God. Oh my God."

"Shh, sweetie." Ethan stooped and sat next to her.

"It feels so long."

"What does, babe?"

"Life."

Ethan rubbed her back.

"In the moment it feels short, but it's really long." Claire raised her head. Her face wet with tears. "I'm only thirty-two. There are still so many days to fill up."

"It's not so bad, Clarabelle."

She wiped her eyes on his sleeve. "How's it not so bad?"

"Well, think of it this way. You've never really been alone. You got married right out of college, you were so young. Before you could be a sun, you signed on to be a moon." Ethan treaded carefully. "Charlie's ideas became your ideas. His opinions became yours . . . but now you're steering the boat."

"Ethan, do you believe in soul mates?"

"I believe in everything. But Charlie was your soul mate the way Bennett from Mamaroneck was your soul mate, and the guy from Gallatin, the music studies major, was your soul mate."

"Gerard," Claire whispered.

"Right, Gerry. You were convinced you'd been married to him in a past life," Ethan said.

"Maybe I'm poly–soul mate."

"We all are, honey," Ethan said, and he stroked her hair. "Derek Jeter is my soul mate. One of them."

"The baseball player? You know him?"

"No. But if we met I bet we'd be soul mates." This got a smile from Claire. They sat like this for an hour, Claire with her head on his shoulder, letting the Seventh Avenue din lull her calm again. And when she didn't feel like crying anymore, and her body ached from sitting, they got up and walked home.

CARTER HINCKLEY WAS waiting for them in the foyer, holding Charlie in the etched bronze urn. "Hi. I'm so sorry, Carter. I forgot." Claire looked from Carter to Ethan. No one spoke. Ethan looked from Claire to Carter, then back to Claire. Ethan took the urn and broke the silence. "Well, you know what they say, a widow without ashes is like a cowboy without a hat." Carter didn't laugh. Claire looked horrified. "Call me if you need anything, Mrs. Byrne. Have a good night." Carter nodded then left.

Ethan carried Charlie inside and sat him on the coffee table, then poured out two long shots of Maker's Mark. Claire was not a bourbon drinker; this was a ritual Ethan had shared with Charlie. But she was grateful when he handed her the glass. Here they were, the three of them again. "You didn't tell me Charlie was coming home today."

"Funny, Ethan," Claire said. "I can't live like this."

"Honey, your problem's just structure," Ethan said.

"Structure?"

"Yep. You need a story arc. You need signs of climax, somewhere, even just the hint of a climb. You need a journey. You need acts."

"I skipped past journey to catastrophe." Claire sipped her Maker's Mark.

"Think of Charlie's demise as your plot point. Where do you go from here?"

"I can't even manage the menu at Starbucks. Where am I supposed to go?"

Ethan ran a hand through his perfectly styled hair, his legs stretched out on the ottoman. "You're too young to be mired in denouement."

The intercom buzzed: chicken parmigiana and Gigi salad from The Palm. Where Claire grew up, people brought casseroles to the bereaved. In New York, well-mannered friends sent high-end takeout. Claire and Ethan ate from the containers with plastic forks. Ethan continued.

"You need divination. You need soothsayers and seers."

"What do you mean, like a fortune-teller?"

"Don't mock, Clarabelle. I'm serious. Here." He wrote down a number.

"Who's this?"

"Beatrice."

Claire wrinkled her nose.

"You know, there's barely any difference between a good psychic and your uptight shrink. Before Freud, dreams were interpreted as messages from the gods. Anyway, call her tomorrow. I'll warn her."

Claire knew of Beatrice; she was famous in Manhattan. She'd predicted the affairs and subsequent divorces of a number of prominent couples and was remarkably accurate about elections. She was also almost impossible to see, but Ethan had developed an odd friendship with her. He went to her apartment once a month for chicken Kiev.

"You'll love her. Take a picture with you, though. She won't read you without one."

BEATRICE WAS NOT what Claire expected. She imagined a turbaned woman with spotted hands. Instead, she faced a long, willowy thing with delicate bones; she might have been a runway model in her youth, thirty years ago. Her face was angular, imposing.

Claire had ignored Ethan's directive and, instead of a photograph, brought Charlie's socks. Out of spite, maybe—at Charlie or at the psychic, she didn't know. Either way, she regretted it immediately. As she handed them over, she could hear the clench of Beatrice's jaw.

"I don't read socks," she said.

"I know," Claire replied. "I suspected you didn't, but they

belong to someone close to me. They're the last living sense of him. A picture . . . the pictures don't seem real."

"I won't read a sock. Next time, bring a photograph of your husband."

Claire hadn't mentioned a husband. These were the first words they'd exchanged. Ethan might have told her, but she didn't think so. Ethan believed in oracles, he believed in divination; he'd had the same Magic 8 Ball for twenty years and still consulted it. Ethan would not have interfered.

"He's not my husband. He's dead."

This was true, wasn't it? How could Charlie be her husband if he was dead?

Beatrice had sharp, judging eyes, like an owl's. She fixed them on Claire and made a rumbling, guttural sound.

"I need to know my arc," Claire said. "I'm on a journey without a plot. I need a story line."

"Give me your hand, then."

Claire clutched Charlie's sock in her right hand while Beatrice read her left. In a charmless monotone, she made her announcements.

"There is a very refined and intellectual air about you . . ."

Claire, initially anxious, perked up.

"You create harmony wherever you go; people are calmed."

Claire smiled.

"You have a cluster of healing and learning planets in Aries. This is the sign of the explorer. It is the opposite of your rising moon. Libra is partnership; it is something you haven't had. You yearn for it."

Claire nodded.

"You have an inquisitive mind. Your journey will be exciting."

"Oh," Claire said. With Ethan's words in her head, she seized on "journey."

"Your health will be good."

Claire scratched her nose.

"And this is a time for you to focus on work."

Claire paused to consider.

"How old are you?" Beatrice asked. It made Claire slightly suspicious—shouldn't Beatrice already *know*?

"Thirty-two."

"What day were you born?"

"Wednesday. May fourth." Beatrice examined her for an unsettling amount of time before she went on.

"This year you will focus on work. You won't find love."

Beatrice looked up and Claire looked down, at her leathery palm. She arched a brow. "Are you sure? I might just need lotion."

"A parade of silver-tongued charlatans and seducers will flatter you; you'll fall prey to one of them. Like the circles of Dante's hell, there will be all types. There will be gluttonous men and violent men and angry and lustful men. What you will not have is love. Not for one year. You are vulnerable to vanity, so beware. Your husband was an egotistical man, and just as the fly returns again and again to the web in spite of certain doom, you sense safety and warmth where you shouldn't."

Beatrice paused and cocked her head as if she heard an unfamiliar noise, then she went on.

"Your work will flourish. You will emerge from a chrysalis and derive satisfaction as a result. You will write this book they are talking about, but you will not write it the way they think."

Claire gasped. Even if Beatrice had seen the gossip in the *Post*, that was still quite a leap.

"Now," Beatrice said, lowering her voice. "I see someone in fuchsia. A close friend. She is taking unnecessary risks."

Sasha, Claire thought. *Only Sasha would wear fuchsia.*

"And a man in a black suit . . . I have not a good vibration, but not entirely bad. A man in a black suit will come into your life and impact it in some way."

Claire considered this. A lot of men wore black suits.

"Still," Beatrice said, as if it needed repeating, "no love for one year."

"Why not?" Claire asked.

"I don't make the rules."

RULE #4: When in doubt, make your own rule.

Claire thought for a moment. "What happens in a year?"

Beatrice's lids lowered and grew hoods like a cobra. "One year."

8

CLAIRE'S MEETING WITH BEATRICE LEFT HER DIS-
turbed. The widow was restless.

Ethan came to dinner on Sunday wearing fur and bearing gifts.
"Pickled vegetables," he said, waving his hand across the jars.
"Cauliflower, cabbage, carrots."

"Why do they all start with C?" Claire asked.

"They're good for you. They're fermented. It's cleansing," he
said. "I drink a shot glass of brine every day."

He arranged an elaborate display on a platter and popped a
dish in the oven.

Claire turned the television on. Ethan went down to Charlie's
office.

"How's all that coming, by the way?" she asked.

He poked his head out the door. "Well, it's not boring. Listen to
this: How do male porcupines hit on female porcupines?"

Claire raised a brow. "I don't know. How?"

"They urinate," he said. "The male urinates on the female, and if she likes him she lets him keep going, keep peeing on her, I mean. If she doesn't like him, she fights back."

"That's very sweet," said Claire.

"It is sweet; it's utterly intimate. We get hung up on our own fears about sex for no good reason. One species' urine is another one's whipped cream."

Claire crunched a piece of pickled cauliflower. "What's for dinner?" she asked.

"Chicken marbella."

"What are you reading?"

Ethan waved a sheaf of papers. "A file of notes on animals. Male garter snakes have two penises, by the way, one on each side of their body. I'm so jealous."

"That must be why cheating men are called snakes. You didn't ask me about Beatrice."

"Shh!" Ethan said. "Rule number one: you never talk about Beatrice! Rule number two: don't talk about Beatrice!"

"Oh, come on. She said something about the book. Isn't that weird? She said I'd write it. I can't imagine." Claire made a face.

She thought about Charlie and his strange passions. He was passionate about many things, but it was comfort, not passion, he felt toward Claire. While Claire wanted to believe that combinations exist, of man and woman or man and man or woman and woman, that can satisfy both sexual desire and love, Charlie refused to entertain such a notion. To him, it was completely absurd.

"Ethan, do you think love and sex are incompatible?"

He walked down the hall and sat next to her on the couch. "I think they're inconveniently tangled up."

"Is that the same thing?"

He popped a pickled bean in his mouth.

"Are you angry with him?" he asked.

"Who, Charlie? About what?"

He waved a hand around in the air. "The other women. All the . . ." He trailed off.

She was silent for a few moments. "They're ugly," she said finally. "Have you ever seen one? I don't get the fuss."

"Have I seen what?"

"A Giacometti. They're bony and protruding."

"I saw the photo in the paper."

"The surrealists were obsessed with sex. They thought monogamy was bourgeois." Claire pronounced the French word slowly, dropping the last syllable—*boor-zhwah*. "They took the penis, in and of itself, much too seriously."

"Not possible!" Ethan said, feigning horror.

Claire smiled. "Anyway, Charlie could screw circles around them—not with me, necessarily, but in general. He was adventurous, let's say. He lived what he wrote. I knew that when I married him." She thought about the end of affection—when does it stop and why? She thought about women who grow contempt for their husbands but love their children no matter what. Sisters who dote on brothers, in spite of the same troublesome tics they find insurmountable in lovers—clothes strewn about, carelessness with food, televised sports for hours on end. She thought about the mercurial nature of art, the wasted talent of forgery artists, how they never receive due acclaim. She thought of Sande, Walter White's lover, who was perhaps living out the last days of her own dwindling fame. She wouldn't think of Charlie's pre-mortem screw. The intercom buzzed and startled her. Before Claire could speak, Ethan jumped up to let in the delivery man and paid him in cash—leafy greens, bright-colored fruits, fatty sardines, and, as a concession to Claire, Diet Coke.

"Food is therapy," he said. "You need supplies."

"I've never heard that."

"Well, maybe it's not, but you're turning into one of those skinny little sculptures yourself. Charlie always had food here. It's comforting. And listen, no one can know what really goes on inside a marriage, but for what it's worth, from what I could see, Charlie's love for you was real. It was as true as he was capable of, and that's no small thing."

"Beatrice said I'm going to have gluttonous men." As she said this, Claire eyed Ethan suspiciously. All he talked about anymore was food. "Also a man in a black suit plays a role, and there might be someone violent." She recalled how angry Richard had been on the phone.

"Honey, that is between you and the divine."

"She made it sound like I'm going to sleep around. She mentioned a lot of men."

"I'm not listening."

"And Sasha in a fuchsia dress."

"Don't say one more word, Clarabelle, I mean it."

"But no love." Ethan covered his ears and started to hum.

"Okay, I get it."

They watched the end of an old movie together, and when Claire fell asleep, Ethan let himself out. She woke up to a jar of pickle juice by her bed.

9

SASHA WAS APPALLED, NATURALLY, WHEN SHE FOUND out Claire had gone to Beatrice. She hadn't been consulted, no one had pleaded she come along, she hadn't been asked for her post-reading dissection. In the classic chic of her uptown sitting room, she scoffed.

"First, Claire, you never answer your phone, so people are worried about you. Second, everyone thinks you're hiding because maybe you've run out of money. Third, no one goes to Beatrice anymore—she's a carnival act. She hustles tourists, she hands her card out at the Empire State Building."

"I'm not hiding, I have money, and Beatrice said I would meet a lot of men . . . charlatans or something, but not have love. I think it was just because I brought socks instead of a picture."

"No one sees a psychic anymore, is all I'm saying."

"She seemed to know what she was doing."

"I just wish you'd talked to me, honey. Ethan doesn't know everything; I have someone, too."

She handed Claire a black card with white print. It smelled of musk oil.

"This is Eve, she's my botanomanist. She saged Thom's office and the apartment after that little thing with his *personal assistant*—the most ironic title ever—and our energy completely changed. But that's not her forte, she's the real thing. She's not a kook."

"How did your energy change?"

"The apartment is turmoil-free now," she said, though her smile wobbled. "Go ahead, take a deep breath, you'll smell it."

Claire took a breath and nodded, though she smelled neither turmoil nor calm.

Sasha took a long, deep breath, too, and waved her arms through the air. "The lack of tension is palpable. Anyway, her first husband died, so she was a widow once. She's perfect."

Ethan said divination. He said soothsayers and seers. How could one botanomanist hurt?

EVE LIVED AND herbed in a railroad-style apartment in Brooklyn. It had a markedly different feel than Beatrice's stark uptown space. She was a small, thick woman. *Squat* was the word Charlie would have used. She answered the door in a black pantsuit with a bright Hermès scarf on her head and, after "Hello," had little to say. She gestured for Claire to follow her and walked down a long hallway into a large, open room. There were comfortable chairs around a table and there was an orange bowl set out on top. A furry white cat curled up in the window like a pom-pom.

She filled the bowl with rosemary stalks and a handful of sage leaves, then lit the strange little pile with a white lighter adorned with the face of Ringo Starr. "Do you like the Beatles?" Claire asked.

"Not especially," Eve replied. "It was a gift."

She added cannabis leaves to the fire, and the space took on a completely different feel. The smoke blurred the shapes in the room. Claire sat down across from a red Rothko that hung on the wall—unsigned, a knockoff—and wondered if all art is ultimately fake.

Eve moved the rubble around with a cocktail stirrer.

"A friend of mine," Claire began.

Eve put a hand up and shook her head. "Not yet. Don't speak. What I see is that what was once a carefully structured life for you has come loose; it's why you're here. The thread has unraveled, the hem has come apart, and you're not a seamstress."

Claire nodded her head in agreement. She was definitely not a seamstress.

"You need help to smooth the ends. It's definition you lack, and proper nutrition."

Eve unfavorably appraised the small body sitting across from her, and Claire was uncomfortably aware of the few pounds, yes, that she'd lost since returning from Texas to find Charlie dead.

"Well, I eat, it's just that . . . I'm a slight woman, I'm small-boned—"

Eve's hand, again, rose up and she went on. "The masses are shocked, you'll learn, if you haven't discovered it already," she said, while still stirring, "to find that marriages interrupted by death were ordinary ones, the same as their own. Good, bad, boring—at best, manageable."

"Right," Claire said. Eve added more cannabis. She looked Claire straight in her hazel-blue, sometimes hazel-brown eyes. "We mythologize. We have odd ways of coping with death, such as it is—a mundane and natural piece of the life cycle. Think of the phrase 'Don't speak ill of the dead.' We don't subject the dead to any sort of postmortem analysis at all. They become common property. There is no longer a marriage that is yours and your husband's to define and engage in and present versions of, there's no private relationship or collaboration between the two of you anymore, because now it's just you. There's a narrative that everyone is free to contribute to. It's supposed to be a pleasant one. It will drag you along."

"I don't know . . . I haven't thought about it so much."

"The stories people buy, Kate, are fairy tales. The man is handsome and empathetic, and the good-hearted hooker can have him; he'll treat her well. True Love. Never-Ending Lasting Love. Lifetime Channel, Frank Sinatra, Michael Bublé, Jen-and-Brad heartthrob love. When death ends a marriage, it interrupts the same petty hatreds and grievances and withholdings of affection that plague every coupling. Death never comes in the respites where everything is, for the briefest bit, resolved. It doesn't come in those rare moments when you have the sense that all is calm and understood."

Eve continued to stir ash.

"Truth gives way to story and there's little to be done about it. You're not allowed, you know this, Kat—"

"It's Claire, actually . . ."

"—to not be grievously wounded by the death of a man, a partner, whom you may or may not have loved. You're not allowed to be ambivalent. You're not allowed to move on. Now you're burdened with a title—you're a widow. You're allowed to be undone by the loss. You can be sexual—the color black is seductive, no accident—but can't have sex. It's your virginity all over again, but worse. You're best off losing it with a stranger and out of town."

Claire was stunned. "That's what Charlie said! About the

virginity. He had this theory that women experience multiple virginities in a lifetime, and for men, collecting them is some sort of glorious pursuit—like finding whole black truffles, or a case of 1963 Montrachet. He said that to get a woman at one of her virginal milestones was like getting high on the Empire State Building with Keith Richards—an intoxicating, unforgettable moment in time."

Eve's eyebrow rose. "Did he get high with Keith Richards?"

"I don't know. He certainly got some virginal milestones, though."

Eve stopped stirring. The cat twitched its tail. A handful of thick raindrops rattled the window.

"What is it? What?"

"Your sage doesn't look good," Eve said.

"No! What does that mean?"

"Sage is the symbol of love and relationships. What I see here is a struggle."

"No, that's wrong, that can't be, there's no struggle. Look at the rosemary. Add more pot."

Eve gently laid the small stick against the side of the bowl.

Claire shifted in her chair. Eve's scarf, what had first impressed her as a striking taste in accessories, had become unsettling. Its orbs and bulbs and embryo-shaped colors, spooning against each other, swimming the perimeter of Eve's clavicle, disturbed her. It was entirely too quiet in the room. She cleared her throat.

Eve smiled.

"My advice, Katherine? Focus on work."

10

THE READING OF CHARLIE'S WILL WAS ANTICLIMACTIC, despite the delay. Besides Claire and Richard and Charlie's lawyer, there was Ethan, and then Grace on the speaker. They gathered in Richard's office the first week of September, just over two months since the day Charlie had died.

Charlie wasn't a particularly complicated man; all of the assets went to Claire.

His final manuscript, incomplete at his death, the one Ethan was now trying to assemble from eight different files he'd uncovered, also went to Claire.

"In the event that my demise happens in the midst of my work, I bequeath all unfinished, unsold texts to my wife. She will write, edit, and annotate as she sees fit, to ready such work for sale through my longtime, long-suffering agent and son-of-a-bitch Richard Ashe." Before Claire had a chance to react, through the speakerphone came Grace's cough. "Richard?"

"Yes, Grace. Right here."

"What does this mean? How much work is there unfinished, unsold? Where is there work?"

Claire looked from Ethan to Richard. Richard looked from Ethan to Claire. She doubted Grace Byrne had read the *Post*.

"Well, there's a book he was working on, Grace. We're not sure yet what stage it's in. There is a manuscript, some papers, some loose things here and there. Ethan is going through documents and files, and will have an accurate assessment for us soon."

"And when is soon, Richard?" Grace asked. Molly and Morton, her large mastiffs, a gift years ago from Charlie and Claire, barked, and Grace admonished them.

"We'll have an accurate assessment one month from today."

The lawyer, dogs, and Grace all departed in succession, leaving Ethan and Claire facing Richard across the room.

"Well, Clarey," Richard said, in an attempt to make the afternoon feel light. "One thing you might do, while you're cooling your heels, is read up on Huxley." With dramatic flair, he plopped his legs atop his desk, leaned back in his chair, and threw his hands behind his head as he watched this sink in.

"What? Why? Aldous Huxley?" she asked.

"Nope," Richard answered, then waited two long beats. "Jack."

Claire looked at Richard and tilted her head the way dogs do, to better hear.

"Charlie was writing a book about Jack Huxley?"

Ethan typed the name into the search engine on his phone and turned it theatrically around to display the infamous face.

"Why?" she asked.

"Why not? He's practically the international symbol for sex."

Is this a joke? Claire thought, mentally booking her plane ticket to Hollywood. Then she almost laughed out loud. Her dead husband had just set her up with Jack Huxley—indecently handsome, movie star, rogue. Charlie was writing a book about narcissism and sex, about himself really, by way of the most famous baller in the world.

11

B Y AUTUMN THE STORIES OF SUMMER HAD SIMMERED down. The names and faces that had riveted the media three short months before had gone stale. Bigger and better scandals had popped up. Celebrities tried to sneak off to rehab, politicians were in violation of the law, Oprah had lost then gained back thirty pounds. The bit players of the Charles Byrne Show had faded to black. Evelyn and Walter White resumed their position on the style pages of the *Times* as if nothing had happened, smiling again at all the galas. The yogi had got a small part in a movie and was dating an outfielder for the Mets. The publicist, Claire had heard, Charlie's last pre-mortem stand, was screwing an editor at *Vanity Fair*, good for her. And the father-son art cons lingered comfortably in house arrest, awaiting a trial years off, their days filled peacefully with chess games and small meals. Paul Bowman, whose eyewitness account of the falling fake had briefly gone viral, was served divorce papers by his wife, who made great use of the anecdotal material anyway. Her colleagues at Rutgers ate it up. It put her, after all, two degrees from both Giacometti and Charles Byrne. Paul Bowman, with his brief, newly found notoriety, was dating a stripper.

RULE #5: Don't sweat it—everyone's fucked up.

The path of Claire's own life, however, was much less clear.

Focus on work, said the seers. She thought about what they'd told her. Beatrice had said in so many words that there'd be sex but no love—ha, it was so Charlie. There was time to kill, and enough money, she didn't really have to do anything. There was a will, but no law, that said she had to finish Charlie's book. She was comfortably idle; it's the ruin of some.

In lieu of a plan, she went to dinner. After three months of moping around, Claire thought it time to get out.

Since the day of Charlie's funeral there'd been a steady stream of invitations: a life that was beckoning her, whether she was ready for it or not. However, it wasn't just Charlie's life that had ended. It was Claire-and-Charlie's life, too—the one they'd strung up together, the one where people counted on him and her, but not just her. There was no longer that. Now there was this. Friends knew they were to do something with Claire, you don't abandon the young widow, but they weren't sure just what. Their own routines were the same, but Claire's had changed. How did they approach this? Could she get around by herself? Were they to avoid certain topics? Could she be seated next to a man—yes, she'd need to be!—but whom? There are never enough good single gay men to go around.

New York needed Claire to be the way she was before— essentially, married. The situation only slowly dawned on her. Invitations piled up, as if widows were in high demand and Claire was a coup for the guest list. She could have had any room at any weekend house in the Hamptons. There were invitations to join book groups, to attend cocktail and dinner parties, to sit at overpriced tables at charity functions—even one at Princeton, which Claire assumed came via Grace, still after her to "honor Charlie's name."

The one she finally accepted, to rejoin the fray, as it were, was on the Upper East Side at the Starks'. Melanie was a real estate agent with a knack for leveraging divorce properties. Howard was a lawyer. The Starks and the Byrnes had been friendly. They'd gone to dinner a few times a year, and they were in the same social circles. Charlie and Howard played tennis at the club. Claire and Melanie had been at NYU at the same time. Melanie was filthy rich and sweetly wholesome. She'd had a schoolgirl crush on Charlie. She liked having an intellectual—a randy one at that—to round out her table. They'd had a harmless flirtation, as did Claire and Howard, for that matter; it was balanced. With four of them together, they'd kept everything in check. Facing the Starks alone, Claire was anxious. She agonized over her outfit ("Black, honey," Sasha said. "What do you think everyone else will be wearing?"). She decided on charcoal, a jersey knit dress with a thin red belt to deflect any mourning.

It was a long ride uptown.

"Claire!" Howard called out when she came through the door. He parted mingling guests, kissed her hard on both cheeks, and took her coat. "You're just in time—we're about to seat." He squeezed her hand. "We haven't seen you since the funeral. How have you been, sweetheart?"

Melanie popped up out of nowhere at his side. "Claire!" she squealed. She looked unnaturally straight in five-inch heels that made her a head taller than Howard. "How are you, honey? You look ravishing."

Claire smiled, nervously. She was suspicious of words like *ravishing* or *stunning*. She touched her face, checking for flaws, discreetly glanced at her chest. Something felt off.

Melanie gave Howard an odd look and squeezed his elbow. "Honey, would you check with the caterer. Make sure we're ready for the first course?"

As Howard walked away, Melanie snatched Claire's arm. "So listen," she whispered, "I have a client here. And he's wonderful. He's *very* successful. An architect, he did a gorgeous museum in Berlin. And, guess what?"

Claire smiled and shrugged.

"His wife just died!"

Melanie was grinning at Claire with big, thrilled, round eyes.

Claire felt her own eyes contract in return. "Oh, wow . . . that's awful."

"Sweetie, he's so darling and charming and I think you're *very* compatible."

Claire's head twitched a little. What? *Compatible?* "You do?"

"His name is Brian!" Melanie's teeth were bright and square and her eyes looked like gel paint. She was too close, too vivid. Her face was making Claire dizzy. "I thought about you two when she was still alive, to be honest. It isn't something that just popped into my head."

"You mean when . . . Charlie was alive?"

"Well, no, I don't mean that. You know what I mean. After."

Claire's vision blurred a little. The room got big, then small, then big again. She felt ambushed. Oh my God, she thought . . . *Is this how it's done? Like Go Fish—do you have any single men? No. Guess again. Do you have any widowers? Yes.* Melanie seemed so sincerely enthused. Claire did her best to smile back.

"So I've put you next to each other, and I'll let him tell you about himself over dinner. He's very, *very* successful, I said that, right? Oh, and he's *Jewish.*" Melanie mouthed the word *Jewish.* "And I don't think he really loved his wife, by the way. She was *sick.*" She mouthed "sick," too. "But he's a good *man.*" For some inexplicable reason, Melanie also mouthed *man* and then mouthed one last word, as a coda—*rich.*

Seconds away from her first fix-up in ten years, Claire panicked. What would she talk about?

Brian, I hear your wife's dead. That's a drag.

"Melanie, this is really thoughtful of you, but . . ."

"I *know*, honey. Girls look out for each other." Melanie winked. "Come on, let's meet your date." Melanie took Claire's hand and led her down the hall into the dining room.

Brian's wife hadn't been sick, it turned out, she'd been old. Like Brian. She was dead from old age. Soon Brian would be, too. The last time he'd seen blueprints, Claire estimated, she was going to junior prom. They compared funerals over the risotto. Brian had used Wanamaker and Sons, too, and yes, he remembered Carter, a very competent young man. Claire didn't tell Brian about her smelling salts, or Sasha's flask, or the way Carter's thighs had looked pressed smooth against his slacks.

They spent most of the osso buco course talking about Brian's dead wife: how they met in college, the summer in Europe before Ann got pregnant, their beach house on the Cape with the children and now the grandchildren. Ann's lobster salads, impromptu game nights, and gin fizzes at the club. The crab bakes, the anniversaries in Paris, their favorite bistro on la rue Saint-Marc with the steak au poivre and Veuve Clicquot. Claire found herself consoling him.

She patted his hand, like a child. *Oh my God, what was Melanie thinking?*

When they'd moved on to another room and digestifs—an apple brandy Claire could barely choke down—a woman interrupted the banal small talk between Claire and the woman's husband with a frosty glance and an urgent matter. Left alone, Claire checked the front of her dress again. Again, she touched her face. What the hell was going on? The same thing happened with another couple across the room. Claire recognized the same wary glance Melanie had given Howard.

They were frightened of her, she realized. They'd only known her to be attached—to Charlie. Now that she was single, and vulnerable, there was a slight shift in attention. Husbands lingered; they hovered too long. Their wives perceived this. She was a threat.

She tested out her theory at a charity cocktail party the following week, and at a gallery opening the week after that—different social circles, different attendees, all people she and Charlie had known, and the same protective response. She felt like a circus animal—everyone wanted a look, but women kept the men carefully out of reach.

Did divorcées go through this? she wondered. She suspected they didn't. Divorce came with baggage, the presumption of issues; a mess. Husbands weren't as interested in what another man walked away from so much as they were in what he unwillingly left behind.

So this is what she was faced with. Interactions laced with either suspicion or pity. There were awkward crossings with people who—unbelievably—did not know her news. "Claire! Great to see you. How've you guys been?" *Oh, I'm not too bad, thanks. But*

Charlie's dead. And there were chance encounters with people who hadn't seen her since the funeral and felt obligated, still, to mourn. The latter involved limp hugs and watery eyes, and usually happened as Claire engaged in the most banal of tasks—sorting through the olive bar at Whole Foods, for instance, or buying tampons at the Korean deli. They used a special tone; they placed careful hands on her forearm. "Oh, Claire, sweetie, how *are* you?"

"Did you love him, then?" asked Lowenstein during one of their sessions.

Love had seemed beside the point. They both knew there was a certain absurdity in the question, not to mention a range of possibilities.

Claire replied, "I think so."

Franz Kafka lusted for his fiancée's best friend, Grete. No one disputes this. Grete's claims, however, that he fathered her son were inconclusive; Kafka wouldn't come clean. There is love and there is sex, and there is some confusion surrounding the two. There are panderers and seducers and men who are vain. There is always, somewhere, a woman in fuchsia courting danger.

"Claire, did you love your husband?"

"Well, I'd become very used to him," Claire said. "And that's something."

12

C LAIRE WEIGHED HER OPTIONS.
    She could follow in the footsteps of the Mailer and Roth wives and write a memoir. She could say Charlie was lousy in bed—they'd line up for blocks to read that. There was his unfinished book, of course: a manuscript that would eventually, Richard hoped, become a posthumous bestseller. She could pick up freelance work again—interview actresses in Los Angeles for *Misconstrued*. It might be nice to get away. She could even write her own book. Why not? One afternoon with a file of notes and a laptop beneath her arm, Claire poured an iced tea and got comfortable in a chair. She had a pile of Charlie's old reviews, excerpts from his books, and the pieces Ethan had found of his new one. Jack Huxley.

    A Google search turned up predictable results. There he was with movie directors, with the president, with his costar on the red carpet at the Oscars. He looked unnaturally self-possessed. Thick hair, boyish grin, dark eyes. There were countless photographs of him with the same girl, this one a blonde, this one a brunette, all of them bikini-toned, long-legged Barbie doll–shaped things, all coached for the camera, clutching his hand like little girls. She understood why Charlie had been intrigued. Like Jack Huxley's, Charlie's ambling prick was at least as famous, if not more so, as his body of work. And he was at least equally proud of it. No doubt her husband had admired the man. Huxley was the kind of guy's guy whom other men could be enthralled with. Good-looking bastard, they might say, and shake their heads approvingly. He was the kind of guy's guy men would be flattered to have sleep with their wives. He was the kind of man both women and children adore, and the kind who is careless with both.

Claire hadn't seen many of his films—though, thumbing through a stack of Charlie's old reviews, she realized she didn't know much of her own husband's work, either. She'd always been unimpressed with *Thinker's Hope*. She'd secretly agreed with Ben Hawthorne: it should have been a flop. The public sometimes flocked to Charlie's books the way they flocked to NR movies, more for the graphic sexual nature than the artistic or narrative quality. But Hawthorne was the only critic to point it out.

In fact, his 723-word review of the book's 723 pages had created a buzz in literary and academic circles, two otherwise dull and isolated communities. Writers spend the better part of their years indoors and alone, or indoors in the same small groups. They live for the occasional scandal—when the poet Elizabeth Dewberry left her Pulitzer Prize–winning novelist husband for a media mogul. Or when Ben Hawthorne ruthlessly skewered Charlie Byrne's *Thinker's Hope* on its tenth-anniversary re-release. Reading Hawthorne's review again now, Claire smiled, impressed. Cute and scruffy Ben Hawthorne had taken on a giant:

Goats and Goethe: Byrne Lost Me at Hello

BEN HAWTHORNE

Charles Byrne's *Thinker's Hope* might have the distinction of being the most ridiculous publication ever reviewed in these pages. Were we at *The Atlantic Monthly* to give serious treatment to a Zsa Zsa Gabor advice book on marriage, it would be no less ludicrous than to assign this salaried staffer to pick up, open, and then fix his eyes upon the first of over 230,000 words, not one of them of much use. Here are otherwise perfectly good words that Mr. Byrne has arranged into a pretentious and unintelligible shape called *Thinker's Hope.*

Mr. Byrne's intent—according to material his publisher sent with the book—was this: to write "an intellectual novel, a work that is both witty and wry and sends up some of the world's greatest thinking men, and great artists, and all of their central philosophies." At the same time, he promised to offer a "frank sexual portrait of the common man, with all of his predicaments and peccadilloes."

Let's start with scene and setting. The story opens in a brothel-cum-massage parlor, circa 1999. The Madam proprietor is Fortuna, a Roman Goddess. She's ancient, but we know the time is contemporary because she's wearing Guess jeans and the artist who was then known as Prince is playing from a boom box. The Goddess turned Madame wanders languidly about the grounds in jeans and black bustier and at this point in the narrative we should be bowled over by the literary brilliance of Mr. Byrne. The Goddess of Fate, in designer jeans, prancing around in 1999 as Prince sings that year's titled track. Great stuff!

The patrons of our modern medieval whorehouse are mostly artists and philosophers, few of whom were alive at the same time—Schopenhauer, Kant, Hegel each make an appearance, as do Matisse, Damien Hirst, and Matthew Barney, which gives Byrne the opportunity to drop the term "Cremaster" repeatedly. It is a reference that is neither original nor fun nor anything that most readers—assuming there are some—are likely to get. It is one of many such references designed to stroke Mr. Byrne's cerebral ego but add nothing to his text. Aside from Fortuna, there are no women in the whorehouse, only caricatured glory holes (among them, Margaret Thatcher and Elizabeth Taylor) and an assembly of clean-scrubbed farm animals.

There. I've just alluded to the only interesting thing in the 723 pages—that Schopenhauer's love is a goat. There is nothing else, really, to say. This is Harold Robbins on a long-winded creative writing assignment—it's staggering, self-abusive, unrestrained. It's Byrnes's *Story of O*, written not to a lover, but to himself. Reading it feels like getting left alone with the bar drunk at 2 a.m., so your friend can get the phone number of the only girl.

This should be the end of my review; anything more than this and you'll be terrifically bored. It would insult you to go on, in the same way that Charles Byrne goes on, and on, oblivious to the value of his reader's time. He might have, more considerately, ended his tale at the bottom of page 232 (a suggestion perhaps too generous to his prose). But there was space to fill up, empty pages. To fill them is the order of the day, and so in that vein I've got (here, right now) 297 more words of this review to go. Soon 289. And my apologies if you're still reading.

There'd been a night at the Quill Awards shortly after the *Atlantic*'s review (Charlie was presenting) when Claire had inadvertently struck up a conversation with Mr. Hawthorne, who was wearing the sort of end-of-summer tan and beach-tossed hair that inspired Slim Aarons books. "You know, I read 'Hustling Woody,'" he said, and she forgot to remember he was an enemy. "I loved it. It was very good." They'd shared a polite but friendly laugh. "Are you working on a book?"

"Oh, I don't know, not really." She'd looked down as she said this, moved her foot in short arcs on the floor, and then she'd looked up, her mouth beginning to form words she instantly forgot when her eyes met Charlie's across the room.

They went home and he didn't speak to her for three days. It was understood, in the Byrne house, that there was their version of a fatwa on the critic's head. Claire had egregiously crossed the line.

Claire had put down *Thinker's Hope* at the exact same page cited by Hawthorne, the middle of 232, interrupting a painfully long dialogue between Hannah Arendt and Albert Schweitzer on the sensual possibilities of Brie. She'd made heroic attempts to finish, skipped ahead, started fresh on the introduction of Kant walking into a pub and promptly banging the busty Irish lass on a bar stool, from the front and then the back as two farmers discussed their potato crop undeterred. Charlie's erotica, Claire had to admit, packed a punch. But there was something blowsy about the rest.

A week after the funeral, she'd taken a worn copy from Charlie's nightstand drawer. She thought rereading it would be a nice gesture. She turned to where she'd left off before they'd married. Chapter 13: "Sartre and the Horny Mikmaid."

"To exist is to scatter one's seed across field and ocean; across continents and brambles, over the knotted topcoat of the Redwoods, or onto the crinkled fabric of yellowed bed sheets."

By the bottom of the page, she fell asleep.

With Charlie spying on her from God-knows-where, with his posthumous endorsement (he certainly never imagined he'd die! Had he written that in his will as a prank?) She was charged with his book, his last one. Claire felt a responsibility.

"Jack Huxley and the Art of the Narcissist" was, so far, a loose group of pages marked up with notes. There were countless references to mythology, of course. Charlie never met a god—including himself—he didn't like. Narcissus was here, and Tiresias, the incurable voyeur who was changed into a woman. The pages were part biography, part fiction, part psychosexual pseudofantasy.

That it was a biography, of sorts, from one of the world's most egotistical men about one of the world's others, was the jig; Charlie's little wink. Claire was beginning to feel the whole damn thing a setup.

She clicked on an image of Huxley to make it bigger. His head was cocked, angled down. He was looking at nothing particular but seemed amused, like someone in on a clever inside joke.

Charlie's infamous book had sold over five million copies worldwide in its first edition, and over twenty million copies to date. He considered it a serious work, but it was titillating enough to find its way into every cocktail conversation from Beverly Hills to East Hampton for a better part of the '90s. Had Jack Huxley skimmed it? Claire suspected he had.

RULE #6: Sometimes a dream is just a dream.

Claire woke the next morning with an epiphany. She rushed breathlessly to Lowenstein. She arrived early and twitched impatiently in the waiting room for her appointment. She'd had a vivid dream and she'd written it down. More important, it wasn't the first time that she'd had it.

"Go ahead, then," the doctor said.

"Okay, this is a recurring one." Claire knew that Lowenstein liked those. "I've never mentioned it, but I used to dream it when Charlie was alive."

"Okay, go on."

Claire took a breath and closed her eyes. "I'm a bug and Charlie sits on me at dinner."

"Where are you?"

"At someone's house."

"Whose house?"

"The Spencers'. Wilt and Sherry. They have bad art and an orange Eames chair that no one ever sits in. Charlie hated their apartment. Anyway, that's not important."

"I don't agree, but go on."

"He sits on me and I'm helpless. Trapped. Under this unending swath of corduroy."

"Did Charlie wear corduroy?"

"Never. But in the dream it's clearly corduroy; there are wales."

"Go on."

"I'm pinned to the chair. No air, no light, though I can hear them all talking. I'm praying he'll need to relieve himself and get up. But time goes on and on and I can't move and I'm forced to listen to all of it for hours. There's no chance to excuse myself, or breathe, or rub an elbow distractedly or even scratch an itch."

"You said this is a recurring dream. How long have you been having it?"

"Well, I used to have it when he was alive, like I said. And I'm not just any bug, I'm a green leaf beetle. Have you seen one?"

"No. But I assume they're green?"

"Yes, they are. They blend. I always blend too perfectly with the upholstery, so I'm never noticed, and he sits on me every time. I'm always perched delicately on the chair as though I've just got there, just landed and am taking the room in, when the solid square mass of Charlie descends. This is awful, it makes it sound like I hate him."

"You felt trapped by him."

Claire picked at a nail.

"Charlie is always the guest of honor in this dream, and his is the only voice I can make out, that's the other thing. I can't hear any other voices clearly, only his, in loud barreling echoes."

"You felt suppressed by him, overshadowed."

"I don't know. I guess maybe I did," Claire said.

"It's not unusual, you married very young."

She watched the second hand on Lowenstein's wall clock tick by.

"Dr. Jung says dreams are an expression of your *current* condition, not a preexisting one. So you *still* feel suppressed by Charlie. Even in death, you can't escape him. You're still overpowered by him to an extreme—you've painted a harrowing account of claustrophobia—one that leaves me, just listening to you, struggling a bit for air."

"You know what I hated sometimes, about most of the social things we went to?" Claire pushed loose hair back from her face.

"Tell me," Lowenstein said.

"No one laughed."

Lowenstein scribbled something down.

"They were stern, or cold?"

"I mean, they just didn't sincerely laugh. There were ironies or intellectual inside cracks that required a familiarity with Nietzsche or somebody's blue phase or Kierkegaard's concept of despair. These were not met with laughter, but instead more of a bark."

"You thought them insincere perhaps."

"I miss real laughter. No one laughs anymore. You know, where it's uncontrollable and sometimes brings tears. Richard's girlfriend, Bridget, laughs sometimes, but I think it's a nervous tic. Sasha's had too many injections to laugh, and Ethan thinks it's a weakness of character. Real laughter explodes without warning, like a sneeze."

Claire produced a magazine from her handbag, a copy of *OK!* with Jack Huxley on the cover. He was wearing a blue sweater and jeans, walking on a sidewalk in New York. His head was down and under a baseball cap, but not so far that you missed the trademark smirk. A four-page spread in the middle addressed the simultaneous claims on his sperm by three different women—a young actress, a dancer, and a makeup artist, in no special order.

"This is who Charlie was writing about," Claire said. "This was the work in progress when he died."

The doctor studied the pictures for an unusually long time. Claire thought she saw her smile. But she handed it back straight-faced.

"You know who Jack Huxley is, right?"

"Yes, I've heard of him," Lowenstein replied. "Why are you showing me this?"

Claire regarded her curiously. Lowenstein looked away; she wiggled her pencil, she pressed a finger to her lip.

"Because Richard just gave me the manuscript, the one Charlie was working on. He wants me to . . . well, finish it. Charlie stipulated in his will that if anything should happen to him I would be responsible for any unfinished work."

After an unnaturally long pause, Lowenstein spoke.

"Let's not be trivial about this," she said. "That is a huge commitment."

She cleared her throat, then continued. Her voice had raised in pitch. "You didn't know what he was working on, then?"

"I wasn't interested. And Charlie never brought his work home. So, no."

Lowenstein set her pen and notebook on her desk and assessed the pictures in Claire's lap. "That is a profoundly attractive man," Lowenstein said. Then she took up her pen again and wrote something down.

13

SEE, THIS IS WHAT I MEAN!" CLAIRE WAVED SUNDAY'S *New York Times* Style section at Ethan.

They were eating brunch and sharing the paper at Pastis. October had dawned cool and rainy, as if to emphasize that time kept moving, even when people were stuck. "Did you read Modern Love?" Claire asked.

"No, honey. It's hard for me to read it when you have it," Ethan said.

"It's from a widower. Five hundred sappy words on why he's already sleeping with someone four months after his wife died. *I needed the distraction. She would've wanted it that way.* Are we supposed to believe his wife wanted him screwing around four months later, and that she'd be happy for him? I'll tell you something, it's not like that on my side."

Ethan took a slow drink of his coffee.

"Did I tell you Melanie Stark fixed me up?"

"No, you didn't. I hope he was rich." He was reading the

Sunday Magazine. A quick glance at the article revealed none other than Charlie's muse: "Huxleys in Hollywood: Then and Now."

"There must be a movie coming out."

Ethan whistled low and shook his head. "That is one pretty man."

"Anyway, yes, he was rich, Melanie's setup. He was also seventy and widowed."

Ethan was scanning the Huxley article.

"May I remind you that I am thirty-two? That's too young for seventy," Claire said, loud enough to make the man two tables over glance their way. "What? You've never heard a woman raise her voice?" Claire snapped at him.

"Whoa, whoa, whoa, honey," Ethan said. He put the paper down.

"My point is that this guy was *old* and widowed less than *two* months and he's getting fixed up with *me.* A husband dies and the world gets just another widow. A wife dies, and a star is born."

"That's catchy."

"Seriously, Ethan." Claire crossed, then uncrossed her legs.

"Okay. Does it bother you?" Ethan asked.

"Yes, it does. There's no protocol for men. It's like breaking up: they're just single again, suddenly, and they run back out and fool around. I mean, what about Scout's dad in *To Kill a Mockingbird*— what was his name?"

"Atticus."

"Right, Atticus. He didn't start hitting on Scout's teacher right after his wife died. He stayed sober and serious. He made his children his focus, not getting laid. This Modern Love guy has a seven-year-old daughter. Can't he just watch porn like everyone else? It's pathetic."

"What's pathetic? That he's in a relationship, and you're not?"

"No. That's not . . . no. It's this ruse of doing it for his wife. He says she told him, 'If I die, I don't want you to be unhappy the rest of your life,' then says she added jokingly, 'just for a couple years.' Well, maybe she wasn't joking, maybe she did want him to be unhappy for a couple of years. These widowers have no respect and it's demeaning to all of us."

"No one's saying you can't have a life, Clarabelle."

"Nancy Drew, there's another one. Her dad poured himself into his work. He didn't start screwing secretaries or, if he did, at least he was discreet."

A pitcher of Bloody Marys appeared on their table. Ethan smiled.

"Smooth," Claire said.

"To the bloody widow." He raised his glass and ate his celery. "Relax, honey. Time figures things out."

WHEN CLAIRE GOT home, there was an envelope outside her door, from Richard. It contained a small white card and a note: "What you need, Claire, is a journey, however brief—R."

Everyone and their journeys, she thought.

The white card said this:

> Griot: New York City
> I will take you on a tour.
> You will end up in a different place.
> 212.555.1284

Claire read the card twice, turned it over, ate a scoop of peanut butter from a jar.

She looked up *griot* in Charlie's battered Oxford dictionary.

Noun: A member of a class of traveling poets, musicians, and storytellers who maintain a tradition of oral history in parts of West Africa. Origin: French, earlier *guiriot*, perhaps from Portuguese *criado*.

She called Ethan.

"What's a griot?"

"A griot? Hmm. Well, he's an historian of sorts. It's a West African tradition that goes back centuries, although they are enjoying a renaissance in Europe. Why?"

Claire studied the card. "Well, Richard sent me the number of a griot. Can they be in New York?"

"East Village or West?"

"You know griots?"

"If it's Derek, in the West Village, you should go. He's got a certain flair. You should follow him. Actually, I think he's a client of Richard's."

"Follow him? What do I do?"

"Just show up where he tells you to go and listen. He'll tell you a story. Remember when your mother took you to story time when you were a kid?"

"She didn't."

"Well, pretend she did. This is story time for grown-ups. He'll know every sad song that's ever played out in this town, big or small. Every drunk, every lecher, every swindle, scandal, and sordid act. If he doesn't, he'll make it up. Derek's a bartender by trade; he's out of work. People drink at home when the economy's bad."

It couldn't hurt, Claire thought. And Ethan said, "If Beatrice wasn't the olive for your martini, so to speak, you should try him."

HIS NAME *WAS* Derek, it turned out. He was abrupt on the phone but not in an unfriendly way—it was a manner Claire recognized. She had a similar anxiety about words spilled through phones, so unstructured and loose and never a natural end. He told Claire to be at Houston and Sullivan Street at nine o'clock Thursday, and when she arrived he handed her and four other people a white card that he produced crisp and neat from his fingers, like magic. It was blank but for his name and phone number in small Helvetica font.

Derek Fountain, Griot   212.555.1284

And then one word in Garamond: LONGING.

Besides Claire, there was a businessman from Kansas, a woman from Great Neck and her teenage son, and a pale man in leather pants and black hair with bright tattoos that snaked from his wrists up into his sleeves on both arms, and which Claire could not quite make sense of.

They walked two blocks in silence, then Derek stopped and read from *Le Père Goriot* by Balzac. After he closed the book and replaced it in his backpack, he produced a tarnished flute and began a Chopin étude, then he walked again. The group followed. They walked for thirty-three minutes until they reached a corner at West Twenty-Fourth Street, where the griot broke down the flute, returned it to his pack, and began to speak.

"That, my friends, is the site of the town house where Evelyn Nesbit first maneuvered her rosy adolescent body onto Stanford White's red velvet swing. White was a wealthy architect. His firm was responsible for the second Madison Square Garden and the Washington Square Arch, among other prominent city fixtures. Nesbit was an artist's muse and an actress. She was the Norma Jean of her time, circa 1903."

The griot faced the rubble that had once been a stately four-floor mansion. He took a deep breath and continued.

"This was not Stanford's family home, of course, but a private lair where he turned vulnerable young women into his conquests. Evelyn Nesbit was the most vulnerable of them all and, subsequently, the most infamous."

He cleared his throat.

"She was sixteen when she disrobed and climbed onto his notorious red swing for the first time. Stanford White, married with children, was forty-seven."

The woman from Great Neck gasped.

"She had the narrow waist and full hips that Marilyn Monroe would later trademark, the famous 'hourglass shape.' She had soft lips and delicate skin that, it is said, rendered Stanford White helpless. Of course, some might think it a stretch to imagine a wealthy and powerful forty-seven-year-old man helpless against a sixteen-year-old girl, but this is how the story's told and what I do here is tell stories."

The griot's small gathering was rapt.

"While White pursued her fervently at first," the griot continued, "he later abandoned her for fresher conquests and she returned—both literally and figuratively—to the chorus line where he'd found her, one of countless young women hoping for a shot at security that the families they came from never had. The working women of Broadway at this time had a short window in which to engage a proper husband—one who could provide them with an allowance and a future shielded from poverty, after their youth had faded."

Suddenly, Claire caught the griot's eye. She'd been watching him, they all had been, but then he looked at her directly. His eyes were clear and blue.

"Some time later, long after the end of her affair with Stanford, Evelyn married the millionaire Harry Thaw. She wore black to their modest nuptials. Shortly after they married, Harry shot Stanford White in the face."

The griot gazed at his little group and then at the site of the mansion. He wiped a hand across his brow—it was unseasonably warm for late October.

"Unfortunately for Evelyn, Harry's family was crazy, too. After her husband was jailed for murder, she was cast onto the street, penniless. She lived a long hard life, finally succumbing at the age of eighty-two, in California—after decades of false hopes and setbacks, addictions, and lousy men."

The griot paused to check his watch. Without a note or a word, he squared his shoulders and walked away. The street corner resumed as if he had never been there.

He had a certain *je ne sais quoi*, a flair. Ethan was right. She found herself thinking about him. A few days later, she called again.

"I'd like to buy a subscription," she said.

"I don't do that. But you can come again on Thursday at nine a.m."

Claire hung up. She wished she hadn't. She wished she'd kept him on the phone. She tried to picture the griot on a red velvet swing.

In the days and weeks after Charlie died, Claire had had occasional thoughts of intimacy with other men. Now, a few months later, she thought of it all the time. She imagined having sex with the brusque man behind the counter at her corner deli, she imagined it with the grocery delivery boy from Fresh Direct. She imagined sex with Jack Huxley, and even, oh my God, Ethan. Now she imagined it repeatedly, and in great detail, and in various locales with the griot.

She grew increasingly concerned with her virginity as a widow. She wanted to be done with it. She harbored the irrational fear that she might die like this—a widow virgin. And her death thoughts weren't the general existential ones, a woman struggling with mundane thoughts of mortality. Hers were neurotic and imminent. Claire began to believe she was going to die any minute. When she crossed streets, she braced for the wayward bus to mow her down. Out to dinner she imagined a deadly virus in her food. She naturally entertained thoughts of objects falling from the sky, and if she woke in the mornings with a foggy head or if there was a twitch in her arm, she couldn't quite put a name to the thing but was sure it was fatal.

Beatrice, who'd been thorough on other topics, did not seem concerned about Claire's death. But it wasn't uncommon, according to Judith Lowenstein, to feel vulnerable after the experience Claire had had. Survivor's guilt, death by proximity, crazy paranoia—call it what you will. If healthy, robust Charlie who had looked just fine that June morning could expire before noon, then it was likely, in Claire's mind, that something would befall her, too. She noticed symptoms, beginning with her faint onto Carter Hinckley's office floor at Wanamaker and Sons. This, she was certain, heralded Parkinson's disease. At the Waverly Street Starbucks, unable to summon the presence of mind to order a drink, she thought she had lupus. When her stomach fizzled and rumbled after a late Sunday breakfast at Sasha's—her cook was sick and Sasha had bravely whipped up eggs—she'd thought it was Asian flu.

Ethan believed these subconscious fears were planted by Beatrice and Eve, by their gloomy outlooks on romance. It was true, the oracles had unnerved her.

The following Thursday Claire showed up where Derek had told her to show, at St. Anthony's Convent on Prince Street. There were three followers this time, including Claire. They exchanged twenty-dollar bills again for Derek's card, which had his name and number and a different larger word, again in Garamond: ABSURDITY.

Derek started by reading the work of poets who'd suffered tragic deaths—Delmore Schwartz (alcoholism and madness), Keats (tuberculosis and a broken heart), and Derek's own second cousin Frank (laxatives).

Then he walked north toward Washington Square Park. He was tall and didn't slouch. He wore his jeans loose but not baggy. He was thin but defined. She dressed and undressed him in different outfits as he spoke—hovering over her in a white T-shirt and denim, then shirtless, then in a tailored black suit. She imagined his hair gelled back, then loose, then cropped short, then wavy and long. She imagined his hands on her waist. She imagined him in front of her and behind. She failed to hear most of what he said.

The griot stopped abruptly on West Third Street and spoke in a low murmur, as if he were being careful to not let someone overhear. "We are standing six blocks from the Provincetown Playhouse where Eugene O'Neill began his career with the short work *Bound East for Cardiff.*" He shifted slightly to the right. "At the height of his career, O'Neill was most noted for the very public affair he conducted with

Jack Reed's wife, Louise. Reed was O'Neill's close friend, and also fellow communist and radical, who was made a household name by Warren Beatty in the movie *Reds*. Louise was played by Diane Keaton who, by the way, is a regular when she's in town at that restaurant right there, across the street."

The griot took two small steps to the right. "We are five blocks from where Henry Miller lived before he fled New York for Paris with his second wife, June. Henry and June carried on a bisexual ménage à trois for several months here with the artist Jean Kronski, which Henry wrote about in his autobiographical work *Crazy Cock*."

The griot spoke as if no one else was there.

"In Paris, Jean was replaced by Anaïs Nin in the Millers' love triangle, which launched Anaïs Nin's longtime patronage of Henry. June Miller eventually left to marry a businessman, who then left her for an actress. June deteriorated. She was in and out of the city's psychiatric system for years and finally died in obscurity."

The griot shifted once more. "We are just over three blocks from where e. e. cummings gave up on capitalization." At this the griot smiled and in reply the three others in the group chuckled. Claire stared at the back of Derek's head, willing him to look at her again.

He gesticulated in one direction and then, without warning, another. Then he spit out an array of trivia like fireworks. "You are three and a half blocks away from where Mark Twain moved after his wife passed away, five blocks from where Henry James was born, and a short distance from where William James—an anonymous man, with no relationship to Henry or to Henry's brother William—fed his obese and bed-ridden wife Oressa a steady diet of arsenic eggnogs in order to off her and marry her young daughter. Oressa

James took a heroically long time to die, but when she did it was gruesome. She expired in a pool of her own vomit and filth and William jumped off the Brooklyn Bridge as police bore down on him, in a terrible cliché of an end." Derek pointed southeast in the direction of the bridge; then he gathered his pack and left. His followers disbanded. Claire was the last to walk away. She was more than slightly undone by the morning's narrative. She was breathless.

Part II

The Widow Gets Laid

14

Let's pause briefly, here, to recap. Charlie Byrne, husband to Claire, writer, sexologist, and notorious man about town has been dead for five months, and his widow's unsure how to proceed. We do not know if Claire Byrne derived sexual pleasure from her husband, though there's a strong indication she didn't. There's the impression that there was love. Still, there was something missing in her life and now she craves it. But what with paraphilia and philandering and pronouncements from psychics, who knows what anyone wants or even which way is up? Is it sex that she wants, or is it something more pure—the state of *platonic amor*, maybe, as Plato understood it?

Claire is a pretty girl with hips in nice proportion to her waist. She's young, in good health, and has money. Her friends seem interesting; her dreams don't seem dull. She is by some accounts, in spite of or maybe because of her husband having died, fortunate.

The griot had said a lot of things, most of which Claire hadn't even heard—she'd been too busy imagining him in bed. She felt frustrated. She longed for an awakening. She wondered if Jack Huxley was susceptible to an almost-perfect ratio of hip to waist. She remembered that Eve said to do it out of town. Thanks to Beatrice, she was on the lookout for black suits. She was ready to be flattered and seduced.

But whether from the monotony of marriage, or by Charlie's ceaseless analysis, or by the theories and the talk and the other women, sex for Claire was not a simple act. She couldn't imagine calling her gynecologist, for instance, to get the name of a good stimulating lubricant, rushing off to buy it, and applying it liberally before mounting the sweaty tumescent man across the couch, as Dr. Ruth had just suggested that morning on *Good Day New York*.

Often, when Claire and Charlie had sex, she felt like a control subject in his research. If Charlie wanted her to stroke something, he would instruct her to do so in a clinical fashion, mentally record the conditions under which she'd done so, and observe the results. She was more lab assistant than intimate.

MOST ANYONE WHO gave it thought felt Claire should hole up the first year, cool her heels, wear conservative clothes. That was the rule, after all, implied by the general public and reinforced by a psychic—no love for one year. Richard, of course, wanted to finish and sell Charlie's book.

"Work on it, you'll thank me. The distraction is good." To that end, tabloid magazines appeared in weekly bundles at her door, the subject of Charlie's book affixed to every one. Always arranged at a dodgy angle from the camera, Jack Huxley refused to be shot

straight on. It was like Claire's captivating author's photo that had
first turned Charlie on.

Life in a three-quarter turn.

Ethan was anxious about change. He was plainly in the cool
your heels camp. Sasha, though, thought it high time to move on.
As she delicately put it, "If there was anyone who would have
wanted to see you get laid, it would have been your dead husband,
God rest his perverted soul."

Charlie had always had a thing for widows, it's true. He would
have hated to see one go to waste. Claire, having been recently
relieved of a husband, was at a virginal milestone. To anyone other
than jealous wives, Claire, much like Iberian ham in Spain at the
height of the season, was a rare delicacy. Charlie would have derived
ecstatic pleasure from the catch; ah, the irony.

Claire picked up her phone, put it down, picked it up, put it
down again. She left her apartment and took a cab to 969 Park.
When the doorman called up to announce her, he paused. His eyes
darted warily toward Claire. He replaced the telecom slowly and
nodded Claire up.

Claire immediately identified the doorman's concern. Sasha
was fixed at one end of her custom D'Angelo sofa, with a cocktail
shaker at her right elbow and a pitcher of vodka on the Adnet table
in front of her. Her torso was perfectly straight; her legs were
looped carelessly beneath her. The scene looked like a Cindy Sher-
man display.

"What are you doing?" Claire asked, alarmed. It wasn't the
presence of vodka in the afternoon so much as the shine of
Sasha's skin, the dark, blood-colored lips and vivid, skintight
leather dress that slightly startled her. Claire remembered what
Beatrice had said.

Someone in a fuchsia dress is taking risks.

"Talk. I can't move, I'll drip. Just talk."

Botox is a relatively innocuous procedure, but Sasha had a deathly fear of needles. Pills before the appointment, drinks with pills after. The leather dress, Claire assumed, was for—

"Let me guess, Dr. Struck?"

Gerald Struck was new in town and taking the ladies' skin scene by storm. He was a former quarterback; he'd played one season for the Jets. He was tall and defined beneath his thin cashmere crew necks and gabardine slacks in a way no dermatologist had ever quite been before him. He walked about in a teasing stage of semi-erection.

"Um-mm." Sasha waved her hand for Claire to talk.

They were all acting like lunatics. It was the autumn of everyone's discontent.

"Well, listen to this. I have a griot," Claire said. "His name is Derek."

"That's nice, honey. What's a griot?"

"It's a storyteller. They tell stories. He recited the entire text of *The Waste Land*, with footnotes."

Sasha's housekeeper came in with a straw for her martini glass. She put the straw up to Sasha's lips. When Sasha had finished sipping, she pronounced her words carefully. "Things must be slow downtown."

"After *The Waste Land* he recited a parallel text he'd written from his own life. His own *Waste Land*. He called it *The Gap*. It's tongue in cheek. He also plays the flute."

Sasha breathed in and eyed Claire dubiously, "What's so great about a griot?"

"Well, that's why I'm here."

Sasha made an attempt to open her eyes wide to show interest, but the Botox had already taken effect. "I'm listening."

"I want to have sex. I want to get it over with, out of town or anywhere, I don't care. I was at the movies with Ethan last week and started rubbing his leg. I didn't even realize it."

"And?"

"And I don't know how to go about it. Charlie wrote an entire book on animal sex that he never published. Isn't that crazy? Anacondas mate for three weeks."

"That's longer than most New Yorkers," Sasha said.

"It's three weeks for one single act. One single fuck. And it takes thirteen males to do it. Thirteen male anacondas wrap themselves around the female and then just hang on until they're done."

Sasha picked her legs up one at a time and laid them out on the couch. She let out a sound that might have been an exasperated laugh if she'd been able to move her lips. "Stick to human seduction. You know, most women would trade places with you in a heartbeat. Marriage is so—you know. And here you are with a freebie, a do-over." She waved her arm in the air lazily, closed her eyes, groped for her drink. The Klonopin was kicking in. "Margorie Dermott's already dating a surgeon."

"Great. Good for Margorie. Who cares? I'm dating, too. That's what I came to tell you. I'm not going to wander around in disrepair. I want to date and I need you to find me someone."

"Thank God. Enough's enough."

"It's been months, not years. I'd hardly call it procrastination."

"Good. I'll live vicariously through you. Marriage is so damn repetitive . . ." Sasha trailed off.

When she began to snore, Claire tucked a blanket around her and left.

THE NEXT DAY Sasha got serious. They sat in her study as she thumbed through Thom's Rolodex, the old-fashioned kind with handwritten cards that spun around in a wheel. She was jotting down notes.

"Here's what I'm going to do, I'm going to assemble a variety pack. You don't know what your taste is because you've been out of the game. So I'm going to start you off with this fun little three-some right here." Sasha was holding three white cards in her hand.

"Alex is a journalist, he's very tall, very nice. Stephen's a billion-aire. Balding a bit, but he's a billionaire. Jake plays hockey, great ass, but not too bright, and then I might throw in Sid. He's an alcoholic."

"Alcoholic?"

"Yes, a high-functioning one. He's a venture capitalist, energy. He's into those windmill farms in the Midwest. Apparently there's a lot of wind in Kansas."

Claire picked the journalist, to start.

"Great. You can just have a drink, no pressure," Sasha said. "This is a warm-up to practice your small talk. It will be easy."

Sasha called Claire the next morning.

"Okay, I gave him your number. He's out of town but gets back tomorrow. He'll probably call—"

"He did already. He called."

Sasha squealed. "Ha! You see? He loves you. I knew it! And so?"

"We might have coffee. This week, maybe? I told him to call me back."

"Call you *back*?"

"Yeah."

"But he just called you." Sasha sounded baffled, as if Claire had told her olives don't pair well with gin. "Why does he have to call back?"

"Call me back later this *week*, I said."

There was a pause, filled by the sound of a vacuum.

"Lydia. Can you *please* vacuum someplace else?" Sasha sounded exasperated.

"Okay. What happens later this week? I don't understand." Sasha was speaking to Claire in the same tone she used to speak to her Westie.

"I'll know about coffee." Claire was thumbing through an old *Paris Review*. Susan Sontag on "The Art of Fiction." She wondered if she ought to have a bisexual phase.

"Sweetie, what is there to *know* about getting *coffee*?"

"Never mind. We talked for a few minutes and I told him to call me back, that's all."

"I hope you didn't bring up anacondas."

"I didn't. And never mind."

"Listen, honey. If you want to play you have to be in the game. I know what you're up to. He'll call, and you won't answer, then you'll call him from a cab or an elevator and get cut off and he'll call again and you'll wait a few days more to call him back; then two months will go by and he'll be too tired to bother with coffee, he won't even remember your name. And in two months he will have had two serious relationships come and go and be into his third and, by the way, she's the one he'll marry. Call him back *now*. And dinner—or at least a drink. Something grown-up."

The truth was, Claire hadn't liked the sound of Alex's voice. It was faint and there were gaps in their talk that she'd felt obligated to fill in. She hated that. *He* had called *her*, after all. But Claire called him back, and they agreed to have dinner. Claire picked the restaurant; the journalist picked the time. The Waverly Inn on Bank Street was easy to get in and out of.

ALEX THE JOURNALIST was tall, Sasha was right about that. And he was slightly disheveled, though it looked contrived: he seemed to have purposely tousled hair. When Claire walked in, Alex was standing at the bar. He greeted her—and took charge right away. There was a table waiting and he ordered foie gras and salads before they sat down. He dashed quickly through three bourbons— was it four?—before they considered the entrées. Claire nursed the house Chardonnay.

"Foreign correspondent," Alex said. Claire was tuning in and out. "Bureau chief, Beijing. *Washington Post.*" Alex was the sort of foreign correspondent who carried a picture of himself dressed in camouflage holding an M16 rifle. He was also the type of dinner date who liked to take it out and show it. Claire nodded at the picture in approval.

"Fallujah," he said.

Alex was newly divorced. ("But," Sasha had assured Claire, "I promise he's not fucked up.")

He'd been divorced for three months and said so more than once. Observations and exclamations popped out of him unexpectedly. He was halfway through a bottle of wine by the time their entrées came—quail for him and chicken potpie for Claire. When his fingers snapped—twice, and loudly—for their waiter, Claire jumped and the waiter appeared. "I can't eat this," Alex said. He was grimacing. His face was contorted into equal parts disgust and alarm. She glanced carefully toward his bird, afraid of spotting a leggy insect crawling out.

"It's bloody," he said through clenched teeth, "can't you see that?" Here, with his fork, he held back a small wing to reveal to Claire and the waiter the unacceptable gore. Claire couldn't see it.

"Take her plate back, too, please," said Alex, through a brittle smile. "Keep it warm until you cook mine." The waiter snatched up both plates. "You don't mind, do you, Claire?"

"No," she said, and took a deep breath. In Charlie, she might have found this scene charming. She was used to Charlie's domineering. He had earned it. "No, I don't mind. Of course not." She smiled.

"More wine?" Alex asked.

It was red, and though Claire didn't care for any, she nodded. The bottle made a gurgling sound as he tipped it into her glass.

Dinner—partly due to the quail, and partly due to long pauses Alex employed between pronouncements and digressions, and lavish stories about bombs—went on for hours; three and a half, it turned out, and during that time they covered the following: Alex's book (*A Parrot in Berlin: The Colors of War*); Alex's publisher ("No fucking clue how to sell a book. What. So. Ever"); Alex's piece in *Harper's* on Anwar Sadat ("At the risk of coming off as arrogant, Claire, it's the goddamn closest anyone's ever got to him"); Alex's ex-wife ("I just fell out of love"); Alex's rowing career at Yale ("We won the '84 regatta against Harvard, the pussies"); Alex's middle name (Letham, after his great-grandfather); Claire's middle name (Marie, she wasn't sure why); and Claire's marital status.

"Do you get along with your ex?"

"Yes, very well, under the circumstances." Claire picked up her fork.

"What—"

"My husband's dead."

"God, I'm a jackass," Alex said, loudly enough that other patrons looked up from their twenty-dollar starters with indiscreet curiosity. The place was a tabloid staple, Claire had forgotten. Ellen Barkin once threw a vodka in her ex-husband's face and hours later the splash found print on Page Six. Claire eyed her drink.

Alex lowered his head and repeated himself, softer this time.

"I knew, I just—I forgot. Sorry."

"It's fine," Claire said. *Not fucked up?* She was for damn sure going to give Sasha some rules before the next date.

"SASHA SAID YOU write," Alex said. "What are you writing?" That the stream of the lofty journalist's consciousness had switched to Claire was astonishing. The widow thing, naturally, intrigued him.

"A book," Claire answered, trying out the feel of it on her tongue.

"Fiction? Memoir?"

"Bio, sort of. It's about a movie star. I don't know if that's technically nonfiction."

Alex appeared to be amused and impatient. "Biography? Can you say who?"

"Jack Huxley."

Alex put down his drink. "No shit."

"The perfect man."

"Ha! Right. Why is that? What makes the perfect man?"

"I don't know yet," Claire said.

Alex leaned in across the table. "Let's make it easier, then. What makes the perfect date?"

"Hmm. I'd say good conversation and coy double entendres and approving glances from strangers, then a balmy walk, some-

thing slightly risqué and impulsive, and a long cab ride to anywhere."

"Sex?" Alex slurred.

"Oh, no thanks," Claire said. "I'm good."

Alex smirked, gulped at his brandy. They were long past the
wine.

"Picture this," Claire began. Sasha had said this was practice, a
warm-up, after all. "It's late at night and a woman enters her home.
She's tired, walks into her bedroom, and begins to undress. She
turns on a light and is startled to see a man on her bed. He's lying
on it, comfortably stretched out and fully clothed, and he's pointing
a gun at her. 'Keep going,' he says, and he makes a gesture with
the gun. She looks scared—not frightened, but startled—and
unbuttons her blouse, then her skirt, then steps out of her slip. He
gets up and approaches her, still holding the gun, and they stand
close, face-to-face, for a minute, saying nothing. The mood is tense.
Finally, she breaks the silence. 'Do you know what I wish?' she asks.
'That once you'd get here on time.' "

Alex the journalist looked blank. "I don't get it."

Claire smiled and sipped.

"Seriously, I don't get it, am I missing something? Is that hot?
To pull a gun?"

"It's the most erotic movie scene ever filmed. Robert Redford
and Katharine Ross? *Butch Cassidy and the Sundance Kid*?" Alex
looked confused. "Nevermind. It's Cinderella. Every woman has
her own version of the prince at the door with the slipper."

"I don't think fairy tales sell well," Alex said.

"Fairy tales are the only stories that sell."

It was late and the tables around them had thinned.

Alex summoned, then signed for the check. He waved off Claire's fifty-dollar bill, then immediately waved it back. "Sorry. I'm on per diem," he said.

They walked outside and Claire signaled for a cab.

"Well, good luck with your book," Alex said behind her as she climbed in the car. Claire blew him a kiss and shut her door.

It was the end, for Claire, of journalists.

15

THE NEXT MORNING CLAIRE WOKE FEELING UNSETTLED and in the slow fog of waking she forgot—even five months later—that Charlie wasn't there and wondered briefly, alone in the bed, if he'd made coffee.

There was a message on her phone. Sasha, of course. She wanted a recap of the date.

Claire texted: Good test. But not sure he worked.

I just fell out of love, Alex had said.

She felt like Charlie was calling audibles from stage left.

The Opposite of Sex—his famous theory. He'd explained it at every dinner party, in every well-appointed apartment above Fifty-Seventh Street. Most New Yorkers in a certain circle could quote him by heart, could even do a fair impression of him leaned back in a chair, hands locked behind his head, eyes on the chandelier.

The opposite of sex, he used to say, is love. Then he'd smile, pause, grin like the Grinch. "Sex and love are the crudest sort of magnets," he'd say. "One north, one south, violently repelling one another, which is why the natural state is to have one or the other but not both." And as Charlie famously wrote in his first book, "Love does not coexist naturally with sex, it is its opposite. We use the metaphor of *fireworks*. When forced together, the two of them, the result is a tempest—unsustainable, unendurable beyond short lengths of time. We simply cannot manage the battle."

Claire had the feeling that Charlie would have liked Alex.

After Charlie and Claire married and the unsustainable tempest dulled, Claire mostly thought Charlie was full of shit. Their lack of storm was certainly not the result of too much love. Charlie neglected to account for the couplings where stormlessness was the product of a dull routine, and different bedtimes.

Sasha's Plan B was a billionaire. She made lunch reservations at the Four Seasons where the ceilings were tall and dramatic, and the maître d' was, too. Sasha, in sequins and already tipsy, was like a fish back in water. She had a notepad, and white wine on ice. Unlike journalists, apparently, billionaires required a primer.

"Sweetheart!" Sasha said and stood up to kiss.

"Hi." Claire kissed Sasha once on each cheek. She was trying out the double kiss.

"If you want a billionaire," Sasha whispered, "it's important to show up where they lunch. It's like the Serengeti." Then even more softly, she added, "Don't look, but speaking of, Bloomberg is two tables left." Then louder: "So Alex is not your speed. He *can* be a bit self-involved. I've got other options for you."

The waiter filled Claire's wineglass and she took an inelegantly large swallow.

"Stephen seems the most likely candidate to me—he's the one I told you about, an old family friend. You met him at our wedding. You might not remember. I don't expect you to, but he does remember meeting you." Sasha and Thom had married at the Colony Club. Claire did not remember any Stephens but she did remember Olive, Thom's namesake and delightfully quirky mother. She'd been named after Olive Thomas Pickford, a Ziegfeld showgirl who accidentally poisoned herself with her husband's syphilis treatment. A topical medicine she'd mistaken for whiskey.

Sasha's in-laws had old family money and lots of it, the kind that gave them the freedom to be eccentric. Mrs. Wyse was the sort of woman, Claire thought, who'd be found nude when she died, swathed in feathers, with bowls of cat food spilling onto the marble floors of her cavernous town house.

"I don't remember," Claire said.

"Well, no pressure. There are others," Sasha said.

Sasha pulled out a pocket-size album of pictures along with a typed bio for each one. There was Jorge the sugar baron—three divorces, grown kids, homes in Spain and Morocco besides the standard places in Miami and New York. Harold—venture capitalist, one marriage, ranches in New Mexico and Wyoming. Luis— old money, ties to royals. Luis, Sasha admitted, was not *exactly* a billionaire but close enough. She'd rounded up.

Stephen's father, Claire learned, reading his bio, had patented the automated car wash, and like Walter White of the Giacometti, Stephen owned a sports team. They were golfing pals.

She studied the pictures. Charlie had been much older than Claire, but he didn't have the fortune these men had. He'd had to rely on other means of attraction—physical appeal, sexuality, charm. Before her were sagging chins, a pallid countenance, a general sense of disrepair. "Billionaires, honey," Sasha said, sensing Claire's concern.

Claire gave Sasha a brave smile. "Fine. I'll take the sports guy."

The day after Sasha gave Stephen Claire's number, his secretary called to arrange a date. Then she called back. Three times. Each time she left the same message: "Hello, this is Vivian in Stephen Mack's office. Please return the call at your earliest convenience. Thank you." Each message, though, was left with slightly more edge to the tone than the last. Vivian was a bully. What did this say about her boss? The next day Stephen himself called. He was brusque and official.

"This is Stephen Mack calling for Claire Byrne by way of Sasha Wyse. I'm under the impression we're to meet. Please return my call."

While Claire listened to his message, her phone rang again. It was Stephen. And when she didn't answer, it rang again. "Hi, it's Stephen. I'm having a hard time getting a hold of you. Uh . . . not sure what else I'm supposed to do. Give me a call." The process was making Claire anxious. The calls came at too fast a clip.

"He's kind of pushy," she told Sasha.

"Claire. He's a billionaire. He has a lot going on. You can't just leave him hanging."

Stephen called again on Wednesday and then again on Friday. This time he left his cell number. Late Friday, Claire called him back and he answered on the first ring.

"Oh, good. So you're okay."

"Yes, I'm sorry. I'm just really new at this and—"

"I had my office call Sasha this afternoon to make sure you were okay."

Claire paused. She had the urge to just hang up.

"Thank you. That was . . . thoughtful."

They arranged a date. Stephen told her he'd send a car.

On Tuesday, a car came as promised and took Claire to a private club on Fifty-Second Street where Stephen and his billions commanded an elaborate corner table. He looked like a man who'd never had to try.

"Well, you're beautiful, like Sasha promised," he said, followed up by a toothy billionaire grin. He was dressed in a plain navy suit. He'd lost most of his hair. He kissed each of her cheeks and pulled out a chair for her. The club was ill lit. Edith Piaf crooned through the walls. Nothing seemed quite in sync. Stephen had a magnum of champagne at the table, and after Claire sat down a waiter brought oysters. Oh my God, Claire thought. *Really?*

Stephen, as it happened, was a Dangler. He spent the evening dangling his wares for Claire. He dangled houses and yachts and exclusive islands and private jets. He dangled the luxury suite of the football team he owned, for Claire and all her friends. He dangled an emerald bracelet that he affixed to Claire's wrist as the night wound to its end.

"Oh, no. I really can't," she said. It was hideous.

"You have to," he said. "I picked it out for you."

"Okay, well . . ."

"It looks exquisite on you. I'll take you home."

Claire did not invite the billionaire inside, but she briefly, politely, kissed him good night.

The next morning he called at eight and two more times before ten.

"Where were you?" he asked when she summoned the nerve to call back. "I've been calling."

"Yes, I know. I'm sorry, Stephen. I don't think I'm ready for this."

"I'm confused. What happened between last night and this morning?" Stephen asked. It did not occur to him that *not ready* was even a possibility. He was a billionaire for Christ's sake.

"It's just too soon, I guess."

"You guess?" Stephen asked. His voice went up a half octave.

"No. I don't guess. I know," Claire said. She summoned her nerve. "You call a lot. Too much. You're pushy and a pathological caller. I can't be the first girl to tell you that."

"Yes, Claire, you are."

Claire mailed the bracelet to his office.

It was the end, for Claire, of billionaires.

16

SASHA WAS UNDERSTANDABLY DISCOURAGED. SHE BECAME convinced that Claire's inability to sleep with or even French-kiss either of her first two dates was a psychiatric condition that needed to be addressed.

"You know what you need? A second opinion, sweetie," she said.

"On what?" Claire asked.

"On everything. When your car dies, you don't roll over for the first mechanic."

"I don't have a car."

"When Snowball coughs up fur, you talk to different vets."

"I don't have a pet."

"But you do have a dead husband; you can't order your own coffee or return a phone call, and Lowenstein disapproves of your every move. You waste half your sessions on made-up dreams. You need a second-opinion shrink."

"I have a shrink."

"Yes, which is why you need a second opinion. To know if your first shrink is giving good advice."

Dr. Evan Gordon Spence had treated the Wyse family, on and off, for thirty years. He had an opening on Wednesdays and an office on the West Side. An attractive man, he had gone to great lengths, Claire could see, not to tempt his female patients: the forced clutter of his office, the dingy beige walls, his athletic frame disguised in houndstooth trousers and a pilled cardigan. The shoes at the ends of his socks were battered and clunky. The gold ring on his left hand was tarnished. Dr. Spence, with psychiatry degrees from Yale, then Harvard, then Yale again, was not about to be mistaken for a sex object.

In the waiting room—one chair, one end table, and a mini-fridge stocked with juice—Claire flipped through the stack of magazines and here was Jack Huxley again. The cover of *Vanity Fair*, an article in *Forbes* ("Hollywood Heavyweights"), and his caricature in the *New Yorker*. He was ubiquitous. He had a small dimple in his chin; you could see it in close-ups. Charlie had insisted that dimples were a deformity and had often noted how it was fascinating, wasn't it, which deformities we celebrate and which make us recoil. In the case of the dimple, Charlie said, it's the symmetry that charms us. "Humans are simpler than they'd like to think, and I don't exempt myself," he said. "We like bright colors, uniformity, nice symmetrical shapes." Jack Huxley was symmetrical.

Claire and the Wyse family's shrink dispensed with introductions and Claire began.

"Here's the thing. My husband is dead and I want to get on with my life. But I'm not sure what I want."

"Let's pick a place in there to start," Spence said. "Tell me about your husband."

"No. I don't want to. I want to talk about sex."

Evan Spence raised a brow. "All right, talk about sex. Fire away."

Claire, to let him know this was serious yet difficult, let out a long, protracted sigh and tugged at her socks. "Well, okay. It's like an elephant in the room," she told him. "Or a gorilla, however the saying goes. There's this very pure expectation, I think. Of widows. I can remarry, but I don't want to remarry. I'm young and I want to, you know, date. But there's this expectation that I shouldn't be sexual because I'm a 'widow' and widows are pure, like virgins, and it's disrespectful to Charlie if I just date, but I was lonely, a little, when I was married and now I'm lonely and not married. And I don't know what to do about any of that."

Unlike Judith Lowenstein, Evan Spence was liberal with eye contact. They were blue, his eyes. Claire thought it careless of him not to wear bookish glasses.

"Why aren't you supposed to have sex?" he asked.

Also unlike Lowenstein, Evan Spence had neither notebook nor pencil, nothing with which to distract his hands or allow Claire time to look around.

"Because my husband died. I'm supposed to only want to have sex with my husband, still. Unless I marry someone. So it's kind of like I'm still married, in a way, except that he's dead. My botanomanist felt that, too, when her husband died. She had to screw an Acura salesman in New Jersey."

"I wasn't aware of these rules," said Spence, in a smooth voice a bit too cool for his orthopedic shoes. Claire imagined him undressing.

"Perceptions, yes, but not rules. Will you hand me that violet beside you, on the window."

Claire took a potted African violet from the windowsill and

handed it to Spence, who began to sift through its leaves and—with two very long, strong fingers and scissors—snip off the blemished ones. He motioned Claire to continue.

"Well, the perception, then, is that I'm a threat now. I'm alone and I don't have divorce baggage, so I'm a bit of a trophy."

"A trophy?"

"Yes. Don't ask me to prove it, but my husband was a sex specialist. He knows."

"Yes. I've read his work."

For no good reason, Claire looked up and there was Charlie's 723-page *Thinker's Hope* on Spence's top shelf, between *The Bell Jar* and *The Nuremberg Interviews*.

"Well. He floated the trophy theory—virginal milestones . . . pregnancy sex, postpartem sex, divorcée—their first time with a new man. Widows rank high. He spread that one around when Glory Loveland's husband died and she was driving everyone wild. I mean, I'm sure you've thought about, you know, a widow."

"My thoughts and desires are not at issue here, but go on."

"Women are suddenly guarded with me, and men are not. It's adultery kicked up a notch. I'm still someone's wife, in a way. So it's naughty and even slightly more brazen than flirting with a divorcée."

"Are you behaving differently?"

"No. I don't know. Yes. Differently than what?"

"Are you flirting more with men? Maybe subconsciously you want affection, whether in the form of sex or not, yet consciously you think it's wrong. It's *not* wrong, it's a natural human urge, but these factors are warring and result in your unconscious prevailing in overt flirtation."

"I'm not flirting, I don't even know how to flirt. I went on two dates. Well, three, if you count Brian at Melanie Stark's. I haven't dated since college and that hardly counts."

"Um-hm."

"The first year of widowhood is specifically set aside for awkwardness—lewd gazes from men and the treacly sympathy of their wives. Friends like Melanie all want to fix me up—they want me married and off the market again. The first year is reserved for clever dinner seating arrangements."

"An astute observation, if perhaps overly generalized, but go on."

"The first year, too, is set aside for details. Those, I'm much better with. There are credit cards to change, bank accounts, mail, subscriptions to cancel. New things pop up all the time. You have to transfer the airline miles, for instance. Most people forget that one— and clean closets out, of course, you know, there's just a lot. I don't know where I'm going with this."

Evan Spence maintained his posture and gaze.

"Did you save anything of your husband's?"

"Well, I kept all of his books, obviously—not the ones he owned but the ones that he wrote. I kept his letters, his papers, his computer with its files. All the wine. He was a collector. I kept all of it, although I don't really drink wine. I kept his shaving kit—you know, the toiletries, his toothbrush. And I kept his robe."

"His toiletries. Why is that?"

"I don't know."

"Where do you keep them?"

"In the bathroom."

"You keep your late husband's toiletries in the bathroom?"

"I do, I guess. Yes. And his robe on a hook, also in the bathroom."

Evan Spence put down his violet.

"This is interesting."

Maybe Sasha was onto something with second-opinion shrinks. Lowenstein had not found this interesting.

"It was brand-new, cashmere. He'd hardly worn it."

Evan Spence took a pen and pad from his small table and scribbled something down.

17

I T WAS 9:00 A.M. WHEN THE PHONE RANG, 8:00 A.M. IN
Illinois.

Claire was awake but had spent the past hour in a dream state,
conjuring future boyfriends, having imaginary conversations.

The Wilkinsons' dinner is Friday, but let's not go.

We have to go!

*Let's not, love. Let's stay in bed the whole damned weekend if we
want.*

But what will we tell them?

We'll say we're away, then we won't leave the apartment!

*Oh, Robert–Nick–Darren, you're perfectly wicked! We'll have
popcorn and takeout. We'll watch* Casablanca*!*

Claire had never watched *Casablanca* but she planned to with
future boyfriends. She never cared much for Thai food but it, too,
played a part in her imaginary future affairs. As did Elvis Costel-
lo's music, card games, Tom Stoppard, and maybe crochet hooks.
Claire thought she might crochet in her next relationship, while

Peter watched sports highlights. Or Harry, maybe. Or possibly Joe.

"Claire, I'll be frank. Your father and I are worried," Betty said. She'd been calling every morning, for weeks, and Claire hadn't answered. She figured it was time.

"Hi, Mom," Claire said into the phone.

"Claire." Her mother's tone was slightly scolding.

"Yes?"

"I can tell you're not up yet, it's not good. You don't answer your phone. You're falling into depression. It's important you stick to a simple but constant routine. Up at eight, to bed by ten. Do something with your mind, as well as regular physical activity. Follow small daily rituals."

"I'm not depressed. I'm tired."

"Were you out last night? Late?"

"No."

"Did you stay up late, then?"

"Not really, no."

A query about food was coming soon. Betty's answer to everything was sleep and food, but not too much of either.

"You're not tired, you're sleeping because you're depressed. The chemistry of depression stops your sleep chemicals from functioning appropriately."

Some mothers spend their lives convinced their children will be whisked off by creepy strangers. Betty's biggest fear was that her children might catch depression, followed closely by a fear that they might lack food.

"I don't know what that means."

"It means that non-depressed people wake up. They get eight

hours of sleep and then wake up. If people were responsible about their sleep habits—eight hours a night, from nine to five, or ten to six, or whatever—and every night at the same time, we wouldn't need alarm clocks because your body knows naturally when to stop. But that's not why I'm calling."

Betty had retired from her teaching career much too early, Claire thought. It gave her too much time to read, and to worry that the sky was falling down. Claire made a *phew* sound.

"Don't make fun. What are you eating?"

Claire's brother, Howard, had moved to Oregon after high school. He went to college, became an accountant, married and bred and led a nondescript life that hummed along. Claire went to New York and married a Byrne, and that, in her mother's eyes, was almost as good as landing a senator. Betty had relished her role opposite Grace.

"You're not calling to find out what I'm eating," Claire said.

"Well, it's not the main reason, no. I'm calling because Paula Wingrove's mother told me that Paula can't have children."

"That's too bad. Did she want any?"

"Claire! She's only thirty-seven. She and Mark have been trying for three years. Ellen is devastated, as is Paula, of course. And it got me thinking. I think you should harvest your eggs."

"Mom, please. I don't even know if I want kids."

"What are you talking about?" Betty said. "Every woman wants children."

"And even if I did," Claire said. "I'd probably get diabetes."

"Claire Byrne!"

"Pregnancy triggers genetic diseases, that's all I'm saying. So thank you for wishing that on me."

"Well, that's a nice attitude. No one's saying you have to have children, just harvest your eggs. I'm sending you the name of a doctor."

"I have a doctor."

"This one's very good."

"I have a good one."

"Are you eating, sweetheart?"

"No."

"Are you seeing anyone?"

"Yes I am, as a matter of fact. I have two shrinks, two seers, two dates, and a griot. I gotta go. Say hi to Dad."

"I'M NOT LOVING these blind dates," Claire said. She'd been summoned to lunch again to consider Number Three.

"He's not blind."

"I'm not on a lucky streak."

"He's not a gambler." Claire scrunched up her mouth as though thinking about her response, then broke open a fortune cookie.

They were at Shun Lee on Fifty-Fifth. Sasha had ordered champagne, which meant she had something to talk about over and beyond Claire's dates. Claire had asked for her fortune before the meal, and the waitress brought her four cookies. It was three in the afternoon and they were the only ones there. Claire sipped the champagne and opened her cookies one by one.

The first two were identical and promising: *You'll have a life full of daring and thrill.*

"The thing is, there's no *thrill* anymore, with Thom," Sasha said. Here was the reason for the palliative champagne. "He goes to work, he comes home, Lydia makes dinner, we stare across the table at each other—no, I stare, he eats—and say the same ridiculous things. 'Is Frank still fucking up the Bankers Trust account?' 'No, he's pulled it together.' 'Hey, is Lydia still going to the same butcher on Madison? Something's off with the steak.' That's a Monday. For Tuesday and Wednesday, substitute 'Frank' with 'Lyman,' and 'steak' with 'salmon.' Then we get stoned on scotch and he watches CNN in the study and I watch *Real Housewives* in my room."

"Which one?"

"New York. Okay, sometimes Jersey. It's not important."

Sasha took a drink of champagne and continued.

"Anyway, then I decided, okay. We need kids." She was twisting her diamond tennis bracelet around on her wrist. She was making Claire nervous. "We agreed, before, early on, you know—no kids—but that's ridiculous. There's nothing to do if you don't have kids."

Claire thought of her mother's warnings about Paula Wingrove. "You should freeze your eggs."

Sasha sighed. "Well, I went to see Dr. Riva. And of course she says I have terrible ovaries, they're appalling. In fact, her exact words were, 'Your ovaries are appalling.' She said I have fifty-year-old ovaries."

Claire gasped.

"I know," Sasha said. "Then she told me, 'You don't want a baby, no one should have babies.'"

Claire nodded. This was Dr. Riva's steady refrain. *Good God, no babies. If you could see what I see.*

She practiced what she preached. Joan Riva had delivered plenty of babies but never had any herself. There were family pictures on her desk, grown children, but Riva had explained it to Claire. They were her husband's children. Ervin's sperm, Ervin's first wife's ruined womb.

"Did you know that every time you ovulate, after the one egg is released thousands more explode in your ovary?" Sasha exclaimed.

"Wow," Claire said. "Intrauterine genocide."

"I'm serious, Claire." Sasha took a large sip of her beverage. "I don't think my marriage will survive childless. We've run out of conversation. We need something else to talk about at dinner."

Their waiter appeared with a basin of live seafood, which Sasha scrutinized slowly and carefully, like a wizened old fishmonger.

"This one," she said, and she jabbed her finger in the bucket. "That one right there in the middle, poached. And we'll start with the prawns."

While Sasha gulped champagne, Claire cracked open her third fortune: *You are true to your nature.*

"I just feel like it's in my nature, you know?" Sasha said. "I am *meant* to be a mother. Don't you think? I'm nurturing. Not every woman is nurturing."

Claire raised a glass to her lips to avoid responding. The waitress appeared, to fill their water, and Sasha snapped; she was on edge. "Will you *please* go away? We will tell you when we want water."

Claire opened the last fortune cookie. This one was ominous: *There will be a dark question that has no answer.*

"Okay," Claire said. "Go ahead and set it up."

"Set what up, honey?"

"My date, the hockey guy. Three's a charm."

18

I 'M TRYING TO DATE. IT'S NOT GOING SO WELL," CLAIRE
said to Lowenstein.

"All right. Let's come back to that. You mentioned another
dream."

"It wasn't really a dream, more like a vision, a hazy sort of vision.
How do you remember things?"

"How do I store certain events—is that what you mean?"

"No, not store them. How do you play them back? Do your
memories have sound? Are they in color?"

It was a pertinent question, because in memory Claire took
liberties. She was thinking of when she first met Charlie in the bar
of the St. Regis, an old throwback of a hotel where men stroked
rolls of bills and wore heavy watches, and women were busty with
tottering hair. Claire had painted and repainted this scene, thousands of times since that night.

"They do and they don't have sound and have color," Lowenstein said. "Our memories are parceled out by sound and color,

yes. When you recall them, they retrieve these links and assemble into a sort of multimedia production, if you will. Memories are pliable."

Claire got out of her chair and paced. She felt agitated. Charlie was everywhere, but not in comforting or nostalgic ways or anything that was mildly reassuring. He raced through her mind like an extra darting out from the crowd, causing the actors to flub their lines.

On weeknights the St. Regis was flush with commuters, in that dreamy period between high-rise offices and Greenwich picket fences. The men stood and the women dangled from stools. Claire had been to the St. Regis just that once, to meet Charles Byrne, yet her memory of it was so vivid, she could tell the grade of jewels on the women's hands when she replayed it. She could see the worn spots on the fabric that cloaked the walls. She recalled the back table where she waited, the warmed bowl of almonds she'd eaten to seem occupied. The gin and tonic she'd ordered, the bruise on the lime. The memory ran through her memory in black and white, and *sérieux*, like a Truffaut film.

"Yes, they are," Claire said. "You're right. It wasn't dingy, or black and white, the room was bright. It was full. There were candles on the tables, and the girls were in short skirts."

"Is this a memory, then? Is it a significant one?" said Lowenstein.

"I'm just thinking of when I met Charlie. What's the point of memory, though, if we change it to suit ourselves?"

"In some cases it's quite useful. Memories are a source of comfort, and they are also flawed. They are affected as we take on new information or add life experience. For instance, this memory of your first meeting with Charlie is likely different now than it was five years ago, based on the experiences you've had since."

"I've turned it into a movie scene: A room of middle-aged men and saggy chins, call girls in leopard prints circling like sharks. Clenched faces, fake alligator bags, fingernails bright red."

"And why do you think that is?"

"I don't know. Either because I'm destined to write a mildly interesting screenplay one day, or I'm just re-scripting my averagely interesting life."

"Are you playing with memory, to make your life more interesting to you?"

"Everything was thick. Wrists, carpet, walls, high-backed booths. The room was dark and table lights drilled down from the ceiling in the shape of cones, like an interrogation room. The carpet was the color of dried blood. Norma Desmond would have fit in perfectly sprawled out on a velvet settee in the corner with a cigarette holder the length of her arm."

Lowenstein cleared her throat.

"Claire, the scene has changed three times while you've been sitting here," she said. "Whether you consciously realize that or not, memories are affected by the information you've received subsequently. When you're having conflicted feelings after your husband's sudden death, don't you think it's interesting that the room decor has gone seedy? This dream-memory stands in for Charlie and for men; you're at a point now where you're seeking out intimacy, however tentative."

Claire looked out the window. While Lowenstein was looking down, she exhaled on the glass and traced her name.

"I don't know if it's intimacy, exactly. Part of me just wants to sleep with someone and get it over with."

"You want a lover. Someone you can place in a different scenario than you see Charlie in."

"I don't know. Eve, my botanomanist, said to do it out of town and don't even ask his name. She screwed a car salesman and then got married eight months later."

"To the car salesman?"

"No, to a tax attorney."

"I see."

"We're out of time, aren't we?"

"Yes."

19

CLAIRE'S THIRD DATE PLAYED HOCKEY FOR THE NEW York Islanders, and she arranged to double with Richard and Bridget to take the pressure off. They met, in various stages, at Bemelmans at the Carlyle Hotel. Bridget was there when Claire arrived, draped loosely around the bar, eating olives.

"Oh my God, Claire. Hi!" Bridget said. A great part of her appeal was her unparalleled fervor for almost everything.

Bridget double-kissed and Claire did not, but they got past it almost flawlessly and Claire assumed a tall chair at the bar.

Bridget was a dog stylist. She outfitted very wealthy dogs. Charlie had casually observed of her once that she was a G-string away from pole dancing, which wasn't saying anything at all except that he wouldn't mind sleeping with her, given the chance. Claire noticed a wobble in Bridget's movement off of, then back onto, her own tall chair. She was drunk.

"So, are you okay?" Bridget whispered it passionately, with her head down, speaking and looking not at Claire but instead straight ahead, like a spy from central casting.

"Yes, I am. Thanks," Claire replied, also straight ahead. Bridget was having martinis; Claire followed suit.

"No, I mean it. God, it's so fucked up. I mean, how did you deal?"

Claire hadn't seen Bridget since the funeral and she wasn't completely sure they were talking about Charlie, but it hardly mattered.

Bridget was eating the olives from her drink, pulling them one at a time from a swizzle stick with her teeth. When she finished, she loaded her glass up again from a bowl the bartender had set in front of her. It was fascinating to watch. She chewed each briny fruit purposefully and with her whole mouth, like caramel-covered candies.

"And now, oh my God. You have to start dating. Doesn't that suck?"

Claire bypassed Bridget's questions and countered with her own, a trick she'd learned from Lowenstein. "How is work going?" If she started on this, Claire knew she wouldn't have to talk for a while. Bridget's eyes popped wide and she sucked in her breath.

"Oh my God, you wouldn't believe it. It's going *so* great. I'm in *Bark* next month!"

Claire had to ask. "*Bark?*"

"You know, the magazine? They did a huge cover story called 'Doggie-Style.' Isn't that smart? We did the shoot in Bayville Beach. It was really amazing. Susan Sarandon's dog was in it. And you know that woman who played Anna Wintour in the movie? Her dog was there, too."

Claire took an olive and contemplated the thought that Bridget did not even know who Meryl Streep was. Bridget went on.

"I'm starting my own line now, too. Entire ensembles focused around verbs. Richard says it's very highbrow."

Claire took another olive, leaving them just two—one apiece—with the bartender nowhere in sight.

"They're not a statement or, you know, a lifestyle or anything like that. They don't say anything about you. They're a verb. So I've sketched out a Sit line and a Come line, and, of course, a Shake. I'm planning to launch six verbs to start and add twelve more next year. I have to finalize my collection by November to get into spring shows."

Bridget picked up the last olive with her thumb and third finger and placed it on her tongue like communion. A ticker tape of new verbs, no doubt, raced through her seamless head. Still looking straight ahead, and not at Claire, Bridget let escape a prolonged laugh. It was a good laugh and it brought the bartender back with more olives.

They chewed and Bridget laughed and they ordered more drinks.

Richard's arrival just then might have been anticlimactic had he not walked in the door with Jake Murphy on his heels.

Claire was gripped suddenly by pet verbs. They had hold of her like an old song on the radio. *Stop. Stay. Heel.* Richard kissed first Bridget, then Claire, and ordered drinks for the four of them. Jake stuck out his hand and Bridget laughed.

"You girls know this guy, of course," Richard said. Claire didn't watch hockey, but she understood the expectation that one was to recognize sports stars. She suspected Richard hadn't known who Jake Murphy was, either, until that morning when he googled him.

"Honey, this is Jake Murphy, best center in the league," he said to Bridget. "We just met in the lobby. And, Jake, this is Claire." Claire smiled. *Bark. Fetch.*

Jake was cute and smartly dressed. He looked like a well-appointed boxer—the dog and athlete both. He was sleek and muscular, his clothes were snug. He looked obedient.

Sasha just then began a steady stream of texts.

4got 2 tell u, J's writing a book! Claire took Sasha's cue.

"I heard you're a writer off the ice. I didn't know hockey players could write. I thought their hands were always all broken up."

Jake held out his smooth, unbandaged hands.

"Memoir?" Richard said.

"Something like that." Jake was looking at Claire intently. "It's about hockey, pretty much. So yeah." Claire flashed a lopsided smile back. Between the chewy olives and Bridget's verbs, she had managed to finish off three martinis. A square-jawed hockey player in business-casual Prada seemed like the next obvious thing.

"This is brilliant," she slurred to Richard. "Sasha's out of her mind." She felt the buzz of her phone: He has profile in Vogue, 2! Nxt month.

Jake was not what she expected. He was soft-skinned and had all of his teeth. He didn't look like a hockey player; he looked like a Chippendales dancer who juggled acting gigs by day. He looked like the Golf Pro on *Days of Our Lives*.

"How'd your *Vogue* piece go?"

"It was cool. Yeah."

"Who was the writer?"

"Can't hear you, honey."

"WHO WAS THE WRITER?"

Jake grabbed Claire's hand. They moved their foursome to a table and Claire followed Bridget's tipsy weave.

"You write or something, too, right?" Jake said. Sasha had prepped him.

Claire, heady from booze, formed a wry smile and geared up. "I write erotica," she said. "BDSM, groups, shemales." She laughed into her drink, looked up at Jake through wispy bangs, then sunk one pinky carelessly in the vodka and twirled.

Richard eyed Claire suspiciously. Bridget took Richard's hand and started laughing again. "It's okay, baby," she said.

"My husband was a sexologist," Claire said.

Jake smiled big, first at Claire, and then at Bridget, and Richard intercepted Claire's next drink.

"It's *okay*, baby," Bridget said again.

By midnight, Bridget's head wobbled, Richard yawned, Claire was enjoying Jake's hand, but talk, for the most part, had died; they'd grown restless. Richard leaned in close. "Listen, you okay?"

Claire gave him a thumbs-up and felt her phone buzz again.

R U still there?

Bridget was nudging Richard to leave. Claire texted Sasha, squinting at the screen on her phone, which appeared to have gotten smaller.

Yes . . . little drink-richard I think worried.

After some gratuitous wrangling, Jake paid the check and Bridget and Richard got in the first cab while Claire and Jake waited for the next. "Where are we going?" she asked, her hands clutching onto his muscular arm.

"Fuck," Jake said. "I don't have my keys."

"What? Okay," Claire said.

"My keys. Shit, I don't have my keys. I left them at the gym."

A call to the gym confirmed it was closed.

"Shit. Oh well."

Claire was too hazy to think through whether this was some-thing he'd planned—the old key ruse. So she took keyless Jake home. She tossed the clutter of take-out containers under the sink and threw open her drapes to let in the city lights.

"Whoa, babe. Nice place."

She opened a bottle of wine and started giggling.

"Beaujolais!" she announced. "Big fruit and leafy smells." She took an exaggerated sniff of the bottle. "I think it's out of season. There's a season for Beaujolais, you know." She could hear herself slurring. She found everything terribly funny. She stumbled and Jake caught her arm. She let her hair fall out of its clip and kicked her shoes across the room. She poured a glass of wine for Jake and kept the bottle. Clutching it, she put it up to her mouth for a long drink and wiped her lips with the back of her hand. This was New Claire now. Claire of the Jungle. Single, young, hot, wild, crazy Claire.

Jake grabbed the bottle and drank from it, too. "You're a naughty girl, I bet." Naughty Claire? She considered it. Should she spank him? Spank herself? What would Charlie have said were Claire to ever have inquired about the terms of being naughty?

"You know," Jake said, rubbing the wine bottle against her throat. *Oh God*, Claire thought. *Am I supposed to do it with the bottle?* "I might be stuck here for the night."

"I bet you say that to all the girls."

Jake asked to take a shower, which seemed perfectly natural. Claire pointed down the hall. It was one o'clock, and they could sleep in or maybe not. They could go for coffee in the morning, or he could leave while it was dark. Who cared? There was a man in her room for the first time in six months, not counting Ethan. She was too drunk to panic. This was easy. This was nice.

At that moment, losing her widow virginity to a hockey player made perfect sense.

But fifteen minutes later Jake reappeared in Charlie's robe. The camel-colored cashmere robe she'd bought him for Christmas just last year, before anyone knew about dying. Their last Christmas, before she knew it was the last.

Claire gasped loudly, then covered her mouth. "Oh my God. Shit." The night was blown. All of it. The flirts, the man, the crazy, naughty Claire.

> RULE #7: Do not keep your dead
> husband's robe in the bathroom.

"What, babe? What's wrong?"

Was this why Evan Spence had made a note about the robe? Why had Claire left it hanging on the back of the door, her dead husband's robe? Why the fuck had she left Charlie's toiletries neat and in place, instead of moving them to the second bathroom down the hall—the shaving supplies, the cologne? One bathroom for Claire, one for dead Charlie. She'd never thought this was anything that would intersect with Jake, with any Jake, with any hockey player, with anyone. How had Jake seen dead Charlie's robe? Didn't he think it was strange to put it on, another man's robe? Shouldn't he have avoided it? Did he think she ran a fucking hotel outfitted with men's cashmere robes?

No, it was Claire who was wrong. Claire had a problem, not Jake.

"Listen, you know what. I'm sorry. I can't . . ."

"Can't what?"

"I need to take you home. Somewhere."

"I don't have my keys to go home. Hey, what happened?"

"Then you need to call someone, a friend. Nothing happened. I just . . . you need to go. I'll walk you somewhere or go with you. I need you to put your clothes on."

"Are you okay?"

Claire's voice was rising like floodwater in a hurricane and she thought she might scream the way a three-year-old screamed—eyes closed, hands on ears, full-throated emotional scream. Claire had that urgent need and hoped she could hold it in until Jake went away.

"I'm fine. I think the alcohol wore off, and I get these headaches and I just want to go to bed."

She was fighting the urge to tear the robe off of him, to snatch it off and kick him and run. She needed to get him out the door and he was moving too slowly.

"Okay, baby. That's cool," Jake said. "I'll call someone, then."

"Can you call them outside, please?"

"It's loud on the street."

"Then in the hall? Please."

Jake was putting on pants, buttoning buttons, slipping on shoes. He looked dazed and confused, and a little sad. He very gallantly kissed Claire's cheek before he left, though. It made a tear of hers run down. "Good night, pretty girl."

It was the end, for Claire, of hockey.

20

I BROUGHT A MAN HOME, TO SPEND THE NIGHT. TO HAVE sex with."

"And how did that go?"

"He put on Charlie's robe and I freaked out."

Spence had an emery board and was very methodically filing his nails. Claire couldn't take her eyes away.

"Why is that? Why did you freak out?"

"I don't know. It felt like Charlie was in the room watching us. I felt like I'd been caught."

"What do you feel today?"

"Um. Annoyed, I guess, a little. Anxious. If I don't find someone suitable in the next couple of months, my married friends will move on. Sasha wants to have kids now. Mothers don't have time for single friends."

"Claire, did it occur to you that each person bears his or her own set of problems? That if you read Socrates, or Hegel, they tell you that the struggle of the ordinary is one of the universal pitfalls of mankind?"

"No."

"It's the every day, the getting from breakfast to jobs to appointments to dinner to bed, all the seemingly minor incidents lodged between big moments, that topple us."

Claire looked at Spence, then looked out the window. He probably got all this crap from Charlie, she thought.

"I just need to get through the first year," Claire said.

"What makes you so certain some sea change occurs after a year?"

Spence had an eyebrow raised, her cue, she knew, to behave. Be fucked up, but do it right.

"A year is as long as you can stretch it. You know, the Jewish year of mourning . . . it's a year. You get a year."

"I wasn't aware you were Jewish," said Dr. Spence.

"It's carefully unwritten into every conversation about death. It's the three-six-three paradigm."

"I'm unfamiliar with it," Spence said.

"For the first three months, everyone's around and attentive, there's great concern, or show of concern, and they conspire to keep you distracted and busy. The next six months are busy, too, though the attention trails off. Widowhood is like any other commodity. It's not enough to just have it. You have to understand its value."

Spence managed to glance at his watch without disturbing the eyebrow, which Claire found fascinating, but she was determined to finish her thought.

"And then the last three months it dies. Tumbleweeds blow by. The old couples' friends stop calling; some new friends trickle in. You start to segue out of one skin and into another. Then you start running into people. 'Oh yeah you, I remember. You're still a widow? How's that working out?'"

She looked at Spence's shoes; they were a horrible shade of red-brown. He should be starting his wrap-up.

"Claire."

"Yes?"

"Did you hear me? I need to reschedule next week. Can we move to Thursday?"

The perfect man will walk through my door one night when the lights are out, Claire thought. And then she heard her mother's voice: *Honey, lock your door. It's New York. People get killed.*

The journalist, Alex, hadn't liked Claire's seduction scene, but what did he know? Stephen had had the seductive power of a rat. Some girls want candles and wine, and that's okay. Some like to be whisked out of town. Some are fine getting fucked in a nice room at The Standard. Charlie covered methods of seduction and sexual fantasies at length in *Driving with Her Head in Your Lap*. Generally speaking, in almost every species, from the bonobo to the fruit fly, there's a template the male follows: show confidence, then empathy, self-deprecation, then go for the kill.

Claire, personally, liked how Robert Redford seduced Katharine Ross. What was wrong with that? "Yes, sure. Thursday is fine," Claire said. When she got home, Jack Huxley was in her mailbox, on the front page of *Variety*. She'd almost forgotten about him. He had just signed on to a new project, opposite Keira Knightley, who'd been offered the highest amount of money ever paid to a woman in a lead. An enormous picture of the two—she in red, a full-lipped bosomy piece of candy; and he in black with his lottery-winning grin—adorned the small article.

21

WHEN CLAIRE FINALLY GOT LAID, IT WAS A DISAS-
ter, of sorts. Not completely, but of sorts.

It wasn't at gunpoint; it wasn't particularly sweet. There was
grunting in place of banter, there were tequila and cigarettes. The
whole thing went down fast. It was messy, and in Claire's post-
marital bed, and with only one shoe. But it was over. She went to
the movie premiere at the Ziegfeld Theatre on Fifty-Fourth because
Richard asked her to. He asked because he wanted Claire to meet
the subject of Charlie's incomprehensible, unfinished book.

It was the season's holiday blockbuster, opening wide the next
month on Thanksgiving Day. *The New Guy* was a rom-com starring
Olivia Wilde as Tracy Dow, an improbably stunning single mother,
and Jack Huxley as Matt Ryan, a gorgeous but emotionally unavail-
able man. Tracy is betrothed to the town rogue, Eric Stone—
played by newcomer Bradley Hess, his first feature film. Eric Stone
is considered a catch—good-looking with money. He behaves well

when Tracy's around but behind her back screws every lonely woman in town.

Matt Ryan is a new mechanic in town. He's handsome but guarded; strong and silent. There's heartbreak in his past, which was obviously written into the story to give Jack Huxley's irresistible wounded look ample time on the big screen.

Tracy, of course, falls for him as Eric reveals his brutish nature, and they have an encounter. She thinks it's one thing, Matt Ryan thinks it's another. There's a comedy of errors—miscues, starts, and stutters. Matt advances, Tracy demurs. He retreats, she takes a chance, he blows it. In the end, of course, Jack Huxley gets the girl.

The story was predictable. Claire expected it to be. But the close-ups were breathtaking. Wilde and Huxley were aesthetically stunning, including one long, beautiful scene of them on a motorcycle winding through colorful New England fall trees. Huxley looked so natural on the bike. Claire wondered if he owned one.

After the premiere there was a cocktail reception, and the drinks came fast and strong. Richard drank scotch while Claire sipped a lemon drop from a tall, skinny glass. The room was visibly restless. Jack Huxley was late.

In his place, Bradley Hess worked the crowd. Disappointment was thick, but Hess was undeterred. He posed with Olivia for the press, he consorted with the cast. He seized his moment, working every photo op in the room. There were a hundred cameras waiting for Jack and they were twitchy, shooting at everything.

Claire was standing with Richard and the movie's producer, Frank Mennant, at the moment the actual star did enter the room. The sudden flutter of hearts was palpable; you could feel the collective jolt. *People* magazine had just declared him the sexiest man alive.

This, Claire thought, might be interesting. He headed toward them, and every eye in the place followed. What had been anxious and anticipatory chatter moments before exploded into a quiet roar of murmurs. Skin prickled and hairlines went taut.

"Jack," Frank said. He interrupted their conversation to greet his prize. The room tipped toward them like the list of a boat that was taking on water. Jack Huxley transformed their bit of floor into a stage.

Frank turned slightly toward Claire. "You've met Richard already, of course, and this is my dear friend Claire Byrne," he said. "Claire, Jack Huxley." As he spoke, Frank's mouth crept into a slow smile that put Claire in mind of a cartoon villain. *Here is a movie star. Here is a woman. Now, if she suits him, he will have her.*

"This is a pleasure," Jack Huxley said—theatrically; was there any other way? Here were the movie star lashes, the leading-man gaze in the same close-up shot she'd just seen on-screen.

He held her eyes and kissed her hand, and Claire thought of Red Riding Hood's wolf. The well-tailored suit, the healthy tan, the white teeth and thick hair and just slightly ruddy hue to his cheek, all the better to screw her with. *Oh brother,* she thought, but couldn't stop herself from blushing. She said, "Thank you."

Claire had seen this before, if on a slightly smaller scale. She'd been married to the most-important-man-in-the-room. Women were lined up and presented for these men like drumsticks at a medieval banquet. Sure, Jack Huxley was handsome. Okay, beautiful, exquisite even. Still.

Frank excused himself, gesturing vaguely to some matter across the room. "I need to catch up with someone," he said, and then he left. Richard followed him to the bar.

"Did you like the film?" Jack Huxley asked Claire. Just like that they were alone and familiar. Jack Huxley knows everyone, everything. Richard watched from across the room, bemused. Claire became anxious. Why had he left her? Why was everyone staring?

"It'll do great, I'm sure. It's a perfect holiday flick." *Oh my God*, Claire thought. *Perfect holiday flick?*

Jack smiled, amused. "How do you know Frank?" he asked.

"He's an old friend. Old, old friend," Claire said. Frank had known Charlie since he was an Ivy League blowhard with no prospects. "How do *you* know him?" Jack Huxley and this was the best she could come up with?

"We used to date. Bad breakup, but we're good now."

Claire relaxed a bit. Mr. Huxley liked to play.

Out of nowhere, someone put a drink in Jack's hand, and then put one in Claire's.

"Claire," he said. "What are you doing with this seamy crowd? You're not an actress."

"How do you know I'm not an actress?"

"Because you're not acting."

"Well, I'm in a very high-end but obscure line of work. You wouldn't have heard of me."

"Here. Give me your drink."

Puzzled, Claire handed him the drink she'd been given—she wasn't even clear what it was. Jack replaced it with a small glass.

"Blue agave tequila. It's smooth, not like what you drank in college on spring break. I shared a bottle with the crew after the premiere of my first film—I was Man in Elevator. I got my first speaking role the next day, so I have a shot after every premiere. I'm superstitious."

Claire clinked her small glass with his, braced herself, and drank it down. He was right; it was smooth. No bite at all. A fuzzy little warmth traced a path from her lips down to her ankles.

"So," she said. "Did you forget to have one after *Danger and Darkness?*"

"So you're one of the eight people who saw it!" Jack Huxley put another small glass in Claire's hand.

"Now, what's this obscure line of work you're in?" Claire had just drunk enough to think, *What the hell.*

"Sex toys," she said. Charlie would have been proud. "I design them." Richard, she thought, looked concerned, though she couldn't quite make him out.

"Really?" Jack Huxley said. "That's interesting. What sorts of toys?"

Claire took another drink and lost more inhibition. "Penetrators, mostly, for men. Anal penetration is an art and in most heterosexual relationships men get the shaft, pun intended, because most straight women are unschooled. They think of toys as something to stimulate the clitoris and vagina, which is very shortsighted."

"How about that," Jack Huxley said, smiling. Claire was enjoying the audience. She went on. "Heterosexuals are actually very ignorant about male sexuality. Most design around sexual aids only considers the vagina. There's a wide range of possibility."

The actor was still smiling. "Take it easy on those," he said as Claire downed her second tequila. "They sneak up."

Because of Charlie, Claire was overeducated in theory, underequipped in the field. She didn't recognize certain mating tics, signals, signs. She no more knew whether this man, the movie star, wanted to sleep with her than whether he was signaling her to steal third. Had she been clearheaded and aware, perhaps the night would have gone differently.

Instead she found herself drinking a third shot of tequila, and then a fourth. In hindsight she should have left the building with Richard somewhere between her second and her third tequila. That would have been the smart move. Instead, she insisted on talk. It was what they did, after all, in the movies. There was repartee, a natural progression. Conversation and small glasses of booze.

Then a notable thing occurred some time between when the movie star entered the room and the dark hours of morning. Claire lost her virginity as a widow.

Let's watch it out of order, because the middle part is best. Here's the scene: Claire faceup on her bed in her apartment, eyes glued to the ceiling, skirt hiked up to her hips. Her legs are pried apart like a wishbone. Her stockings have slouched and her garter's askew. A bottle of tequila is on the nightstand alongside her antique hand mirror.

She was struggling with a headache. She was struggling to know what happened. Where was she, how did she get here, what did she do, and who with? Jack Huxley had been wearing a dark suit, she remembers that clearly, but it wasn't the one that was crumpled on her chair across the room. Jack Huxley from the magazines in waiting rooms, the man her dead husband was writing a book about, the object of human desire, of Hollywood, the rogue nephew of Aldous, was in a dark suit at one point and they were talking. And now a different man was on top of her.

"Come on, baby, put on the shoes," he said. It was Bradley Hess. It was the romantic rival, the jerk in the movie, the supporting actor, not the star. Bradley Hess' jacket was on her chair. *What?* Fuck!

He had one of Claire's shoes in each hand, not the ones she'd been wearing, but two different shoes from her closet. They were both red but mismatched. Between thrust and parry, to-and-fro, he tried to shove them onto Claire's feet, one at a time. It made her motion sick. Songs about shoes rushed through her head—"Red Shoes," "Blue Suede Shoes," "Goody Two Shoes."

RULE #8: Make sure you're having sex with the right guy.

"C'mon, honey. Put on the shoes."

Hess was handsome enough in his own right, and in any other universe, coming around like this in a bed, not yet clear on everything but clear enough to know you are having sex with Brad Hess, would not have been unpleasant. But where had he come from? Brad Hess was not Jack. As her widow cherry popped, Claire attempted to piece it together. Jack, yes. They were talking, he'd left early. Claire drank tequila, a lot of it. Oh my God, quite a bit. He said to go slow, and she didn't. Why not? She used bawdy language. She remembered saying *ass-fuck*.

Jack Huxley left and Brad Hess stayed. Now he was here in Claire's apartment, stripped bare to his socks. Charlie would never have left on socks; God knows Jack Huxley wouldn't. Here, however, was the actor who plays Eric Stone in *The New Guy* with his socks on; the hardwood floors in Claire's rooms were cold. Behind him, her television was on Channel 1079 and it was costing her fourteen dollars an hour. He succeeded in getting one shoe on her foot.

Claire became absorbed in the images on the screen, two women and a man. One woman, a blonde, was on top of the man, bouncing up and down without expression. Claire wondered if she was happy or sad. The other woman rubbed the blonde's back, squeezed her breasts as they bounced, reached her hand around to where the man's penis went in and out. The blonde threw her head back and let out a high-pitched noise. Huxley said something to her, before he left. What did he say?

"Come on, baby."

Right: Bradley, the shoes. He got the other shoe on, finally. He quickened his pace for a few moments, then stopped. His face contorted, he breathed in sharply, then let his breath back out slow. He was still for a few moments and then he dismounted and moved to Claire's living room. Left alone, Claire surveyed the wreckage. In addition to the tequila, an ashtray on Claire's dresser held the remains of a joint.

Minutes later, from the living room, music pierced Claire's four-in-the-morning air. Singing—big, booming, operatic singing. She recognized the song. She got up to peek out her bedroom door, and Brad Hess was sitting naked on her tiger-print couch, bellowing out "Jesus Christ Superstar" like Pavarotti. On the coffee table sat Charlie in his urn, silent and condemning—or else laughing his late ass off.

" 'Jesus Christ, Superstar.' "

Claire lit up the half-smoked joint, choked inhaling, and tried to process the scene.

Brad Hess looked over at her. "I'm classically trained."

She felt dizzy, but in a nice way. It could have been worse. There was a handsome naked man sitting upright in her living room, with good posture, feet shoulder-width apart, chest taut, singing show tunes. He had a water glass in his hand.

Oh my God, Claire thought. *What just happened?*

22

CLAIRE WENT NOT TO LOWENSTEIN WITH HER NEWS, but to Spence. He had the radio on low. He was trimming a primrose in a small pot on his lap.

"Okay. Well, I met a man at a movie premiere last night, an actor. The star, actually. Well, I met the star and then also the supporting guy, who I guess isn't a star but is still in the movie."

"Yes."

"So we flirted, a little, afterward, after the premiere at the reception. And then we had sex."

Spence put down his plant. "Well, this sounds like a welcome turn of events. This is what you've been talking about, isn't it? You've been tormented with this idea of virginity hanging over you."

Claire smiled weakly but didn't answer.

"Who did you have sex with?"

"The actor."

"The actor you were flirting with."

"No, no. I didn't. Well, I mean, I did."

Spence looked puzzled.

Claire took a deep breath.

"I flirted with the star. And then I had sex with the not-star. It gets . . . blurry."

"Okay."

"I think I blacked out. I'm pretty certain I did. Actually, I did. And when I woke up it was like I was in the middle of a scene. One minute we're in a room of pretty people, dressed and bantering, and I'm flirting with Jack Huxley—"

Spence put his hands together atop his lap and made no attempt to respond. He'd earlier that morning had dental work, Claire knew, and was putting great effort into the movement around his mouth; it was still partially numb. He moved his hand there, unconsciously, several times in the course of a minute, and to her it appeared that he was trying not to laugh. She fidgeted in her seat. She looked around at the walls and windows.

"So, yeah. Jack Huxley. It was the premiere of his movie. And there was tequila. And he kept, well, someone kept giving me little glasses of tequila. And then the next thing I know we're on my bed flanked by, well, marijuana . . . and more tequila, and he's shoving my feet into these shoes. Only it's not Jack's suit jacket on the chair, it's a different one, and then it's actually Bradley Hess shoving my feet into the shoes. I can't even piece it together very well."

Spence picked up the primrose again. "Well, the substances are a concern, but let's shelve that for now. This is directly tied to what we're working on. You want intimacy, but you also want sex. You fear you're incapable of blending the two—you've been told this, in fact, by your late husband, who stood behind research. So, how do you feel about last night?"

"I'm not incapable of blending the two. Charlie was. Charlie said it wasn't possible."

"Do you think it's possible?" Spence uncrossed his legs.

Claire thought he seemed smug. "I don't know. I think so."

"Okay, so you're ambivalent."

"I kept thinking how absurd it was. I mean, he's an actor, it seemed unreal. From what I can recall, it felt like we were just doing a scene on my bed. A disastrous one—I never would have written it."

Evan Spence did not take a note and did not look down; he just looked at Claire and waited. Was he captivated or bored?

"I was trying not to laugh. He wanted me to put on these shoes . . . and then later, he sat naked in my living room, on my tiger-print sofa, and started singing."

"What was he singing?"

" 'Superstar,' you know, from the musical. He has a very nice voice. I wasn't expecting that . . . but I couldn't stop thinking about my neighbors across the hall, waking up at four in the morning to a bellowing Brad Hess. The entire transaction, from the premiere party to the sex to the singing and his exit was seven hours. It was completely unplanned. I went to the premiere to be introduced to Huxley and ended up screwing his costar. That's fucked up. Maybe I need a sex therapist."

"You might be getting ahead of yourself."

"My dead husband had a pathological obsession with sex. Can you get it from a partner?"

"Obsession is not a communicable disease."

"Then it's learned behavior. His, and now mine."

Spence tilted his head slightly, narrowed his eyes, continued the conversation. "Charlie affirmed all of your internal doubts about yourself and your relationships with men, and then he left before you had a chance to dispute him or prove otherwise. He made it okay for you to be this way. You made it okay for him, as well. You said he had one or maybe two other girl-friends?"

"Sure. For comedy's sake, let's call them 'girlfriends' and let's say 'one or two.' "

"Perhaps he hadn't found anyone who would accept this in him until you. Someone who would let him remain emotionally with-drawn but still be loyal. You looked at Charlie and saw yourself, and the two of you were attracted to that in each other. Now that he's gone, the trouble's been where to restart."

"That's all I want to know."

"You've recognized that you want to have intimacy, both emo-tional and physical."

"Maybe I'll have a promiscuous phase."

"Having a sexual encounter does not equate with promiscuity."

"He doesn't know my number; it will be awkward if we meet again. He's probably done this a thousand different times."

"Is Jack Huxley aware that your husband was writing a book about him?"

Claire shrugged. "I'm not really sure. We didn't get to that."

Spence nodded.

"I liked the water glasses," Claire said.

"The water glasses?"

"Yes. Afterward, after he was singing, Brad Hess smoked a cigarette. He asked if he could smoke in my apartment, and then he did, and then he had a glass of water. We both did. We both drank out of water glasses, and then left them there. So when I woke in the morning, there were water glasses on the table. Two of them."

"And?"

"And I liked that. Maybe that was what I wanted."

PART III

Love Is a Drag

23

THE FOLLOWING TUESDAY, WHILE SASHA DROWNED her childless angst in a proper old-fashioned—cubed sugar, muddled bitters, three shots of Canadian Club—Claire went back to Beatrice. *What the hell*, she thought. *What do I have to lose?*

What the hell, indeed.

There, in the stiff-backed chair of Beatrice's sterile little office, Claire handed over a photograph. It was the one from *New York* magazine, it was the one with her soul in her eyes, the one that Charlie had confused with her talent. Beatrice studied the picture; she held it at different angles; she held it close to, then away from, her face. She was intent. For Claire, the bar was lower now. She was just killing time. But Beatrice was a career gal, a professional. She took her job very seriously, and she was on the clock. Her long fingers jerked and twitched as she squeezed Claire's hand and then relaxed. She mumbled things as she studied the picture, things that Claire could not understand. Claire did see her smile. There was a smile on Beatrice's face: a small, smirky smile that began to stretch out into a broad one. She squeezed Claire's hand once more, quickly, then released it. The excitement was spiked with the claustrophobic air of Beatrice's office. Claire gasped. Something had clearly happened.

"Yes!" Beatrice shrieked. She actually shrieked. This was not the same Beatrice that Claire had experienced before. "This is good. Before you see me again, you'll find love!"

This time it was Claire who was skeptical. "Love?"

"Yes. Love."

"Where? Who?"

With intense concentration, Beatrice studied Claire's hand. "I see it, it's remarkable. Your cheeks are flushed pink. You're sitting at a bar, and you're wearing a flower-print dress."

IT WAS SIX days since the night Claire, legs askew, wore mismatched shoes for someone she thought was Jack Huxley. Predictably, Bradley Hess hadn't called. She didn't own a flower-print dress. Her phone rang on her way home, in the cab. *Unknown.*

Did she believe in fate? The universe? Coincidence? It didn't matter whether she did; Charlie and the events of the thin man had spoken for themselves.

"Hello?" she answered, cautiously.

"Claire!" It was Richard. He wasn't the caller she thought he'd be, but he wasn't unwelcome. "How would you like to flee this cold, cruel city for warmer climes?"

He continued without waiting for an answer. "I've just had a call from the manager of one Huxley, Jack. Seems he was impressed by you, especially when I dropped the fact that you're working on a book about him."

Jack Huxley, it turned out, was finishing up on the set of a new movie, *Chaos Effect*. He'd invited them to L.A. the following week to be his guests at a party he was hosting. He was curious (or so Richard claimed Jack Huxley's manager had claimed) about Charlie Byrne's book. Neither Richard, nor—Claire hoped—Jack knew about the night of the mismatched shoes.

It took two calls to Ethan's voice mail, one to his landline, and a text to his new boyfriend to track him down. He hadn't been coming around as much. "Where have you been?"

"Sweetie. Daddy's got things to do, people to see."

"Well, I need help."

He was there within the hour bearing gifts—stockings from Kiki's, a colorful pile of fitted tees, a well-thumbed paperback of Erica Jong's *Fear of Flying*.

He gave Charlie's urn a loving pat—Claire cringed. Then he stretched himself out in Charlie's chair. "Okay. Let it out."

"I had sex."

Ethan's eyes popped open wide.

"With a person?" he said.

"Don't judge me." Claire said and paused for a moment. "It was Bradley Hess."

Ethan's fingers rubbed his chin, his eyes narrowed.

"Sasha's accountant?"

"No! Brad Hess. The actor. You know . . ." Claire couldn't think of the name of a movie he'd been in. "Well, he's in a new movie right now. It opens soon."

Ethan rubbed a hand through his hair. He was loving this.

"An actor," he said. "Well, that's nothing to shake a leg at, Clara." His smile spread slowly across his face like an oil spill.

"You said you wouldn't judge and, by the way, he's going to be big. It's Jack Huxley's new movie."

"This is an interesting twist."

He folded his arms. He was making Claire nervous.

"It was fun, and it's over, and that's that."

"It was fun?"

"Well . . . I think it was. There are gaps."

Ethan got up and walked to the kitchen. Charlie's weekly delivery from Gourmet Garage was still coming. It was on the counter. It had come just before Ethan arrived. Mixed winter greens, smoked trout, infused vinegars and assorted herbs, and a hormone-free grass-fed leg of lamb. Ethan rubbed his hands together and perused the wine selection in Charlie's stash.

"It's a lot to take in, sweetie. We might need to whip something up for this," he said. He opened a red, took an appraising drink, and brought a glass out to Claire.

"It was complicated anyway. No, I mean, not really. It's fine. I don't want to analyze it."

"You always want to analyze. That's your thing," Ethan said putting emphasis on *thing* to make his point.

"Well, I don't want to now." The smell of onion and garlic was relaxing to her. She'd taken it for granted for so many years, the fragrance and bustle of a kitchen. Of someone preparing and serving meals. The Malbec made her brave.

"I'm going to L.A."

"You're going to L.A. Well, you can't make someone fall in love with you but you can stalk him and hope he panics and gives in. I love it!"

The small kitchen began to sizzle. Ethan pulled out his iPod and plugged it into Charlie's speaker. Maria Callas singing *Tosca*. It felt reassuring and familiar—like a prelude.

"Nobody's stalking anyone," Claire said. "Richard told Jack

Huxley about Charlie's book. I think he's trying to muscle me into finishing it." The music grew louder. *Vissi d'arte, vissi d'amore.* Claire raised her voice to be heard over it. "Anyway, he invited us for a meeting."

"Who invited you for a meeting?"

"Huxley."

Ethan tasted a shallot off the end of his fork.

RULE #9: Always judge a book by its cover.

"Wow. Nicely played by Richard. When do you leave?"

"Next week," Claire shouted. Ethan turned down the sound. "So I need your help with the manuscript. I've looked through it—it's a mess."

Ethan pulled out his phone. "Honey, you don't need manuscripts, you need shopping. Have you learned nothing from me? It's never the product, it's always the packaging."

Six hours and one decadent lamb stew later, Claire was armed with a little black dress, Giuseppe Zanotti heels, and a Halston jumpsuit that Ethan swore would turn him straight—things it felt ridiculous to be buying when the temperature in New York was forty degrees, things that would be perfect for L.A.

She returned to her apartment shell-shocked by the crush of early holiday shoppers. She watched the rain fall down the long picture windows that Charlie had never liked. The smell of pine and sage snuck under her door. Couples were opening bottles of wine; they were warm and at ease. They were flirting, and kissing, and making soufflés, and watching *It's a Wonderful Life.*

For the next week, Claire worked diligently on Charlie's book. She fleshed out Huxley's character. She reread old profile pieces. She marched through conflict, then resolution, then conflict again. Jack Huxley had wild affairs both off the screen and on. Jack Huxley was the nephew of one of the world's most intellectual men. Jack Huxley played a charming brooder in big box-office rom-coms but funded independent films of Alister McGrath on the side. Jack Huxley was an enigma. Rogue. Heartthrob. Womanizer. Check.

But was Jack Huxley also serious? Sensitive? Real? Claire was getting mixed messages. How much of Charlie's manuscript was true to Huxley's life? Would the story evolve as she got to know its subject better? Richard was selling this as Charlie's book, under the guise that it was for the most part complete, with Claire just cleaning it up. But the project was turning out to be a lot for her to chew on.

24

C LAIRE DID NOT OWN A FLOWER-PRINT DRESS, BUT
after Beatrice's pronouncement, she bought one. And while
Huxley said his lines in front of a replica of a Turkish mosque
on the Paramount lot, Claire Byrne batted her eyelashes on a Boe-
ing 757, which touched down in Los Angeles at 11:03 a.m.

Frank Sinatra crooned through her iPod. It was seventy-five
degrees and the air felt light as she walked from the plane into the
pleasant buzz of LAX. Even baggage claim, through Claire's new
sunglasses, looked pink. On the drive to her hotel, there were tall
palms and green grass, there were bright colors and open spaces
and panoramas. Here, it seemed, everyone was entitled; there were
enough sunny riches to go around.

"We have dinner tonight. Eight," Richard said.

"Okay," Claire said, from her room in the Hotel Bel-Air. "Dinner with Huxley. It sounds like a movie title." She was picking rai-
sins out of breakfast cereal, comfort food. She was rattled, but
Richard couldn't see this through the phone.

Jack Huxley. What would she say when she saw him? What would he say when he saw her? She didn't remember him leaving that night. God, had she been a complete mess? Did he know what happened afterward?

"The three of us, then? The four of us?" Claire asked. Richard had brought Bridget along.

"Oh, I doubt it. Huxley won't come alone, he'll have people there—his agent or lawyer, or assistant. Just be charming and professional. Be yourself. I'll have to meet you there, I've got a meeting with one of my film agents; we might be able to option the rights to something now that Charlie's dead." He cleared his throat. "I'm sorry, honey. That was insensitive. I'll have a car sent to take you to the restaurant. Don't be late."

Claire hung up the phone and dialled Ethan.

"I'm nervous," she said. She lounged across the California king.

"You'll be fine. Just picture him naked."

"You're not helping," Claire said. "Do you think he knows about Brad Hess? That whole *situation*?"

"The 'situation'? Sweetie, you're just having dinner."

"Right, I know. You're right. I'll be fine." Claire hung up the phone and pressed the button marked CONCIERGE.

"Hello, Ms. Byrne, how can I help you?"

He sounded young and well built, and Claire thought of all the ways in which he might help, but settled on hair. "Can I get into the salon for a blowout at four o'clock?"

"Of course. Will that be all?"

"Yes. Thank you." She hung up the phone and flopped across the bed.

The tide was turning. Claire felt the shifting of sand. For nearly six months she'd been "the young widow." But something had changed and she had the unsettling sense she wasn't reading things right. It was dangerous, perhaps, to fiddle with a narrative too soon into the story.

She was prepared to be aloof. To coolly reference the night or to not reference it at all. She was prepared to go all Joan Didion on Jack Huxley. Unflappable. Inscrutable. She'd be a cool customer to his Hollywood dog and pony show.

If she had any luck at all, she'd go to dinner with Richard and Bridget and also Jack Huxley. He'd have his *people* there, they'd exchange pleasantries. She would be amused with his self-absorption, his boorish stories. She'd see he was just another stuffed ego and chalk him up as a souvenir. She'd rehash the details for hours with Ethan. Then she'd file him away as anecdotal material for parties, stories her future lover might prod her to tell. "Claire, tell about that time you met Jack Huxley."

Yes, that would be best. Then she'd scrap the book—it was boring her anyway—and she would never see Jack Huxley again, except on a movie channel here and there, as she flipped around on sleepless nights when her future lover was gone on business.

If Claire had any luck at all, the night would evolve like that. But Claire was sometimes unlucky. Her husband was knocked dead by a fake bronze, don't forget. She'd neither moved on nor picked a charity, as Grace had suggested; Charlie's ashes still sat imposingly atop their coffee table. She flounders.

RULE #10: If you see your type coming, run.

Claire dressed for dinner, but she was careless. She forgot all about Beatrice. Like the heroine in a Hitchcock film, she forgot the one crucial thing. She made the obvious mistake. Instead of the flower-print dress, which she'd recklessly shoved to the bottom of her bag, Claire Byrne wore the Halston. She didn't know it—it didn't occur to her as she relaxed in the chair during her blowout in the salon that afternoon—but she was about to take a turn for the worse.

It was Aristotle who said it: "All human actions have one or more of seven causes," and then he named them: chance, nature, compulsion, habit, reason, passion, and desire.

Charlie had used this idea to open the sixth chapter in *Thinker's Hope*, the chapter in which Aristotle was attacked by postmodernists.

It was by *chance* that she'd met Charlie, it was our *nature* to not be alone, it was a *compulsion* to have sex, it was a *habit* to smoke. There was no *reason* to anything; *passion*, Charlie had said, mutually excluded the rest: and *desire*, yes, desire—desire was Jack Huxley. It was the point of Charlie's book. No one in the entire modern world would have tried, even briefly, to argue against that. Jack Huxley launched a thousand ships. Jack Huxley smiled and it was one of those rare smiles, the smile Fitzgerald gave to Gatsby. Jack Huxley dazzled—no, wait, it was much more than that. He smiled and an angel got his wings. He smiled and women on other continents became heavy with child; he smiled and mayflies started screwing in the dead of winter. Jack Huxley smiled and watermelons burst from frozen ground.

"Every action has an equal and opposite reaction." That wasn't Aristotle, it was Newton, but it was about the forces of two bodies. Charlie and the *Man Walking*. Walter White and Sande. Claire and Charlie. And now Claire and who? Jack Huxley? Jack Huxley's smile spun ordinary objects into jewels.

Jack Huxley was the uncertainty principle.

Jack Huxley led to the room of smoke and mirrors.

CLAIRE WAS LATE, it turned out; not deliberately, but she was glad it had worked out that way. When she walked into the restaurant there was one man in the room who was instantly recognizable—that was Richard. There was another man who was not. She'd sold him short in recollection. She'd met him, they'd flirted, she'd thought he'd brought her home, she may have been a complete ass in front of him, she didn't know. His aura should have been dulled; instead it had amped way up. The air around him should have staled; instead, it was rarefied.

Jack Huxley looked up, and Claire watched him watch her cross the room to their table. In a romantic comedy she would have tripped and spilled somebody's wine and he would have looked on benevolently. As luck had it, though, she traversed the room unscathed and it wasn't indulgence Jack Huxley showed, but curiosity. Ah, the smile. Claire's heart stumbled, stopped, then caught itself again.

The power of a smile—the crazy, dizzy, electrifying, and completely disproportionate unreality of a smile. It's just a smile, for Christ's sake. It's facial muscles, a contraction, a reflex, it's a mindless social tic. But when it's done right, Tony Bennett starts to sing in the background of one's mind, and on his heels, Barry White. Claire Byrne felt her breath pull in and let out. She felt her heart rise and fall like a Ferris wheel, round and round. All of this from a glimpse of white teeth. If it was a shock of pale ankle that set off the Victorians, for Claire it was a smile, this one here. His eyes stopped on her eyes; they connected. A meteor, the great star formerly known as Jupiter, the northern lights of possibility, came shooting out through the man's eyes, and his teeth, and his strong square solid chin. There was a flutter, a crinkle, the unveiling of kryptonite in the hypnotic power of all this.

Caution was sucked from the room, Claire heard the *fwoop*.

"Hello," Claire said. Jack Huxley stood and took her hand. "Claire," he said, and he kissed her cheek. "You look lovely."

"You're late," Richard observed quietly. But his irritation, tonight, was charming. Life and all its petty inconveniences were for her amusement. Richard stood, too, kissed both of Claire's cheeks—she offered them graciously. Bridget grinned, that sweet childish grin, and took Claire's hand. Richard had been wrong. Jack hadn't brought an agent or a lawyer or an assistant or a friend. He'd come alone. "We've ordered starters," Richard said. "And drinks."

Claire felt deliriously calm. Gravity relaxed its hold on her. Something could happen or nothing could happen, and either way, in this room, it was fine.

They sat down; they exchanged pleasantries. Claire wondered if Jack knew about the rest of that night. Bradley Hess had never called her. Did men boast to each other of these things? If he knew, he was coy, asking questions about Charlie's work, about Claire's writing. He asked question after question, he listened, he watched her eyes. Bridget sucked on the olives from her martini.

Their conversation was fine-tuned like a symphony, the pauses were all on beat, the laughter was harmonic, the anecdotal chords were stacked in thirds. They ordered an assortment of foods and passed them around, there was nothing bloody or undercooked. The waitstaff arrived and left unobtrusively, treating this dining party as if they were heads of state. Jack Huxley sat close to Claire, he poured wine into her glass when it was low, he offered her bites of his food, he participated in the general conversation but kept his attention on her. He said wonderfully smart things, he moved between gravitas and levity like a rattlesnake through brush. He spoke of things Claire loved to hear, of the sheer perfection of the burger at In-N-Out, of Leonard Cohen and Graham Greene, of great love affairs. They sipped their drinks: Claire's, a bubbly wine; Jack's, a wheat-colored beer. He was *down to earth.* The reason for the presence of Richard and Bridget became less clear. Claire took an extravagant drink and exchanged a coy glance with her dead husband's agent as he passed her a slice of pâté.

"Thank you, Richard," she said, then met Jack's smile as best she could with a doe-eyed gaze.

"I'd like to read something you've written, Claire," Jack said. Everything seemed transmitted from him by a breath and when he spoke the breath was strong and sure, and it was also minty-fresh.

"Oh," Claire said, thinking it was the story not yet written that was proving to be most intriguing. "There's a lot in progress right now."

"Then tell me what makes a great story."

"You're patronizing me; you make your living on stories."

"I just act them, I don't write them down. Half the time I don't even know what the story is."

"Well." She drew out the word and took another drink from her glass. Was this her third, her fourth? Slow down, sweet Claire. Remember what happened with tequila. Stories. Right, that's easy. Pick your characters, dress them for the weather. Send them to sea in an impossibly small boat and then you bring them back home.

"The *best* story is one about love, sex, and death, but not necessarily in that order," she said. "Somewhere in between—from about page seventy to one hundred and forty-three in a novel, or I suppose pages thirty to sixty in a script—there ought to be a crisis of confidence, a crippling one." Richard nodded approvingly. "A girl meets a boy, they connect and then disband. There's a coupling, an entanglement, and then it all comes undone. There should be sex and the opposite of sex—a healthy dose of confusion. There should be a boulevard that is littered with broken dreams, and the futile pursuit of something . . ."

Claire let out a deep breath and laughed, and then took another drink of wine, from a full glass that had been set before her.

Jack Huxley's shoulder was touching hers.

"Oh my God, that's so amazing! The part about the littered dreams?" Bridget said.

Richard and Bridget now seemed completely unnecessary. Jack leaned over to whisper in Claire's ear. His voice was not too even or too deep, it was meaty but not scratchy, masculine but not dominant. The timbre of his vowels sent chills from the knees to the necks of every girl from here to the San Bernardino Valley, then back again.

"Maybe next time you'll tell me a bedtime story, Claire," he said. He seemed genuinely caught up in her. His lips, as the romance writers would say, brushed her ear.

Claire left the restaurant at the corner of Trouble and Desire in Hollywood, let Jack Huxley put her into a car, and returned alone to her room. But she did not leave, from the dinner, unscathed.

25

THE NEXT NIGHT WAS JACK'S PARTY. "DON'T SAY I NEVER gave you anything," Richard said on the phone.

"I don't know what you're talking about."

"He called me today and asked about you," Richard said.

Claire gasped, then swallowed. *Didion. Cool customer.* "Oh. So what did you tell him?"

"I told him your husband is dead, and you're a mess."

"Richard!"

Laughter on the phone, Bridget's, from behind him.

"I told him you are an amazing woman," Richard said, then added, "But be careful. We'll see you tonight."

Be careful?

Less than twenty-four hours after landing in L.A., Claire had had a wildly successful flirtation with the town's biggest star and now she was attending a party at his home. She wore the black off-the-shoulder dress that Sasha had made her buy "just in case." Thank you, Sash. She wore her crystal drop Swarovski earrings. It was possibly the first time since she'd met Charlie that Claire felt—she wouldn't say the word, but she thought it—beautiful, in her own right. She felt grown-up. Charlie had enveloped her, had squished her like the bug on the chair of her dream, but tonight Claire felt power. She felt a measure of control, Jack Huxley or not.

Her size 4, nearly perfect hip-to-waist frame was waiting for Richard and Bridget in the lobby of the Bel-Air when her confidence suddenly wavered. Sex is one thing. Sex is easy, it turns out—for all that angst about virginity, it's over quick. She thought of tequila and red shoes. The trouble is those other two: hope and its mean cousin, heartbreak. The problem is how to deal with those.

Claire and Bridget stood in a corner of Jack Huxley's tastefully appointed living room, furnished in what appeared to be mid-century Edward Wormley. Diane Keaton lingered in the kitchen, Jude Law was by the pool. Bridget was wearing a bias-cut cherry dress that she'd had tailored to match her Fetch line. Her hair was piled up shiny on her head; it was exquisite but looked as though it might topple her if she leaned too far one way. The possibility worried Claire. She rushed through her drink to put it out of her mind. A jazz quartet played soft standards. The outfits were glittery, the shoulders were tanned. Everyone looked smaller in person than they did on-screen, and most of them smoked.

"You should have stayed with Jake," Bridget said. Richard was working the room—celebrity memoirs were easy money. Innocuous women circled efficiently with flutes of champagne and decorative bites of food. Jake? The hockey guy? This came out of nowhere.

"I wasn't really with him—"

"He has a big dick, *and* he's funny," Bridget said.

She popped a tiny pill in her mouth and offered one to Claire.

"I'm good, thanks," Claire said. Bridget put it in her purse, then shrugged her shoulders.

"How do you know he has a big . . . ?" Claire asked.

Bridget laughed, which made her head bob around, which made Claire nervous, again, about her tower of hair.

"Claire! Don't be a prude!" Bridget said.

Claire didn't pursue this. "It's not like he called me," she said.

"He said you told him not to call. We had dinner with him the next week. I'm just telling you, you shouldn't have dumped him. He really liked you."

Jack Huxley was across the room now, in a white shirt and charcoal-colored suit. He was casually unbuttoned. Claire looked away. "I didn't 'dump' him," she said. "We weren't in a relationship. We just didn't go out again."

Russell Crowe balanced a small plate of food on his cocktail glass.

It was one of the stranger scenes Claire had ever witnessed, and she'd witnessed some strange ones. Like the dinner two lesbian artists—friends (lovers?) of Charlie's—had hosted for him shortly before he died. Virginia painted vaginas, and Katie, her partner, wrote penis-shaped haiku, and during the dinner they gave a slideshow presentation of their work.

It took two hours—Claire had checked her watch more than once—to finally get to Jack. He was surrounded at every point. It took another hour after that before they were alone, on a long cushiony sofa, in a room of various stages of drunks. By then it was one in the morning. Bridget and Richard had left at midnight. One of them, Jack or Claire, had started a silly little thing of guessing the lyric. It was something Claire and Ethan used to do.

"Who left the cake out?" she asked.

"Donna Summer."

"In the rain," she said. "I wasn't finished. Who made love on the dashboard?"

"Easy. Meat Loaf."

"You are the—"

"Eggman."

"Wait—what's the one thing Meat Loaf won't do for love?"

"Lie?"

"He won't cheat. Who's frightened by his lack of devotion?"

Jack rubbed his chin thoughtfully. "Tina," he said. "I used to be much better at this. Or you're cheating."

"I'm not cheating," Claire said, feigning indignation. "How could I cheat? I just happen to possess a wide and encompassing knowledge of seventies pop songs."

They were the last ones in this particular room. There were rooms of people somewhere else, Claire assumed. She had waved off Richard's offer of a ride. She heard voices, laughter from somewhere, but Claire and Jack Huxley were alone here for now. The couch was big and encompassing, a very masculine couch, and Claire felt tiny against the back of it. Jack was on the floor. He had an arm on her knee. He was slurring his words a little bit, but happy.

"God, it's late. I'm not even tired. Do you want to get married, Claire?"

She liked that he was drunk. She could observe him, unnoticed. She'd long worked off the effects of her two glasses of wine.

"Sure, let's." She felt like Molly Ringwald in *Sixteen Candles*.

"Let's go get married," he said. "But let's have another drink first."

"Yes, let's have a drink first."

There are no small parts, only small directors. She'd heard someone say that once. However insignificant this particular moment in time might be, it felt like a big part and she was a small director. Now that Jack Huxley had left the room to find them a drink, she could work on her breathing again. She tried. She gulped. Seconds ticked by and she panicked. He was gone, she'd never see him! How would she get out of here? There was something about this scene, the dichotomy: A man says, "Let's get married," at the perfect moment of a perfect night. It must spell doom. Jack Huxley was doing a scene: "the perfect good-bye." He walked back in with an open bottle of wine in his left hand, something in a short glass with ice in his right, then he lay down on the floor in front of her, his head propped on one elbow and eyes like a little boy's. He giggled.

"I'm drunk, Claire," said Jack Huxley. "Let's be a little drunk."

Claire wanted to be. She should be right now, with him. She threw her head back, stretched out her neck. She took one long great swallow of wine. She hoped it looked sexy. "Okay, let's be drunk," she said.

Jack Huxley laughed and reached a hand out and covered her foot. He put his glass down and rolled onto his back, smiling his beautiful smile; even drunk, his movements were graceful. The awkward noises, the cracking sounds of flesh and bone shifting in movement, the pauses and gaps, the breathing sounds of ordinary men: she had either filtered these out or for Jack Huxley they didn't exist. With Jack it was all dubbed over, as if someone had already fixed the dailies, leaving her the soothing little crashes of crystal and ice and the faint rustle of his six-hundred-dollar shirt, wrinkled and half-tucked. Claire had the feeling that after tonight he might throw it away—he seemed the type. It would be easier, more pleasing, to finish up with the shirt on a nice note than to bother with the burden of cleaning and drying and fixing it up again. *His housekeeper*, Claire thought. *She'll know to be done with it. She'll know by wherever he lets it fall to the floor.*

Jack had been talking. She hadn't heard him. His hand still covered her foot. "There's some knuckleheads still out in the guest-house," he said, "but I've got security. Come with me."

The next three days were a blur. Claire didn't go back to her hotel. Jack Huxley sent a car to get her things; he called and took care of her bill. They stayed in at night and watched movies. Jack Huxley cooked dinner, made pancakes for breakfast and elaborate salads for lunch. They lounged in the sun and drank French '75s.

If Bridget and Richard said good-bye before they returned to New York, she didn't remember. They wound up there ahead of her. There were voice mails from Ethan that she didn't return.

She remembered mostly Jack's bedroom, the firm strength of his mattress, the double shower, the Jacuzzi bath in its own separate room. She remembered each and every time they had sex, and every sentence—she was sure of it—that they spoke. She ran them back on a continuous loop for a week. *The Razor's Edge* was his favorite book (hers, too!). Somerset Maugham was brilliant, they'd agreed, and they both thought people who said "further-more" were ridiculous. They liked potatoes mashed smooth but not baked and thought the obsessive search for happiness was fruitless. They agreed that people are magpies—Claire had said it, and then Jack had seized on it—all drawn to the shiny object. We are not so complex. They agreed that Picasso was overrated and Edward Hopper was not, and that a salad is not a salad without croutons. Introverts, they exclaimed, should pair with extroverts, but never with each other, and all of that is hell on seating arrange-ments. They both disliked people who claimed to be both "hum-

bled" and "overwhelmed." "How can you be both?" Jack said.
Then turned her face to his with his hand and said, "Claire, you and
I will save the world." And she continuously replayed *that*.

One night they watched a marathon of George Cukor films—
Gaslight, The Philadelphia Story, Adam's Rib. Huxley was humble
but well versed in his field.

"That's Cukor right there," he said, and gestured carelessly
toward the wall. "With my uncle." Claire hesitated, then approached
the framed photograph. Aldous Huxley in his unmistakable Coke
bottle glasses. "Oh wow," she said, and traced a finger across the
face. She'd almost forgotten. Mr. Hollywood shared DNA with
one of the greatest minds of our time. No small part of why Charlie
had been drawn to him. Every high school syllabus in the country
included *Brave New World*.

"Don't be impressed. I never even met him. He died when
I was teething." Jack laughed. "I use the photo to get smart girls
into bed."

She turned back to look at him. He sat in a chair, one leg slung
casually over the arm, like he'd been arranged that way by someone on set. *Okay, more slouch. Roll your drink around softly so the
ice clinks. Tilt your head to the right. Perfect.* "Hey, don't act
impressed for my benefit. I'm the Hollywood hack nephew of a
writer. You're a *writer*, who shared a life with one of the world's
most interesting men." He was flattering her, and she accepted. He
was a stranger and out of town. He was exactly what Eve had suggested. He was perfect.

On the night before Claire was to leave, Jack broke down the
details. "I have a car coming early in the morning, sweetheart.
I have to be in San Francisco for a couple of days. But you don't
have to leave. You don't even have to get up. I have another car

coming to get you for your flight. Don't lock up or clean or do anything. I want you to sleep until noon."

"What time is your car?" she asked dreamily. They'd had the best chicken marsala she'd ever tasted and then a bubble bath. She felt like the stagehand in a dream.

"Five, sweetheart. I'm sorry. I know."

Claire tried to smile. She turned the corners of her mouth up, she could do that, control her muscles, but—as he'd observed of her the first time they met—she was no actress.

Jack turned onto his side and held his head up with an L-shaped arm, resting all on his elbow. *Right out of* Pillow Talk, Claire thought. "Right out of *The Thin Man*," Jack said.

Her eyes popped wide open and he kissed her.

RULE #11: Never kiss a man who will
look better than you in the morning.

26

"WHAT?!" SASHA SCREAMED INTO THE PHONE. NO hello, no lead-in. Claire had just barely hit SEND on the e-mail when her phone rang. How do e-mails get there so fast?

"What?" Claire replied, mock innocently.

"You know what. Honey, Thom's sitting across the room with his thumb in his pants and you're telling me you fucked—"

"Ahhhhhhhhhh. Don't say it. Laaaaaa, la, la."

"Okay, you . . . whatever. Are you serious?"

"I didn't say I did."

"No, you said, 'You'd be impressed.' Here it is right here, I'm scrolling down. I say, 'I'm not impressed until you sleep with him,' and you reply, 'Okay, then. You'd be impressed.'"

Claire had decided, for a number of reasons, to start her story with Jack—at least the one to tell Sasha—right here in Los Angeles. In Jack Huxley's house, while she waited for her car to pick her up. There was the night, still, of the movie premiere, the accidental coupling with the wrong guy, but because that was not how

Claire would typically start off any sort of thing—with a tequila blackout and mismatched shoes—she rewrote it slightly, for Sasha, on the fly.

"Okay, but it's not like that. He's very . . . *smart*. He's *interesting*. And funny, he's very funny." She could hear Sasha rolling her eyes. "There's not a single subject he can't talk thoughtfully about and it's because he knows. He's curious about things, he's not a braggart. We talked—I know this sounds ridiculous—but we stayed up and talked all night, every night."

"And, just to be clear, you had sex with him?"

"Yes, but—"

" 'But'? Honey, why are you boring me with all this other stuff?"

Claire ignored her. "We downloaded music, we sang show tunes. He had a disco phase. Donna Summer, we sang the whole *Live and More* album. Oh . . . my God. What have I done?"

"Don't worry about it."

"I don't want to think about him."

"Well, that's not going to happen. Everything will make you think about him."

It was true. When she got home, everything Claire saw made her think about him. He was everywhere, and nowhere to be seen, like God. Magazines, billboards, grinning from the side of every single crosstown bus. She was flipping past *Access Hollywood* and there he was, right in her living room. And again, at eleven o'clock that night, there he was.

Perceptive selection, she thought. *That's all it is. He was everywhere before, and he's everywhere now; it's just that now, of course, I notice.*

Meanwhile, the days ticked by loudly. They hadn't made a plan.

Claire was waiting in line at CVS one day, with her toilet paper and toothpaste, when she realized that it had been three weeks since she'd met Jack Huxley in L.A., and Jack Huxley—oh God, she thought, she cringed at herself . . . don't think it, don't think it . . . Jack Huxley hadn't called. She was suddenly appalled at the things that spilled from her arms—deodorant, shampoo, paper towels, Goobers. Goobers! These were not the sort of things the girls Jack Huxley called would buy.

They wouldn't buy Goobers.

With Charlie, Claire had never bought Goobers. What was wrong with her?

Maybe this whole thing with Jack was an aberration, Claire thought. Jack Huxley doesn't date small-breasted, old-fashioned girls. He dates the girls who laugh, unprovoked, at all of his jokes whether they've heard them before or not. Girls who never roll their eyes, or eat. Not girls who shop at CVS.

Jack Huxley's girls can while away hours—hours and hours—and not miss a single one of them when he's tied up on set. They can try, then remove, then try again every single shade of mousse cheek glow at the cosmetics counter before stopping at Starbucks. They can wear a scarf through the loops of their jeans without feeling the least bit self-conscious. They can hold hands with their "girlfriends." Jack Huxley's girls don't laugh at anything, ever: they giggle.

They wear push-up bras in junior high, Claire thought. And when they moved on to sex, they knew right where to go. The jock first. Then the musician, a local politician, somebody's mogul father, and then Hollywood. These girls are able, somehow, to walk straight up to the sorts of men who command industries and yachts, and who only live when the cameras roll, look those men in the eye, and somehow, without demeaning themselves, lead them away.

Claire couldn't walk straight up to the news seller on Fourteenth Street. She was hardwired to wait for men to come. She was hardwired for courtship. It was the Midwestern in her. It was genetic. Her mother, Betty, had waited. She'd waited for men to call, to court, to send flowers, to ask. She had waited to have sex, and when she had it, she waited for it to end. Claire, like it or not, had inherited her mother's wait. She'd married an older man, from a different generation, one who expected to lead, who pointed her everywhere, who had all the decisions made before she knew there were choices. She didn't walk up to Charlie; he found her and she dutifully followed him home.

27

Y OU LIKED HIM, THEN?"
"Yes. I guess I did."
Dr. Lowenstein discerned a noticeable shift in Claire since Jack
Huxley had come on the scene. Where typically their sessions had
been filled with a disingenuously wry back-and-forth, Claire now
spoke randomly, speeding up and slowing down, letting no two
thoughts connect.

One ten-minute story began in the middle and went nowhere,
about Jack Huxley and a *Slate* article he'd read and how Claire
Byrne, when he'd mentioned it, realized she'd read the exact same
article, that exact same week. What were the odds? There was
something about Jack Huxley's eyes being in focus, and then not,
and then in either case being very dramatic and darkly brown.
"You look into them," Claire said, "and it's like you've found a
wonderful secret place. You feel like Alice falling into Wonder-
land, only it's warm and you're not scared—they're the safest eyes
I've ever seen, they should head a cult. Then your stomach starts to

tickle from the inside and you find yourself giggling for no reason at all; it's like smoking pot."

"Looking into Jack Huxley's eyes evokes a feeling similar to that of smoking marijuana, then."

"Yes. Or, like flying really high on a swing. Whatever it is, somehow gravity takes a pause."

"A pause."

"Yes, for a moment as you look in Huxley's eyes, gravity steps aside. The peripheral sense, too. For a moment that feels like forever, there are only the eyes."

Lowenstein nodded to indicate that yes, she understood. He had a great pair of eyes.

The second thing Jack Huxley had said to Claire after "Hello" was this: "Claire, forgive me, I know this, but it's slipped. Tell me again what you do. Something with vibrators?" This is what he'd said. He was funny. He'd remembered from the first night. There had been no long-winded anecdotes, no performance or puffed-up stories, no pronouncements about the state of film, no scanning the room. There was no excessive facial movement or language, not one wink.

"He was different than I expected. That's all."

"Different from what? What did you expect?"

"He was like the lead in a Godard film—sweet and cool, vulnerable and rogue all at once, and backed by a brilliant sound track."

"What did you expect, then?"

Claire hesitated. She picked nervously at a nail. "I don't know. A flatterer and seducer. A charlatan, I guess." That's what Beatrice had said.

RULE #12: Ignorance is bliss.

28

THE HOLIDAYS WERE A BUST.

Claire capitulated to Grace and took the train to Connecticut for the Byrne Christmas Eve. Grace had been widowed for nineteen years. Franz, or The Judge, as his friends had called him, had died of a heart attack, a much more conventional sort of death than death by a Giacometti. It is helpful, Claire had discovered, if the things that happen to you in life are things that *people can understand*. People don't understand someone getting killed by forged art.

Franz Byrne was no less present in the family home for being dead because after he died, Grace took up Catholicism, which to Claire seemed to mean that Franz was furtively lurking around.

"Don't worry, dear. Charlie is watching you. He's taking care of you. He's up there with his father now. They'll take care of everything." Grace gestured aimlessly at a space above her head. She'd said a version of this on the four occasions Claire had seen her since the funeral. Claire's eyes followed Grace's hand nervously.

Grace, along with The Judge's sister, Agnes, seemed to know the exact location in the sky where everyone was seated. They appeared to have kept in close touch with Charlie since his death. Grace was a better widow than Claire. She had likely not touched a vibrator, much less a man, since The Judge clutched his heart and was transported by gurney to *his time* at St. Vincent's hospital. She put a strong, skinny arm around Claire's shoulder, "Follow me, dear."

In a sitting room at the front of Grace's house was an elaborate shrine. Charlie's ashes—Grace's share of them—were at rest in a huge embossed urn that sat on a tall marble table, flanked by bookcases full of his works: a small but impressive library of sex. Framed family photos and press photos of Charlie littered the walls. There were two armchairs and a chaise. A Chippendale table held the candles.

"Light one with me, dear." Grace pulled an expensive-looking gold lighter from a bowl on the bookcase and lit a candle, then handed the lighter to Claire who lit another. "Join me."

Grace clutched Claire's hand and recited a Gloria and Hail Mary. When they were done Grace returned to her guests and to Claude, her handyman turned bartender. He shook up two Manhattans and topped them each with a bright red maraschino cherry.

"Don't forget your cherry!" he said, looking at Claire.

She found the whole night unsettling. The *Times Magazine* had included Charlie in its annual obituary issue—"The Lives They Lived"—and Grace was reading passages of it aloud.

Claire couldn't get the idea of Charlie staring down at them out of her head. She didn't want Charlie watching her all the time. Good God, had he seen what had happened in their bedroom with Brad Hess? She certainly didn't want Grace to know that Charlie was watching her if he was. What if he reported back?

Charlie's family was notorious for being better than everyone at everything, and widowhood was no exception.

"So, Claire, are you seeing anyone?" Charlie's cousin Dane innocently asked and Grace swatted his hand as if he'd just tried to grope her. "Good Lord, what a thing to ask!" She gestured, again, to the ceiling.

Grace gestured throughout the night. And around ten, after too many brandies, when Grace began to veer, Claire snuck out. She called a cab to the train station and, while she waited, cousin Dane escaped, too, and offered her a ride.

"So, I know we aren't . . . I mean, we've never been very close," he said in the car. It was true. They'd only ever met here, at Grace's Christmas Eve. They'd never gotten beyond small talk. ". . . but how's everything going for you, Claire? I mean, really. Has it been hard? Jesus, I'm sorry. Stupid question."

Claire considered her answers. The stock one: *It's been hard but I'm doing okay.* The drunk one: *No, but it could be, big guy, whyntcha come over?* And the truth: "It's been . . . hard, yes. And also kind of . . . weird. But I just met someone. And I miss Charlie, don't get me wrong—but there wasn't a lot of . . . spark in our lives. He wouldn't disagree if he were here. Still, I feel bad saying it. And now, maybe, well I think I might have met someone and it feels nice."

She went with the truth. Dane, who'd had her back just minutes ago, pursed his lips and was silent. Not one word from him until the train. "Here you are," he said curtly. No promises to stay in touch, no hug. "Be careful."

Claire was home in bed by eleven p.m.

ONE WEEK LATER, on New Year's Eve, Jack Huxley gave a ten-year-old boy twenty bucks for a cup of lemonade in Culver City and every paper in town ran it bold on the front page like they'd scooped world peace. The drink heard round the world. *Here, kid. Keep the change.* It had been five weeks since Claire was in Los Angeles. The holidays had steamrolled through New York with forced expectations and fake cheer. She stayed in alone New Year's Eve. Sasha called to suggest they have an anti–New Year and order in Chinese.

"You're sweet," Claire said, "but I'm fine."

She and Charlie never made a big deal of the holiday. Charlie called it amateur's night and refused to leave the house. They had their own tradition, which hadn't seemed like a tradition until now. In retrospect, it seemed so indulgent—and sweet. Charlie would cook an elaborate dinner for the two of them. Cooking relaxed him. He'd spend hours on the dish—a chicken galantine— deboning the bird, sewing the savory mixture of meats and herbs back into the skin, accompanied by Rachmaninoff, which set the tone for the evening. They feasted on his work over television trays in front of a string of old movies, then switched to ABC shortly before midnight, to count the night down.

What was Jack Huxley doing? This year she fell asleep with the television on, shortly before Anderson Cooper dropped the ball.

Claire woke uncharacteristically early the next day and used the extra hours to write. She was determined, or at least on the first day of the new year, to focus, as Beatrice divined, on her work. As she fidgeted in her chair a single image loomed large in her mind, quite possibly because Dr. Ahearn, her college literature professor described it frequently, and that was of the young Thomas Wolfe at work. Dr. Ahearn told this anecdote about Wolfe, which may or may not have been true: that he wrote standing up, in his kitchen. He was very tall and had difficulty finding a comfortable position in which to write, so he had his papers stacked on top of the icebox and stood in front of it writing. As he finished his pages, he slid them off onto the floor. Dozens of pages, she imagined, such was the prolificacy of Wolfe. Tens and dozens of pages fluttering to the floor like leaves shed from trees in October.

Now Claire wanted to be epic and careless and in love with the world again. She sat slouched at her desk, filled pages up spuriously in longhand, and flung them wildly off to the floor.

The problem was that once she'd flung four or five, she couldn't stop herself from gathering them and neatly stacking them up in order. Inevitably, she returned to her computer and, thwarted by abandon, worked with the digital representations of Charlie's curt words: stiff letters on a cold, flat screen.

His smile: when he smiled he captured the room. Huxley had a sharp eye for the absurd; the paradox of the career he'd chosen didn't escape him. He kept a signed copy of Brave New World *on a shelf— signed not to him, but to Bruce Bozzi "with fondness." He'd bought it on eBay, $37.99 his final bid. Like all practiced narcissists, he considered himself self-aware.*

29

WHAT DO YOU MEAN BY THAT, 'FURTHER ALONG'?" Lowenstein wanted to know. "Where, exactly, is further?"

It was sunny for January. There'd been snowfall; it was melting. Claire's socks were damp through her boots. Sunlight streamed through Lowenstein's hair; she looked ablaze.

"We didn't start with my dream."

"Yes, all right, your dream, then."

Claire was beginning to tire of this doctor, but she feared her enough to stay. Lowenstein had adopted condescension in her manner. She seemed impatient. It made Claire think she wasn't worthy enough to leave.

"It's okay. I don't have a dream. It's just that's usually where we start."

"What would you like to talk about, then?"

"I'm irritable today, that's all." Claire crossed, then uncrossed her legs.

"Yes."

"And I feel like a helium balloon that's half-deflated. Or half-inflated. Which one is better?"

"Why do you feel this way?"

"I'm hovering. I'm lingering. I'm suspended in air. I don't know that this is worthwhile."

"We've gotten nowhere with your dreams." Lowenstein said this haughtily, almost hostilely. It stung.

"Where were we supposed to get?"

"Tell me this, Claire. What makes you think you're so special? What progress, exactly, do you think you ought to have made?"

"I don't know, I just think . . . Well, Charlie's cousin Sara, for instance. I saw her Christmas Eve, at Charlie's mother's. They were all there, Charlie's mother, his cousin, his aunt Agnes—a room full of widows. The surviving men just looked shell-shocked. Anyway, Sara's husband died only seven months before Charlie, he had a brain tumor, and she's already engaged. She's engaged! It's been barely a year. She's getting married, to a mechanical engineer. I mean, her first husband owned two Koo Koo Roos and now she's marrying a mechanical engineer. No one even knows what that is."

"What is it about that scenario that disturbs you? Do you think you should be engaged?" Lowenstein's face was alarmingly still.

"No. I mean, it would make things easier, but I don't think it's the—"

"Do you define yourself by whom you're betrothed to, Claire?"

"Well, a little, I guess. Doesn't everyone?"

"We define ourselves by many different things, some of which may or may not include a mate."

"It's just, a consistent lover would be nice, or someone to get coffee with or read the paper with."

"And where are you, exactly, with Jack Huxley, then?"

Last week Lowenstein had complimented Claire on her perfume. This time they began at the possibility that Claire's unconventional new relationship was not a positive development in her treatment. Lowenstein had been erratic since Claire had returned from L.A. But Claire did not know how to go about breaking up with a shrink, so she didn't.

Instead, after her session, she called the griot.

The sidewalks were slushy; it was uncharacteristically warm for a New York winter. There were a tourist, a young hippie, a man with a backpack, and a dwarf. The griot was late and the small group lingered uncomfortably, fiddling with phones through their gloves, feigning interest. After fifteen minutes, two men, one of whom she recognized, could be spotted on the sidewalk, two blocks down, on the opposite side of the street. They were talking animatedly, which means they were using their hands and arms. The man with the griot, Claire recognized him as they got close, was Ben Hawthorne—funeral-crashing, Charlie-bashing, scruffy-haired Ben Hawthorne. For a brief, unguarded second, she smiled. She was surprised, but happy, to see him.

He smiled back—he had a nice smile. Ever since Huxley, Claire took greater notice in smiles. It was an awkward chance meeting but not entirely off-putting.

The griot passed out his card. The word today on it was *Unfulfilled.* They stood on the northeast corner of Twenty-Third and Seventh.

"What are you doing here?" she mouthed to Ben.

"Shh," he signaled, a finger to his lips.

The griot was a stickler for quiet.

The griot began. "We're looking at the site where, among others, Mark Twain, Thomas Wolfe, and Simone de Beauvoir—when she was in town—stoked their creative and lascivious powers. We are near where Dorothy Parker wrestled with alcoholism and the defeats of a lifetime, and failed. Where Arthur Miller, the playwright, wrestled with his conscience and Dylan Thomas, the poet, died from whiskey. Sid Vicious famously bludgeoned his girlfriend in the bathtub here, after a drug-fueled night. Sid was twenty-one years old and his girlfriend, Nancy, was twenty. He overdosed on heroin four months later in a different lover's bed."

Then the griot began a personal story. It was about his grandparents, Millie and Oren Crews. They were married for forty-three years, raised four sons, and were respected in their small town in Oklahoma. Millie was active in her church and Oren was on the city council. They'd managed a comfortable existence and after their children were raised they traveled some. But then Oren got an itch. He came into a small inheritance and began frequenting the saloons in town. There were rumors that he'd taken up with the town prostitute, Flore Collins.

"When Grandma Millie got wind of this, she got an itch of her own. She took Oren's shotgun to the hotel where Flore worked and used it to get the desk clerk to let her into Flore's room, where she found an unlocked cashbox and several salacious notes in her husband's familiar handwriting. She took the three hundred dollars and change from the cash box. Then she took the shotgun to the Buckaroo Room where Oren's pickup was parked and she waited. He walked out at two in the morning and as he relieved himself by the side of the building, she shot him with his own shotgun in the scrotum." The griot put his fingers into a gun shape and aimed them at his own crotch. "And then, after an excruciating wait, Millie shot him again in the head. When Flore heard the news, her heart stopped and she died on the spot. Grandma Millie lived out the next ten years, happily for the most part, in a county jail. She was teaching herself Portuguese when she died."

The griot and his village walked a few blocks east listening to traffic. The walk was serene, like being the passenger in a car on a scenic drive. Claire paid no mind to where they were headed but relaxed in the journey.

Ben Hawthorne broke the silence. He'd hung back, and Claire had been so entranced with Derek's story, she'd forgotten he was there.

"Well," he said after the griot played his flute and scurried off. "Great material, right? Do you follow him for inspiration? Who was it who said, 'Love and death are the only things worth writing about'?"

The few followers, as was their custom, had dispersed.

"I think it was Maugham, and I don't have a clue what any of that means. You were walking with him, and talking to him. Do you know him?"

"Derek, yes I do. He was an intern at the magazine last summer. Now he does this. We're doing a story on him. I'm not writing it, but I wanted to catch him at work."

"Oh," Claire said. "That kind of spoils it."

Ben Hawthorne laughed. He had a nice laugh, inviting. "Come on, we won't ruin him. And it isn't going to run for another six months. You'll have moved on by then."

There was an uncomfortable pause. Claire felt Charlie glowering, frowning at her from somewhere.

"We should call a truce," Ben said. He held out a hand.

Claire shook her head. "We're not in a fight. I hardly know you."

Ben contemplated her for a moment. "Good. Take care, then, okay."

And Ben Hawthorne, without fanfare, went off.

30

AND THEN HE CALLED.

Time had moved uncertainly since Claire's second encounter with Jack Huxley and she had spent it in a jumble of long, wandering walks, drinking wet cappuccinos, and carelessly buying sidewalk trinkets she had no use for. She continued to work on the manuscript—dabbled was a better word. But the absence of the flesh-and-blood Huxley had been disturbing. Now there was a phone message that she didn't know what to do with, so she booked a double session with Spence.

Spence wasn't the worst way to kill time.

"I'm sorry I'm late."

"That's fine," Spence said, tapping his pen against his notepad.

"I was going to cancel," Claire said and sat in the chair.

"Can I ask why?"

"Today is Charlie's birthday."

"Are you acknowledging it?"

"No"

"You shouldn't hide from your life, Claire. You try to watch it from around the corner, then you avoid having to engage."

Claire fidgeting in her chair.

"But I'm engaged in my subconsious dream life."

"I'm not sure what you mean."

"I already covered this with Lowenstein."

"Who is Lowenstein?"

"Never mind."

Claire hailed a cab from Spence's office, but she didn't feel like going home.

"Ethan?" she said. "Can you meet me for a drink?"

RULE #13: Don't bear the weight alone
when you can dump some on a friend.

They went to Jack Demsey's, with no *p*, in Midtown. It made Claire think of a sign the Worrells, her neighbors growing up, had kept hanging by their pool. WELCOME TO OUR OOL. NOTICE THERE'S NO P IN IT. LET'S KEEP IT THAT WAY.

The bar was a comfortable mix of daytime drunks, college-aged tourists, and mid-level executives. They ordered stout beers.

Claire licked the foam from the top of her glass.

"Cheers," Claire said.

"To birthdays?"

"Yes. To Charlie. Happy birthday."

They clinked glasses and the dark liquid sloshed out of Claire's cup.

"The Devil Went Down to Georgia" was playing full blast and a picture of Don King with a manic grin hung in front of them.

"To scoundrels, too," Claire said, nodding at the photo. "And flatterers and seducers, to the best of them."

"To those, too."

The bartender brought a plate of crackers and sardines and Claire wrinkled her nose.

"Vitamin D, Lollipop. One of these little babies is like a month in the Bahamas for your endorphins and libido. They don't taste as bad as you think."

Charlie Daniels gave way to Johnny Cash.

"You know where that started, right?"

"What?"

"The clinking of glasses, the cheering."

"Um, no. I don't."

Ethan was looking around the room, distractedly.

"Is this a gay bar?" he asked. It was a fair question. Claire alone represented her gender.

"It's from the Middle Ages, because they were always poisoning each other. So before anyone drank, they hit their glasses together to make the wine slosh out and into other glasses. This way, if there was poison, they were all going down."

"How about that."

Claire examined the room, too. The bar was dark. The energy was low. The patrons did not look gay.

"Ethan, do you think I'm boring without Charlie?"

"Sweetheart," he said, and kissed Claire on the cheek. "It's different without him, that's all. He was big and bold and swaggered into rooms. You're small and chic and you move like a cat. It's just different. You were two different people."

"*I* am two different people now," Claire said. "It's weird, I don't know how to be without him. Like losing a sidekick. I never thought of him like that, or me like this, but we had roles and mine was a supporting one and now I feel desperate up onstage sometimes. Like a stand-up comic who's bombing."

"He was the flower and you were the gardener. The sun and the moon; the beach and the waves."

Claire looked confused.

"The train and the station." Ethan continued, "Complements. Those are the only relationships that work."

"Those are song lyrics."

Claire took a bite of sardine. It was salty and delicate. He was right—it didn't taste bad.

She chewed on the crackers as she talked. "There was the Claire of Claire and Charlie, and I feel obligated to try to maintain her. But it's unfair because it was a double act. Like Martin and Lewis and remember what happened when Jerry Lewis went solo?"

Ethan motioned to the bartender. "No, I don't. I'm thirty-one."

Ethan ordered another. Claire was only halfway through her first. The bartender—a stocky man with a long nose—faced her, wordlessly, waiting for a cue. She shook her head no. Two Madison Avenue types were talking loudly behind them about a woman named Jennifer.

"You could still know who they are. You know Oleg Cassini and he's been dead since you were two. Anyway, Jerry Lewis really sucked without Dean; he nearly blew his whole career. No one wanted him by himself. I don't know how to go solo. No one ever makes it."

"That's not true. Cher won an Oscar after Sonny, and Sonny won a congressional seat."

"I'm just saying, it's hard. That's all."

From the bits Claire picked up in the conversation, the larger and less attractive of the two men had slept with Jennifer. *Women*

*value certainty, in sexual pursuit, much more than any physical charm
or characteristic of a mate, or whether or not a potential sexual partner
is nice to his or her mother.* Charlie wrote it in *The Half-Life of Sex.*

"This is great stuff, Clarabelle. But I bet it all has to do with not
getting a phone call. I bet it's as simple as that."

She had, in fact, gotten the phone call. She decided not to tell
him.

"I need to run off soon. Atlanta tomorrow morning. Haven't
packed."

"What's in Atlanta?"

"Kevin."

"Oh," she said brightly. "Good for you."

Ethan finished off his stout. "I miss him, too," he said.

RULE #14: Don't confuse love and sex.
One is a feeling, the other an event.

Charlie was not who she was thinking of.

Late that night Charlie's literary rival, Jonathan Rochet,
called the apartment, on Charlie's phone, the one in his office. It
woke Claire and without thinking she got up to answer it. Jonathan's words ran together. He was drunk.

"Listen, Claire, I'm really sorry . . . calling, so late. I've been
thinking—"

There were sniffles on the other end, and the pitch of Jonathan's voice fluctuated wildly.

"It's not the same, it just isn't. Fuck."

Charlie had hated Jonathan, and Claire was sure the feeling had
been shared; she guessed Jonathan Rochet missed having the perfect nemesis.

Last month, when the *National Book Review* panel granted

Charlie a posthumous lifetime accomplishment award, Claire had gone to the ceremony to accept it. There were cocktails after, and dinner. The chicken was unreasonably bland. The bottles of wine were opened at a ferocious pace.

Jonathan Rochet had cornered Claire right away. He politely raved about Charlie for ten minutes—the man, his talent—then took a minute more to inquire about Claire. Then he came out with it. "I've always wanted to fuck you."

Claire politely demurred. "It's not me. I'm just the straw man."

She didn't take it personally. It's easier, sometimes, to fuck than it is to talk. It was just another method of expression. There were people she herself longed to fuck, for similar reasons, though Jonathan Rochet wasn't one of them. Claire had learned from Charlie never to take sex personally. Although, look at her. She was doing just that with Jack Huxley.

"I know," she said into the phone at one in the morning on Charlie's birthday. "I miss him, too."

31

THE CALL THAT HAD PROMPTED CLAIRE'S DOUBLE SES-
sion with Spence, and Midtown beers with Ethan, had been
from, yes, you know already, Jack.

He summoned her and she came.

She booked a flight and reserved a car. She took the 6:30 p.m.
American and upgraded to business with Charlie's frequent flier
miles, now hers. She read fifty pages of *The History of Loves*, ordered
a vodka and tonic, and took one sip before falling asleep. She woke
up as the captain announced their descent.

Her phone rang, in the rental car on the 405 North to Sunset
from the airport.

"Hello?" she answered.

"You're here," he said.

The phone added years to their relationship. His voice, in just
two words, took on the voice of a man who had known her all her
life. The boy next door, who'd gone away and come back looking
for her.

Here she was. "Yes. I am. I'm on the Four-Oh-Five. Ten minutes from—" They hadn't discussed where she would stay. It felt awkward to assume anything. She had made arrangements at a hotel just in case.

"Good. Perfect. I'm headed back, too. I'll meet you at my house in fifteen. You need to eat. I have a great place to take you to."

"Okay." Claire hung up and dialed the Bel-Air. "I have to cancel my reservation. I won't be needing the room. Something suddenly came up."

If only, Claire thought, she could channel Lena Olin. Have longer legs, an accent, keep her lips always parted just so. Instead, she had clammy airport skin and imperfect hair; she was in jeans and old Converse sneakers and the faux foxtail poncho Ethan swore was big this season.

She made it to Jack's house. She pressed the buzzer at the gate; it swung open, and she parked her car at the far end of the driveway. She brushed out her hair in the rearview mirror, then messed it up again. She put concealer under her eyes and added a smudge of lip gloss. She threw her sneakers and the poncho on the passenger seat and grabbed heels from her bag in the back.

Jack Huxley, he'd told her, is never late. If he'd been fifteen minutes away, then he would already be here. She walked carefully up the long driveway. It was quiet except for the snappy click of her heels, and barely lit. The last thing she needed was an unplanned somersault dumping her at his feet. There was a truck in the drive, delivering to Jack Huxley; a housekeeper emerged from the house to retrieve the package. There was a white van near the garage that read HOLLYWOOD PARTY RENTALS. The side door was open. A man placed crates of glasses inside, then closed the door. The van pulled away, and then the delivery truck pulled out. And on the other side of that, after everyone had pulled back: the reveal. There was Jack Huxley leaning casually against a sports car. Arms folded, legs crossed, his back against the driver's-side window. A little two-door Porsche that looked all wrong for him, and yet all perfect. He was smiling up at Claire. Claire smiled back.

"Hey. You didn't have to park so far away," he said. "Sorry. I should've given you time to catch your breath." His smile dazzled, his eyes twinkled, his whole body seemed tuned exactly to her. She felt if she moved too far back, or left or right, there'd be static. He was the Sandman, Mr. Darcy, and Josh, her first prom date, all rolled into one.

In the car he talked in a steady stream, as if there was so much he had saved up to say; there was nothing required of her. She heard all of it and none of it. She absorbed the smooth, chocolate-coated sound of his voice and parsed through the creamy richness of his words. Words. What Claire lives on. His words, strung together like Christmas lights.

"I don't mean to rush you, it's just that there's this great little place and I know you'll love it. I've been dying to take you to it and I don't know if we can make it tomorrow. They get crowded on weekends. They have the perfect pasta with red sauce, the way you like it."

He turned to her and smiled. He rubbed her knee.

Claire had never eaten out with Jack Huxley, but the detail seemed minor.

"I thought we would order in. I'm in jeans—"

"You look great." He paused, then leaned over—they were at a stoplight—and kissed her cheek. "You look beautiful."

She turned toward the window so he would not see her blush.

"Tomorrow we'll order in. I don't usually go out on weekends, unless I have to—unless it's for work. We'll get a pizza and I have *Love in the Afternoon.*"

French art films and pizza. If it were anyone else she might think this pretentious, but it wasn't just anyone else. It was him.

Musical themes played in Claire's head when she spent time with him. Each one came with a different fantasy. For the *Love Story* version, the pleasant lilt of Francis Lai. For the Redford and Streisand *The Way We Were* versions of themselves, Marvin Hamlisch's haunting melancholy notes.

Jack Huxley left early the next morning for the studio; he left a note. There was fresh orange juice and bagels and the paper folded neatly. He left a driver to take Claire anywhere she wanted to go.

Uh-oh, Claire thought. *I could get used to this.*

32

AFTER THESE VISITS, ARE YOU IN TOUCH WITH HIM?" asked Lowenstein back in New York.

"He texts. Not every day. He calls now and then. We text back and forth, mostly."

"Why texts?"

"I don't know. I mean, he has an unusual schedule. And there's the time difference."

"Do you think this is something positive for you? Or do you think it's hurting something real you could be having?" Lowenstein looked up from her notepad.

"Really? I'm having a little romance with an extremely attractive man. What's not positive?" Claire didn't wait for Lowenstein to answer. "Listen, he's the first person who hasn't brought my dead husband into the room. I mean, there was no trace, no hint, not the slightest remnant of Charlie around. I felt so completely relaxed. No ghosts."

"Does he talk about Charlie?"

"There's no reason for him to. It already happened, and it has nothing to do with him."

"But Claire, the reason you met, the reason you even know Jack Huxley at all is because of your late husband."

"Well, there's that, sure." Claire was uncomfortable at the mention of the book.

"He looks at me without seeing Charlie. Like he's just an old boyfriend there's no reason for him to think about. I don't feel guilty. I think that's it. Everyone here, in New York, has this look in their eye, like they can see someone over my shoulder, watching them. You know, like Jolly. In that Sally Field movie . . . what was it? . . . *Kiss Me Goodbye.*"

"I don't know it."

"Well, her husband, Jolly, dies and she wants to marry Jeff Bridges and move him into her house, but then Jolly's ghost shows up and starts talking to her all the time."

"Do they marry?"

"Barely. Jolly was very charming. She starts falling for his ghost. But only Sally Field could see him, and it's the opposite for me. Everyone else seems to see Charlie, but I can't see him and I don't know what the hell he's telling them. We're almost out of time. Do you want to hear my dream? I had an interesting one," said Claire.

"Yes, then," Lowenstein said.

"So Jack and Charlie are both my husband. They lavish their kisses on me. Charlie weeps, kisses my hands, and says, 'See, darling, how beautiful it is now?' Jack is weeping and kissing me, too, and we are all very happy. It seems, finally, to make sense."

"Um."

"But when I woke up, the dream weighed on me like a nightmare."

"That's very nice, Claire. Though Anna Karenina, as I'm sure you know, already had that same one."

"Really?"

"Yes."

"That same dream?"

"That exact same one."

"Well, it's a good dream."

33

J ACK HUXLEY CALLED AGAIN THE NEXT WEEK.
"Meet me in Charleston," he said.

IMAGINE THE TWO of them—Jack Huxley, Claire Byrne—on a
giant split screen as they carry on their conversation. On the left
side, Jack holds a phone to his ear and tosses a tennis ball in the air
over and over with his free hand. On the right, Claire holds her
phone with one hand, while her other hand traces letters on a book
cover, absentmindedly.

Claire is wearing a long beige sweater over jeans. Jack has on a
blue nylon sweat suit. "Massachusetts?" she says, moving from the
book and table to her window seat, tucking her legs up beneath her,
and staring out her long window at dirty snow piles on the street.
She is trying to be cute. He knows. His laugh is soft and warm, like
her sweater. "No. No. South Carolina. I have to be there all week
and I want you to run away with me." On the one side of the
screen, his movements are fast and jerky—a hand darts to catch the

ball, he stands up, walks to the bar in his den. On the other side, the movement is languid and slow. It is late at night; it is out of the blue. Claire feels she should be put out, just a little. Shouldn't she?

"I can't just leave," she says. "I have work."

On the left side of the screen, Jack Huxley's demeanor has changed. It becomes clear that his attention has shifted; he's wrapping up. An assistant brings him a stack of papers; he mouths "thank you" to her and starts to skim them.

"You can work," he says. "I'll have the best paper flown in. I'll have a case of the finest pens."

"Let me think. I can't think."

"Ritz-Carlton. Use my code name at the front desk."

Jack Huxley is gesturing to someone offstage we can't see. His side of the screen begins to fade.

"What's your code name?" she asks, quickly.

Huxley pauses, one final frame to catch his smile. "Larry Darrell. I'll see you tomorrow, Claire."

She likes the way he says her name.

"Okay, Larry Darrell. I'll see you tomorrow."

"Well?" Claire asked Ethan impatiently. She already knew what Sasha would say. "Did you get my e-mail?"

"Yes."

"That's it? Yes? What am I supposed to do?"

Sigh.

"Don't breathe at me. Do I just keep following him around like this?"

"Can you get to Charleston direct?" Ethan asked. "The question is, *is he worth a connection?*"

"You're right. This is stupid. Flying around the country," Claire said. Then softly added, "Is it?"

"I'm kidding. Don't be silly. You have to go. You are the one who doesn't get to decide."

"What does that mean?"

"It means, you don't get to decide. You don't get to decide when it's over, where it begins, what it does in the middle."

"Yes, I do. I can ignore the whole thing."

"You know you'll see him, so see him. You'll agonize over it and end up going anyway. Your strategy in all of this should be to waste as little time as possible in unnecessary angst."

He had a point.

"Sweetie, don't overthink it. People can spot 'overthink.' You don't wear it well."

"I don't want to see him."

"Of course you don't."

"I mean it."

"Unnecessary angst. Cut it out."

CLAIRE WENT TO Charleston. Jack, of course, was never alone. Their private encounters to date had been red herrings. He was Jack Huxley, nephew of Aldous. Hollywood royalty, candy store smile, eyes like pools of water at midnight under the moon. If only 80 percent of the people in America believed in God, all of them believed in Jack Huxley.

When she arrived, he was in the lobby and so was everyone else. The mayor and his daughters. Cast and crew from the film. Tall and short women; old, young, and middle-aged; thin and voluptuous women—there was an entire chorus line of cleavage.

Black women and Asian women and white women, and they all looked to Claire like zombies, as if a spell had been cast, and they were all perched on the edge of orgasm waiting for Jack Huxley, the hypnotist, to say the word.

Claire was fascinated. Charlie would have flipped out. She understood suddenly why he had never finished the book. Charlie couldn't compete with this level of adoration. It would have driven him mad. "I'm glad you came," Jack said, and kissed her cheek.

He introduced Claire to a dozen or so people; he kept his hand on her elbow; he guided her gently this way and that. He moved her deftly away from critique. He knew what women were subject to. She certainly wasn't the first he'd protected. He was too good at it.

There was a laborious dinner of salty courses and competing anecdotes, each and every one requiring some sort of performance laugh. Claire felt the heat in the room. She was, she knew, a mild nuisance. She was the victim of an unwarranted amount of curiosity. *And what do you do, Claire? You write. How interesting. What do you write, Claire? Is there any money in that? You probably don't get out much then, to something like this, do you, Claire? You're a widow. I'm sorry. What did you say you were doing again in Charleston? How did you say you know Jack?*

Their tongues fluttered like butterflies. Their bodies were plucked and soft, their voices hard. The men among them hung back. There were the soloists and accompanists, there were slightly weathered-looking session players and dewy-lipped women vying for the lead. It was like a *Vanity Fair* layout—The Women of Huxley. They twittered and trilled, and hoped to land somewhere close. There was the woman who'd been in feature films ten years ago and was trying to make a comeback. Her lips did not close together straight. They were crooked in a way that on a man would look like a sneer but that, on this woman, looked sultry.

There was a young girl—she looked seventeen at most—whose father was a senator. "My father's a senator," she said. That's how Claire knew. There was the wife of a producer who was having an affair with a young pop star, if you believed the tabloids. There was the sister of someone, the former child actress with new tits; there was a woman who played the lead in a popular video game. And there was Claire.

Here was a room of people who were in movies, in the movie business, a room of people who were (mostly) paid to entertain and, with the obvious exception of Jack Huxley, Claire thought, not one of them was lovely to watch. There was the director who had just wrapped a remake of *Mothra: Nemesis of Godzilla.* There were two Oscar-winning producers, and a theater actress who refused to speak to anyone but the men. There was a musician, a playwright. Creative, free-spirited people, all of them, and yet the whole night managed to feel dull.

The *Mothra* director was coming off promotions for his film. It was to premiere the following week, and he was budding with stories. The film had been reported as going way over budget and there'd been no early release for the critics. Claire had seen a trailer. It featured Mothra removing the limbs—legs and arms—of a giant tortoise. Nonetheless, the director was allowed to tell a story, and as he began Jack gave him his full attention, and a hush fell as the table followed suit.

"One of the things," Mothra began, "that keeps my heart beating for this job is the wow moments." He seemed unaware that impeccable manners kept the movie star listening, and the others were simply taking his lead. Glances at the table flicked from Jack to the director. As long as Jack maintained eye contact, so did they. Mothra cleared his throat. "In Australia when we started filming, there were a handful of us in the room." He paused and looked down the table, gave a slight nod as if he were assessing it—yes, a table, an ordinary table, one just like this.

"Some of those in the room were filmmakers, giants, and as the lights went down, I became aware . . ." Mothra used artistic license here to full effect, took a swallow of his wine, kept the glass in the air, pitched his head forward a bit, causing the room to unconsciously lean in. "This" he said, "is a moment, I'm thinking to myself, I will *ne-ver for-get*. We all shot each other a look right then, at the same time, as if to say, 'Don't Forget This.'"

Jack nodded, and like dominoes around the table other heads nodded and then shook side to side. One man began to rub his companion's back. Claire picked up her wineglass, and so did the former child star. She swirled it softly and the comeback actress swirled hers. Jack Huxley's face went from wry to bemused.

I'm screwing Jack, is what I'm doing in Charleston, she should have said.

All of it ended swiftly and immediately, just at the point Claire thought it never would. Then Jack was shuttling her into an elevator that stopped at a private floor.

"I have to tell you, whatever it is you do to drum up that fascinating little circus, it's worth it," Claire observed, watching Jack Huxley's lips on the inside of her elbow.

"Yes, fascinating," he said.

"A nonstory about the remake of a horror film as if he had been witnessing the Paris peace talks."

"Exactly. Movies are bigger than peace." Jack kissed her shoulder. He kissed her neck, and then behind her ear, and then back

down her neck to her shoulder again. Claire knew what to do—
she'd watched the movies. Richard Burton slides one strap of the
dress off, then the other. Elizabeth Taylor steps out. Later, Claire
thought it odd that she couldn't remember a sound. Not a single one.
Not the sound of breathing or clothing rustled, or even the soft pad
of a slow foot on carpet. None of the standard noises of hotel
rooms—heat, muffled movement from other rooms. There was no
noise anywhere, as though the sound hadn't yet been dubbed in.

"If you sleep with me tonight, you'll hate me."

"Why tonight? That's a bit fatalistic, isn't it?" She laughed.

"You will. I'm afraid of it."

"Third time is not the charm?" Claire unbuttoned his shirt.

"I'm bad at endings," he'd said.

"Relax," Claire said. "You're jumping ahead."

Just don't tell me how it ends, she thought. *Not just yet.*

34

Is sushi okay tonight?" Jack asked, before heading off to the set the next morning. "There's a little place downtown no one knows about." He put his arms around her from behind. "And bring something to read to me."

Claire turned in his arms. "I can't do that. I'm not far enough along, with anything." She cocked her head—saucy Claire. She put her arms around his neck. "Do you believe in fairy tales?" It was something she wanted to explore in the book, though she wasn't sure Charlie would approve.

"Of course. If there's no hero or someone who needs saving, what's the point?"

"Right."

"I wouldn't have a job if people didn't like fairy tales." He grabbed a polished red apple from a bowl near the door and examined it. "Work here, in the room today. The light's great in the morning. Order something to eat. I forget, does the prince get the poison apple?" He took a bite. "I'll be done at five. If you're running around Charleston I'll come get you. I'll be starving, literally. We have to go exactly when I call."

"Exactly," she said. "I'll plan accordingly."

"I'm not leaving." He pulled her closer, twined his fingers through the ends of her hair.

"I see that."

"I have to go."

"I'll see you later," she said.

"Call if you get lonely," he said. "Claire?"

"Yes?"

"Miss me."

She held her composure intact. "I'll see you later."

He kissed her on the forehead and the door shut, in the heavy, permanent, self-shutting way of hotel doors.

Claire pulled out her laptop. She hadn't been entirely honest: the manuscript was coming along, but it wasn't ready for Jack's eyes; she wasn't sure it ever would be. The title page read "by Charles Byrne." Claire put the laptop away. Claire despaired.

At five o'clock or somewhere near there, the fairy tale returned, but then dark clouds descended—it was the coach turning back into a pumpkin, the forest of thorns strangling Sleeping Beauty's castle. With a glistening piece of tuna held tight between chopsticks, Jack Huxley said, "So here's the thing."

Here's the thing. That's never good.

Claire switched her expression to bemused and waited.

"What are we going to do about this?" he asked.

"About what?"

"About this, here. This." He took a bite and watched her while he chewed. Waiting. Claire felt like she'd missed something.

"What?" She smiled tentatively, not sure of the joke. "I don't know," she said. She lifted her own piece of sushi and chewed, looking askew, not directly at him.

"I don't know either." He let his smile come in slow. "I guess it's like *The Lost Weekend*. We seem to keep replaying it."

"Right," Claire said. *The Lost Weekend*. Billy Wilder. A movie Claire's never seen, so she didn't immediately get the implication. She knew enough, though. She didn't like the word *lost*. She knew she didn't want to lose any weekends.

"Let's just play the scene out," she said in her best sultry voice. She dipped her head toward her plate and looked up at him through loose hair. "We're good at that," she said.

The next morning Jack was due on the set by seven but he called in late and left at ten. He ordered breakfast, they ate in bed, they showered together. Nice.

Before he left, he handed her a scrap of paper. "This is my secret number," he said. "The double-zero spy phone." She wasn't sure if this was a joke. "It's the only one I answer. For friends."

"Oh," Claire said. The word *friend* stuck in her throat. "Okay, thanks," she said.

"Have a good trip, sweetheart," Jack Huxley said. He was close to the door. He had his jacket on. Claire leaned against the arm of a chair in a T-shirt. It was painfully clear who had the advantage. He gave her a long, soft, Hollywood kiss, tipped his baseball cap, and then left, walking backward, out the door. Kicking the heels of his ruby slippers.

CLAIRE MADE IT to the airport for her 2:00 p.m. flight. She had time to return the rental and browse magazines. She had time to find a book. She had time to kill. She had time to see, on the cover of *Star*, that Jack Huxley was in a love triangle with two starlets.

It made her think about Charlie, and the book, a book that was as much about one as the other. *Is Jack a boy?* Claire thought. *Was Charlie a man?* The difference, it seemed suddenly obvious. A boy says, Have a good trip. A man says, Call me when you land.

When she got into her apartment, she wrote Jack an e-mail. Then she deleted it and wrote another one. She deleted that and wrote a note, then tore it up, then wrote another note, then crumpled it up and called the Ritz. She asked for his room, then hung up. She called the "friends only" number he had given her and it went to voice mail. *Beep.*

"Hi, it's me. Call me when you get this. Or not, I guess. I just, something was bugging me, and I wanted to say it. About your question last night. Well, just call me. Or, you don't have to. I don't need to talk to you. I just wanted you to know—I meant to say it last night—that I should watch more Billy Wilder, and I will, I promise, but even before I do, I know that I don't want a lost weekend, for what it's worth. I want to see you again. I don't think we should rule it out. Wait, that's not even what I mean. I just mean, simply, I want—"

You have exceeded your recording time. To play back this message, press two. To send, press pound. To delete this message and record again, press three.

Claire took a deep breath. She couldn't do that all again. What then? Erase it? No, she wanted him to know. But she sounded so scattered. Who would want to get that message? Redo it. She couldn't redo it; she'd screw it up more. She tried to remember where she'd been cut off—was it an ending, or close enough to one? Would he be able to fill it in? *It sounded fine*, she told herself. *Send it*. But then what if he didn't call? She'd never know if it was because of the message. She'd told him he didn't have to call, but how could she not expect him to call? Oh fuck!

To replay this menu, press star. To send this message, press pound.

Claire pressed pound.

35

THE WORST THING WAS THE YAWNING CHASM OF TIME from point A—a wonderful, sweet weekend with a boy, the kind that made Claire think of butterscotch Life Savers—to point B, an undetermined, and maybe completely nonexistent point in the future. The few days following the weekend were upbeat and hopeful. He'll call, she'll see him again. Or, she supposed, she could call, she thought, but she didn't know how to call—she'd already botched that once. And if you don't know what you're doing, you shouldn't be in the business.

THERE WAS A wedding three weeks after Charleston: Emily's. Emily was a photographer Claire had worked with on and off for years on different freelance assignments. Now Emily was producing a reality show and marrying an ex-priest. Everything was going according to plan for her. Claire, on the other hand, had a dead husband, lost weekends with Jack Huxley, a diviner and a sooth-sayer, and too many shrinks.

Claire couldn't bear to go to the wedding alone, so she made Ethan her plus one. He was coming from Miami. His new boy-friend, Kevin, was a flight attendant, which made flying much more fun, first class all the time. So Ethan came from the airport looking relaxed as one only can when they've been served warm hand towels and chocolate cookies with their champagne. Claire, on the other hand, had taken a crowded subway and tromped through puddles of gray, melting snow; she was frazzled.

At Le Cirque, she was seated between a much younger photographer—"He's single and totally hot," Emily had told her—and a new mother. Across from her, Ethan was wedged between the new mother's mother and a middle-aged cousin from Seattle. Emily was right, the photographer was gorgeous, but he said, "Oh, like Kevin Spacey," when Claire said she'd recently been to Charleston. "Remember, in *Midnight in the Garden of Good and Evil*?" And Claire said, "Yes, although that was Savannah," and picked at her salad.

Sooner or later, as it always seemed to in a group susceptible to idle celebrity gossip. Jack Huxley came up.

"He's into strippers. It's an open secret." This from the Seattle cousin who was on her third vodka.

Claire had missed how this started but now her ears were attuned. She affected disinterest.

"That sounds right," the new mother next to her said. "He says in every single interview he's just waiting for the one. He was on *Entertainment Tonight* and they asked about his love life. He squirmed around in his chair like a child."

Claire doubted this. Jack never squirmed.

"He always gives the 'I'm at a good place, happy, making movies I like.'" The new mother snorted. "Are you kidding me? He sounds like he just pledged a fraternity."

"I hope he's gay," the gay man at the table said.

"He's forty-one, never married," the new mother's mother said. Claire tried to hold her peace.

"Maybe he likes to screw around." This from Ethan. He smiled mischievously. Claire glared back.

"Who wouldn't, if you could?" the photographer said, and laughed. "The only reason men get married is that most of them can't live that life." It was good he wasn't giving the toast.

"Maybe he's old-fashioned," Claire said. A table of people who had forgotten she was there now all turned to her at once. "Maybe he takes commitment seriously."

"Yeah, that's it," the new mother said with derision, looking at Claire like she was crazy. "He's just another gorgeous jerk who wants to have his cake and eat it, too."

"Maybe he's just misunderstood," Claire went on.

Ethan gave Claire the cut sign across his neck.

"Maybe he's waited so long because he wants to make sure it's the real thing, maybe he's looking for that but hasn't found it yet. I mean, he could have been married five times by now. Maybe he's more sincere than all of us. Maybe he's just not settling."

The wordless round of glances among them continued. The new mother took the reins and moved on.

"Well, whatever the case," she said, "there is obviously something wrong with him, and it will surface eventually. It always does. Did you see who Emily sat at the head table?" She addressed this to her mother. And then the lot of them moved on.

RULE #15: The secret to marriage—
separate bedrooms, and blow jobs.

36

YOU WOULD NOT *BELIEVE* WHAT A BASTARD HE TURNED out to be!" Sasha swore. She swept through the doors of Nico's in an ermine cape. Claire followed in wool plaid. They'd met up on the sidewalk outside. February had roared into New York like a wet, shaggy lion.

Sasha lowered her oversized sunglasses and peered into the dimly lit restaurant. The maître d' stepped back from his podium, startled.

"My God," Claire said when Sasha turned her head. "What happened?" Beneath her left eye was a large and misshapen dark bruise.

Sasha returned the sunglasses to her nose and said to the maître d', "Wyse. Reservation," then turned back to Claire. She shook her head slightly, as if gathering courage, and Claire was certain she could hear tears in her voice. "It's horrible, isn't it? I can barely leave the house!"

They followed the maître d' past white-clothed tables decorated with amaryllis, to a table near the window that looked out on Lexington.

"I have to get away from him," Sasha continued. "I can't let him do this to me. And my God, I can't trust that it won't happen again. How can I go back there?"

They removed capes and gloves, set purses near their feet. The maître d' pulled out their chairs. He lingered a moment longer than necessary. With his burly build, slicked hair, and expensive suit, he looked like he was answering a casting call for *The Sopranos*.

Claire scanned the wine list. As soon as they were alone, she leaned across the table. "Thom did this?" she said, in a low, horrified voice.

"Honey. No, not *Thom*. Dr. Struck!" Sasha sniffled. Claire had never seen her so upset.

"Dr. Struck *hit* you? Oh shit, please don't tell me you're having an affair with him."

Sasha shook her head. "I wish! He was supposed to inject a tiny bit of Juvéderm to smooth my undereyes, and *this*—*this* is what I end up with!"

"Oh," Claire said, exhaling with relief. "Well, thank God. I thought . . ."

But Sasha started sobbing into her linen napkin. "I think—I think I have cancer. It's my ovaries . . ."

"What? Oh, sweetie." Claire reached a hand across the table. "No luck with Riva?"

Sasha shook her head.

"What did she say?"

Sasha waved a hand. "She went through the whole thing— speculum, swabbing, prodding. 'Dere ees no cancer.'" Sasha imitated Dr. Riva's stodgy German accent. "'You don't vant babies. Vhat they do to your body! Vee are meant to have baby at sixteen, not thirty-five.'"

This made them both laugh. Claire wondered, not for the first time, why Dr. Riva had chosen gynecology.

"I left there feeling worse than before, so I squeezed in a last-minute appointment with Dr. Struck. Life's just not fair," Sasha said. "*You*, at least, have the chance to find a man who will fall in love with your personality"—Claire's brows arched; *Thanks, Sasha*, she thought—"not someone who expects you to look like you did at twenty, forever. God, I wish Thom were dead."

The maître d', approaching their table, stopped in his tracks. Around their table, silence descended. Sasha had spoken a bit louder than she'd intended.

Claire couldn't help it—she laughed again. Then Sasha laughed, too. "*You're crazy, honey!*" Claire whispered.

"We'll never have Paris together," Sasha deadpanned. "You stayed; I went and look what good it did. It got me an impotent husband and you a dead one."

They were laughing so hard now, they gasped for breath. "Stop it, people are looking!"

The maître d' smiled in relief; the din of innocuous conversation resumed. They ordered wine, then cassoulet. By the time they got to coffee, the conversation had turned to Claire. And, inevitably, to Jack.

"He was filming. I went down to Charleston for a weekend. We went to dinner with his friends. You know what he did?"

"What?" Sasha looked like she'd been anticipating something slightly more scandalous.

"He intercepted for me. God I forgot how nice it is. To have a buffer."

"What did he buff?"

"Twice he did it. In the lobby, there was a big group of us just having drinks and someone asked me who I was. 'Who are you?' this woman asked. I can't remember if the emphasis was on 'are' or 'you,' but you know. She probably just wanted to know what film I was in or what I was doing there. Anyway, he was standing next to me, talking to someone else and he intercepted. I love the intercept."

"What'd he say?"

" 'Claire's a writer. She's *extremely* talented.' I mean, who says that? And then he introduced me, and then he stayed there. He stayed in the conversation. You know, like he sensed hostility, something to protect me from, and he wasn't going to let this snotty person have a shot at me alone, so he didn't let himself get pulled into something else. Which is impressive in itself—everyone around him claws at him nonstop. I can't tell you how nice that buffer is— it's like sinking into a soft, feathery pillow bed."

"How gallant."

Claire frowned. "You sound snide."

"I'm not." She watched as Sasha *clink-clink-clinked* her spoon against the coffee mug, but she forged on.

"We left after that. I think he wanted to get me out of there. The first sign of danger and it's like he thought, *She doesn't need this*, and he took me away."

"Like I said, how gallant."

"Don't make fun. Then we watched a documentary on the History Channel."

"That's not hot."

"It was, though, that's the thing. But the more I think about it, the more it's like he's an opener. This is what he does. He's got the first act down, dazzles his audience, leaves them rapt. Then he tries with the second act, right? He tries to introduce conflict, some drama, a romantic obstacle. That's why his calls are arbitrary."

"I suppose."

"And me, I'm just a sucker for the opening act. Charlie was an opening act, too."

They pushed back their chairs and stood, donned their capes, and trailed back past white-clothed tables and coiffed hair.

On their way out of the restaurant, the maître d' stopped Sasha and discreetly handed her a card.

"Please," he said, "call this number."

As they hailed taxis, Sasha preened. "Well, maybe I'll give Dr. Struck another chance. Have to keep my options open, you know."

Sasha headed uptown. Claire headed downtown, thinking about Jack Huxley and narcissists, the subjects of Charlie's book. Narcissists, she reflected, do the best opening act ever. That's how you can spot them, by their opening act.

How was she supposed to feel, she wondered, as she passed a corner newsstand, when Jack Huxley was on the cover of every tabloid flanked by models. Should she wish him happiness, or wish he'd call?

But she didn't have long to wrestle with that thought.

A month after Claire flew home from Charleston, Jack Huxley resurfaced, and Claire's regularly scheduled menstruation did not.

37

WHEN HUXLEY RESURFACED IT WAS TWO IN THE morning and Claire was struggling through Edna Ferber. Charlie had always insisted: if you want to be a writer, read a writer you don't understand. So Claire was reading a portion of the same sentence in a loop: *Selina DeJong, darting expertly about her kitchen, from washtub to baking board, from stove to table, or, if at work in the fields of the truck farm.* Ferber's long and laborious sentences wore Claire out. All those words to convey one thought: *at work in the fields of the truck farm.* What does that even mean?

And then the bell sounded, loud and clear and startling, on her cell phone. *Dinggg.* It sounded like a promise, like silver striking crystal—she never tired of it.

Dinggg . . .

what r u wearing? Elmer Gantry

It took Claire a few long seconds to process. Then she felt

someone was watching her and looked around. *It's a setup, a trick.*
Adrenalin, followed by a nervous but not unpleasant fluttering in
her lower abdomen.

Elmer Gantry was the first role Jack Huxley ever played. He
told her about it the night they'd met, at the premiere. LaSalle
High's spring production of *Main Street.*

What are you wearing?

The warm little fluttering that crept low.

Oh God, Claire thought. It was eleven o'clock if he was sitting
in L.A. It was some other time if he was not. He didn't typically
stay up late. It was Saturday. Eleven o'clock. What is he doing? Is
he home? Bored at dinner?

Dinggg . . .

whatevr it is take it off

Dinggg . . .

ive been thinking about you.

If Claire had not been paralyzed with fear and, at the same
time, a base animal lust—if, too, she were the sort of impulsive,
carefree girl she wanted to be—she would have grabbed a
trench coat and overnight bag and taken a cab to the airport. She
would have walked up to the ticket counter at American—no,
wait, JetBlue had a better flight to L.A. Oh, but it went to Bur-
bank and American didn't have food and she'd be hungry. Nothing was open in the airport this late, though, maybe she'd sleep,
but then they always woke her on JetBlue. American would have
the best red-eye. Regardless, you see, a moot point. She wasn't
that girl.

So here she was with neither spontaneity nor snappy comeback.
Her face washed clean, her hair in a ponytail, over here.

And Jack Huxley, with his aw-shucks smile and strong hands, was over there.

Thinking about me . . .

There was nothing to say. Claire turned off her phone and went to bed.

38

STENDHAL SYNDROME: A PSYCHOSOMATIC ILLNESS THAT causes rapid heartbeat, dizziness, confusion, and even hallucinations when the individual is exposed to an overdose of beautiful art, paintings, and artistic masterpieces.

Jack Huxley called the next day. "I need to see you," he said. "I'm in Toronto but want to see you when I'm back."

Claire's heart skipped. She wished it didn't. "That sounds great," she said.

Miss me. She had a note from him leaned up against a stack of books on her desk: *Widows in Contemporary Time*; *The Widow Wears Black: How to Bury the Past*; *Widows and Sexuality.*

Two words: *Miss me.* A directive. Simple. Neat. No promises, no plans.

"I feel like a cat," Claire had said the night before she left Charleston.

"On a hot tin roof," said Jack.

"Should I jump?" she asked, and then hoped he hadn't heard.

"Not yet."

She couldn't stop talking about him. "We read *Death in the Afternoon* in a big bubbly tub."

She was walking with Ethan through the park. He wanted a hot dog. He had a favorite vendor near Strawberry Fields, and the late February day was sunny and unseasonably warm.

"What?"

"We took turns. He read a chapter, I read a chapter. We had a bottle of wine."

"Who is that, Thomas Mann?"

"Hemingway."

"Oh, Hemingway. That's original."

"Don't be patronizing."

"Sweetie, you screwed him in the bathtub. You need to start calling this thing what it is."

"God, you are so unoriginal. We read to each other, in the bathtub."

"Fascinating." Ethan squeezed mustard onto his hot dog.

"For two hours, maybe three, I think."

"Doesn't the water get cold? And is that even sanitary?"

"Are you jealous or just being mean?"

"I don't know what I'm supposed to say," he said. Ethan missed Charlie; these conversations were difficult for him on many levels. "It's great. You're moving on. It really is."

"I'm having fun. Who cares?"

"I care, honey. I'm just having trouble with the visual. And I really don't know if I like him, to be honest with you. I liked him months ago when I thought he was a onetime thing. Where is he right now?"

"I don't know. His schedule is not like yours or mine."

"You've become one of those girls, you know."

"What does that mean?" Claire stopped short and grabbed his arm.

"One of those girls who turn a few dates into a meaningful relationship as if he *may be the one*. We hate those girls."

"That's not fair, Ethan. I only have you to talk to. Sasha feigns disinterest. She can't bear that I live out some fantasy she still clings to. She mentioned our thwarted Paris plans the other day."

"Clarissa."

"What?" Claire felt like she was going to cry.

"Let me take you to dinner and remind you how remarkable you are."

"No."

"Then let's go to the zoo."

The Central Park Zoo was only a few hundred feet away.

"Okay."

"And you can tell me how remarkable I am."

Claire laughed.

"You haven't been around much lately. Can I guess it's because your airline steward is reading you Hemingway in the bath?"

Ethan smiled. He looped his arm into Claire's and they walked while he ate a second hot dog.

"My period is a week late," she said.

Without skipping a beat, he said, "You'll have the most famous kid in the world."

39

H E CALLED AFTER TORONTO, AND CLAIRE WENT TO L.A.
The flight was delayed and she arrived late so they slept in,
and then he brought a tray with fruits and sparkling wine and said,
"I hate it when people say this to me, sweetheart. But I want you to
meet someone." He laughed at the cliché. "I've been promising
lunch to her for months. I really want you to meet her."

They dressed and he drove them to Ann Holloway's house.

Ann Holloway had a notorious home in the Hills because she
was a notorious woman. She was a Hollywood legend, tucked back
into jacaranda trees and rosebushes. Although she'd long ago
retired, lines still formed at her door. Her name was still passed
around town in hushed tones.

Her home gave off an eerie sense of remoteness. Jack's small,
dark sports car hummed up the hill, hugging the windy driveway,
and neither of them spoke. He looked happy, relaxed. Claire was
half giddy, half anxious, at this unexpected adventure with him.

* * *

ANN HOLLOWAY'S NAME, in certain circles, could open and shut more doors than any of the past four presidents. She was retired, yes, technically. She rarely if ever left her house, but from up here, in her dark rooms, in her hilltop house with its quiet servants attending to all her unspoken needs, she could still topple careers on a whim. She was Zeus, Apollo, Athena all rolled up into one feisty Jewish ball.

Her home was the sort of out-of-reach and altered universe where someone like Jack Huxley could while away an afternoon unnoticed. The first step through Ann Holloway's front door exposed the trappings of a recluse—ornate columns, shag carpets, deep-red upholstery. There were windows, but it looked as though they hadn't worked in years. The decor's primary function, it seemed, was to soak up the light.

The man who let them into the house was dressed in black tie. Jack shook his hand and clapped another hand on his back.

"Alfred, how've you been?"

Alfred? Could that be his real name? He took their coats and Jack peeked out of the foyer, dutifully standing put. Claire glanced down a long unlit hallway, a series of doors. She was waiting for Rubirosa to step from one, a disheveled Monroe from another.

Nothing in the house projected warmth, yet Ann Holloway herself, sitting solid and square amid a swirling cloud of smoke like a sorceress or genie in a floor-length caftan, her cigarette waving around in the air, was oddly—despite the reputation and barking voice—inviting. In her prime, she'd been routinely referred to as "the cunt"—so much that it seemed an endearment.

"Hurry up, get in here, dear. For God's sake, what are you doing?" A voice, gravelly with carcinogens, scratched out the order.

Jack had brought a box of French macaroons, her favorite. She took two out and gave the rest of the box to Alfred. She turned her cheek for Jack to kiss but didn't stand. Her eyes were on Claire.

"I like her already."

Ann Holloway smiled slow and wide, like a wolf.

"Make us a drink."

Jack looked at Claire.

"Okay, but be nice, Annie." Jack bent down to kiss Claire and whispered, "You're going to love her," then left the room.

"So, let's not be coy. I already know all about you."

She did? Claire's stomach took a giddy little hop.

"He tells me you're a writer. What do you write?"

This meeting had been discussed, at least a little bit. Claire had been talked about. It caught her off guard.

"Oh, I don't know." She stumbled a little. "I'm working on a book now. I sometimes write articles for magazines."

"I knew your husband." Ann Holloway took a drag on her cigarette.

"My late husband." Claire said.

"Dead or not, I knew him. I knew him when he was still earnest. Once he got some fame, the academics mocked him, but I always liked his work."

Claire, without warning, blushed, a small, unexpected pride. "Well. That's very nice. Thank you for saying it."

"You should write about *me* sometime. You'd make a fortune. They've have been trying to get my memoirs for years."

A woman brought in a tray with two martinis. It was eleven forty-five in the morning.

"I-I'm sorry," Claire stammered. The martini glass turned her stomach. "Would you mind, could I just have iced tea?"

Ann Holloway looked amused.

"I would imagine Jack's on his way with one." She knew everything. "You know, Claire, there's a story—it's a famous one in Hollywood—that I once fucked a producer to get a client. Because the client, it's said, wouldn't sign with me unless I guaranteed him a certain part." Ann laughed and took another long drag of her cigarette.

"A little twist to the casting couch fable. It's been going around for years, and like most good stories, it isn't true. But you could write it. It's the truth, about me. Had I ever been presented with that option?" She took another long drag and exhaled slowly, in four large rings. "It's exactly what I would do."

Claire took a sip of the martini and coughed.

Jack Huxley reentered, on cue, with iced tea. "I've got to make a call but I'll be quick. I'll be right back." He laughed. "Promise."

"We're just getting to you, dear. Take your time." She turned to Claire and leaned forward holding a slim cigarette. "Would you like one?"

"Oh no, I'm trying to quit." Claire had no idea why she said this except that she had wanted to impress this woman.

"Me, too, for the past twenty years." Then Ann Holloway's face turned serious. "That man is just about the worst thing you can do with your life. You know this, don't you?" Before Claire could answer, Ann went on, her face soft, her eyes on the ceiling, "Oh my, and at the same time, he's the very best, you know that, too, of course. It's why you're here. But the worst of him will kill you before you get the best."

Ann Holloway put her cigarette out and pressed a button, and the woman who'd delivered the martinis came in again with an ornate box on a small silver tray. Ann opened the box and took out a slim and perfectly rolled joint. She lit it with a large glass lighter and took a long drag. The sweet lazy smell made its way slowly to Claire and she took a deep breath, and Ann passed her the lit piece. "Here, then. In lieu of vodka." They took deep drags, passing the thing back and forth. The little hand on the big clock on the wall had moved two places. When had that happened? Where was Jack?

"Why does the worst have to come first?" Claire asked.

"It's survival, Claire. It's nothing more. People are very simple, it turns out, for all the nonstop analysis. You can uncover every mystery of human beings, everything you need to know, by watching rats."

Claire's eyes were closed, her head fell back. She was sleepy in the big velvet chair.

"We're like lab rats in a maze," Ann said. "If you move the cheese, we run different routes to find it. If you introduce a pleasure sensation when we take a certain route to the cheese, we'll remember and run that same route again. If you introduce pain when we take a certain path, the next time we'll avoid it. But here's what is fascinating." Ann Holloway leaned in. "What is fascinating to me is when the pleasure sensation is induced repeatedly, in disproportion to the pain. Do you understand what I mean?"

The pot had made Claire dramatic; her eyes got big and round.

"No, I don't think I do. What happens?" Claire asked.

"The rat," Ann said, "loses perspective. An overload of pleasure mitigates the need for food. The pleasure satisfies the rat's hunger. If you keep stimulating the rats with a pleasure sensation on a certain route,"—it was clear that Ann enjoyed this—"then move the cheese so that they have to take a path *around* the cheese to get to the pleasure. Do you know what happens then?"

"No," Claire said, her eyes still big. "I don't."

Ann sat back in her chair. "The food is right there, they know where to find it, but they run right past it. They starve to death, for the pleasure."

"Of course, people aren't rats." Claire laughed nervously.

"Don't kid yourself, honey." Ann took a long drag of the joint and held it in, quietly let it out. Claire was picking at her shirt-sleeve, pulling it down past her sweater.

"I like you. And I'd like it if you would come back to lunch with me sometime. I'd enjoy it very much. All of that is why I'm going to tell you, Claire: he's ruined for women."

Claire didn't look up, and Ann went on.

"He's fucking two other girls right now, for instance, just this week."

Claire shifted uncomfortably in her seat. The warm pot feeling was starting to ebb.

"It doesn't matter, Claire, it's only sex after all, and he's careful. He won't put anyone at risk. It's not that, it's that he gives a little piece of himself away to each of you every time. He doesn't know how not to. He can't just fuck, he has to give something. He doesn't protect himself, in that way. He does like you. He holds you in high esteem. But protect yourself."

She picked up her drink and tinkled the ice cubes around— Claire hadn't noticed that the martinis had been cleared and replaced by something else. Ann Holloway started to laugh. "If you can accept that we're all rats, Claire, then you might have a little fun."

Claire thought she might burst into tears. Suddenly there was Jack.

"Claire, Ann has this back room I want you to see."

Claire gasped at his voice, right behind her, his head lowered to her level on the chair. How long had he been here? At some point music had been turned on; they were listening to Sarah Vaughan. Ann Holloway's words pounded in her head like the background to some sick Hollywood thriller sound track. Jack Huxley's character would lead her to another room now, lay her down on a cold marble table, and the two of them would drink her blood.

"I don't think so," Claire said.

Jack's head jerked back just slightly. "All right." He stood up.

She tried a smile, but Claire Byrne was no actress.

"Is anything wrong?" he asked.

"No, nothing. It's fine. I just have a headache. The martini." They both looked at her barely touched drink. "Maybe I could just go—"

"Go?"

"Maybe we could just go back to the house, if that's all right. I get headaches. Sometimes. I just need to lie down."

They were in the car ten minutes before either one of them spoke.

"Listen. Claire, I'm sorry. For whatever she said in there. She's a bit unfiltered."

"No, she's not. She's just honest."

Jack pulled over and stopped the car. He took a deep breath.

"There was another girl, Claire. I'm sure you already know that. There are papers, television shows, magazines, I don't kid myself, I know. I'm sure you've seen it."

Claire's heart pounded. She wanted him to stop talking and she didn't know how to ask him to without sounding pathetic.

"She's not in the picture now."

"In the picture? One girl?" Claire wanted to start laughing. It was so absurd. And Ann Holloway was right—it's not about the sex. Charlie was right. Love and sex can't coexist. Jack Huxley was never going to get that, any of it.

There was one more day before she was to leave. Jack had left early in the morning, with some vague detail to take care of. Claire's small body coiled up beneath his goose feather comforter, eight-hundred-thread-count sheets. Still she shivered.

There was a book face down on the pillow next to her. Claire turned it over. *The Razor's Edge*, first edition. Signed by Somerset Maugham. She couldn't imagine where Jack had found it. Was this his own personal copy? Now given to her? Inside was a note:

> C—
>
> Our book. Now yours.
>
> —Jack

He gives a little piece of himself away to each of you, every time. Ann Holloway's words rang in her ears.

> RULE #16: Relationships are like writing; the
> hardest part is knowing when to stop.

40

AFTER CLAIRE GOT BACK TO NEW YORK, SHE GOT HER period. So much for that. She relaxed, then obsessed, then met Sasha and Ethan at Bar Pitti for post-Jack analysis.

Claire handed Ethan her coat. She told them about the visit to Ann Holloway and their awkward last day. She didn't tell them about the book. They wouldn't understand.

"I don't have an exit strategy," she said.

"Oh my God, it's not love, honey," Ethan said.

"How do you know?" Claire asked.

"At best, it's oxytocin," Sasha said. "It's the bonding hormone. Women release it during sex and childbirth. Dr. Riva says it can take up to two years to detox from high levels of it."

"You're ridiculous."

"I might be, but I'm not the one claiming to love a hologram."

"A hologram?"

"Yes, you see him in front of you but when you reach out to touch him he's not really there. I hadn't wanted to tell you, but this whole thing you're doing is not you and it's not good for you either."

"Don't preach, Sash. Last week you said you wished Thom was dead."

"What?" Ethan said. "Did I miss something?"

Sasha glared at Claire.

"Never mind," Claire said.

Panderer and seducer, flatterer and alchemist—the embodiment of everyone Dante bumped into on his zippy little foray into hell. That was Jack Huxley.

"You should sue him for breach of affection. He's squandering affections you should be investing somewhere else. He's sabotaging your future potential. He should pay you restitution."

"That's not very helpful, Sasha," Claire said. "I'll just forget any of it ever happened. Who cares? My husband died. I'm thirty-two and I don't have a clue about life or love or men."

"Clarabelle, sweetie. Take advantage of your freedom. Go out with me tonight. Maybe you'll meet someone normal—a ballet dancer."

Claire pouted. " 'Freedom's just another word for nothing left to lose.' "

"That's a song lyric." Ethan said.

"Song lyrics are true. Joan Baez was a poet." Claire took a sip of her wine and distracted herself with her menu.

"You didn't just say that." Ethan pulled Claire's menu down from in front of her.

"Janis Joplin!" Claire said and laughed. "Just testing you."

41

I T WAS THE MIDDLE OF CLAIRE'S DISCONTENT. SHE WOKE
up at three minutes past nine in the morning. There was a phone
call from Richard.

"Claire. Sorry to wake you. Did I wake you?"

"No. Yes."

"Knopf is asking for the first one hundred pages of Charlie's
book. If you stall, they'll lose interest and then we're back at square
one. Do you have something?"

"Hmm. I guess."

"Something I can give them?"

"No."

"Okay, first fifty."

"By when?"

"As soon as you can. If you give me something reasonable, I'll
tell them and they'll be okay if they have a date. The catch is, you
can't miss it."

"Tell them a year. Maxwell Perkins used to—"

"I know about Maxwell Perkins," Richard said. "But you haven't written *For Whom the Bell Tolls* yet. So until then, they want to know how much of the book is going to be Charlie and how much you. They want to know they're going to be able to sell the booksellers on it."

"I need more time, Richard."

"I'll tell them first few chapters and a synopsis by June. They'll take that. Stick to a schedule. Get up and eat some fruit and get to work. I want to see some finished pages next month."

Claire was tired of Charlie's book. She had been taking up space at the National Arts Club, going every day, staring at walls, watching Don DeLillo come and go, counting down the remaining days of Charlie's membership, and e-mailing people she hadn't talked to in five years. She had not, technically, done much work on Charlie's book at all.

THE CITY, AS if to shame her, felt unnaturally upbeat. Unapologetically happy. It rolled right over her. Ethan invited her to a cocktail party on Thursday, and Jonathan Rochet was there. Claire made it a point to overdrink. She choked down the house bar's signature margaritas in big gulps. She made a terrible insult to Ethan's friend, then excused herself to wobble back home.

Another week down. Three million to go.

The first day of spring, Claire took a taxi to the Empire State Building and bought an all-day pass to Big Apple Tours—a doubledecker bus that drove up and down the city, over and over, like a giant narrative taxi, infusing its passengers with useless bits of island legend and gossip and lore.

She took the first bus in the line and handed her ticket to Derek. Yes, Derek. Claire's griot. Islands are small.

He began in a quiet, conspiratorial murmur. "Right now you are six blocks from where Thomas Paine died. Paine, the infidel, the author of *Common Sense* and *The Crisis*, two of the most political pamphlets of American history. Both written during the American Revolutionary War. Thomas Paine returned to fifty-nine Grove Street to die somewhat disgraced soon after being imprisoned by Robespierre in Paris during the French Revolution."

He made no suggestion of knowing Claire, and she was glad. There was no awkwardness. She sank back in a seat and watched. The griot was animated. His arms gesticulated in one direction, then—*swoop, whoosh*—in the other.

She sat and listened, and at the first stop she stayed on. She stayed on through the Village, through Chinatown and Soho, up to Times Square and Museum Mile.

By late afternoon Claire was hungry and considering getting off when the tour bus slowed at Sixty-Fourth Street as it made its way up Madison Avenue.

"Here," the griot began. He was solemn. Claire sat up straight.

"Here is where just last year one of the city's finest minds was felled by one of its most expensive works of art."

He didn't say Charlie's name. He didn't mention the fake. No one asked any questions. But he did catch Claire's eye.

She stood up as the bus approached the stop at Grant's Tomb, 122nd Street and Riverside Drive. He was in the middle of a story about the number of times Grant proposed to his wife before she finally agreed to marry him. Claire left with her heart warm and walked the long, long, long way back downtown.

At the corner of Broadway and Fifty-Ninth, at Columbus Circle, she stopped to catch her breath. There was a newsstand on the corner. In the same way that Michael Corleone didn't look but still sensed the headline that said his father had been shot, Claire sensed it.

She did not want to turn her head, but she did.

Jack Huxley was on the cover of *People*, *OK!*, *Us*, the *National Enquirer*, and, of course, the *New York Post*.

"Preggers!"

Claire walked up to the newsstand under the pretense of buying gum. She pretended to dig through her wallet. She tried inconspicuously to read the magazine.

"Right," she said softly.

"You want the paper?" the brown-haired man asked impatiently.

"Just gum. Doublemint."

She looked up and down Eighth Avenue. She looked across at the park where couples where swinging small children between them, lifting them up off the ground and letting them back down.

No one in the city could possibly register the Richter measurement that had just rocked Claire Byrne.

Preggers!

RULE #17: Once you have non-monogamously dated a man, step aside for other women to non-monogamously date him.

She left a dollar bill on the counter, snatched up the *Post*, and walked fast and angry the rest of the way home. Then she called Sasha.

"Someone's pregnant."

"What? Who is? Wait, hold on a second."

Claire took the phone into her bathroom and examined herself in the small mirror. Charlie's bathrobe was still hanging on the door. Her hair looked too long, too brown, too old. Her face looked too plain. She had very small breasts. Charlie had liked her. Hadn't he? *No one is ever going to like me again*, she thought.

"Honey, I have a situation going on," Sasha said. "I'll call you right back."

Instead of calling, though, Sasha came through the door thirty minutes later. She walked in with wine bottles.

" 'Remember when I was young and so were you-ouuu. And time stood still, and love was all we knew-ewww.' " Claire was singing loud and off-key and didn't realize either of these things until she looked up to see Sasha staring. Claire took an earplug out. "What?" she said.

"Lock your front door, Claire, and what are you listening to?"

"Alan Jackson."

"What is wrong with you? Are you crying?"

"No."

"You are. Oh my God. Honey, what the hell is going on? Alan Jackson?"

"I'm not crying. And why do you have wine? I hate wine," Claire said.

"It's good for you. Antioxidants. Where'd you see it?"

Claire had already processed the information; she didn't want to go over it. At this point, it didn't really matter how or who or what was pregnant.

"It doesn't matter. He's like a rat who won't move for cheese. Ann Holloway explained it very clearly to me. I just didn't know someone would get pregnant, but of course someone eventually would. You have sex, the sperm and the egg, sometimes they meet up. Who cares? Why aren't you saying anything?"

"Because I doubt anyone's pregnant. I'm sure the girl is a nut, she's trying to set him up, manipulate him into thinking he should care about her and his fake unborn baby."

"And what if she is?"

"Since when do you believe tabloids?"

"Since I started reading them."

Sasha sat down next to Claire and slipped out a gold cigarette case from her purse. "Listen," she said and lit up a pink menthol, "I saw the pictures. She's not going to risk losing that body."

"That's, for some reason, little comfort."

"It's the oldest trick in the book, that's all I'm saying. You get pregnant or, more likely, say you are, you land the guy or at least get his attention." Sasha handed the cigarette to Claire. "It's a desperate move but girls do it because, guess what, it works."

"Like negative campaigning?" Claire took a drag of the cigarette and handed it back.

"Exactly. The energy shifts back in her direction and then, suddenly, a fake miscarriage." Sasha stood and walked into the kitchen. She got halfway there, then turned back and grabbed the wine bottles. "Men will never get it. Listen," she added. "You need to really find some better medication. I didn't want to say anything . . ."

"I'm fine, with medication. What do you mean you didn't want to say anything?"

"What are you taking?" Sasha called. Claire could hear her opening a cabinet and pulling out glasses.

"Nothing. An Ambien sometimes if I can't sleep."

"Klonopin for anxiety then, maybe." Sasha popped her head out of the kitchen and gestured with a corkscrew. "In my purse. There's a prescription. Take two."

"What do *you* know?" Claire said, as Sasha's head disappeared.

She set the cigarette on an ashtray, then dug around in Sasha's giant leather purse and surfaced with a small, unmarked white pill bottle.

"Movie stars fall in love with regular girls in the movies—it's so sweet—but you're not in a movie."

"Okay, Sasha, I get it."

"In real life, you're lucky you even had one. It's like a shooting star, or finding a new leopard species in Borneo or a four-leaf clover, or maybe winning a fucking Pulitzer, I don't know. But there's a half-life, honey." Sasha could be brutal.

"A half-life?"

"Yes, the pleasure of the experience is cut in half in direct proportion to the likelihood of it happening. In other words, let's find a nice investment banker next time."

Claire popped open the bottle. Sasha continued.

"He's not real. He doesn't even know who you are when you're not in front of him. You probably have to keep telling your fucking story over and over to him every time you get together. Right? And then he picks up a detail and plunges into it, because that's what he does. It's a role, and he nails it because that's his job and why he gets the big parts, and then you misinterpret that for some greater quality of humanity that you have never quite found in someone else and the reason you have never quite found it in someone else is because it doesn't exist. Real people don't have those qualities. Screenwriters make them up and people in Kansas pay ten dollars to fantasize for a few hours."

Claire glanced down at an old *Daily News* she'd saved. It was sitting on her coffee table next to Charlie's urn. It was the photo of a movie star buying lemonade from a little kid. Jack was reaching down, handing him a bill. "Jack Huxley's $20 Lemonade."

Claire had just dropped three pills into her palm when Sasha came into the living room, wineglasses in hand, took one look at Claire, and shrieked. Both glasses dropped from her hand and shattered. Claire watched as red wine cascaded like blood across her hardwood floor. She stood up. "Jesus, Sasha. What is wrong with you?"

"Put those down," Sasha said, eyes wide, rushing across the room. She took the pill bottle from Claire's left hand, then took her right hand and tipped it over the ashtray so that the three little yellow pills spilled out next to the pink butt. Sasha backed away from them as if they were radioactive. In the background, on cue, Dr. Oz began a story on prescription drugs.

Claire stared at the ashtray. She stared at Sasha, who was wobbling on her heels. Sasha never wobbled in heels.

"Those aren't Klonopin," Sasha said. "They're ketamine, special k, fucking tranquilizers."

"Jesus, Sasha. Are you trying to kill someone?"

Sasha went pale. "Oh God. Sweetie. Do you remember a few weeks ago—that bruise under my eye? Dr. Struck? I might have been a little upset that day we had lunch."

"Understatement," Claire said. "But go on."

"I might have accidentally given the maître d' the impression that my husband had beaten me and that I wanted him dead."

Claire laughed. Sasha did not. "I've heard of maître d's hooking customers up with coke or sex. But horse tranquilizers?" Claire knelt to the carpet and began picking up the glass. "And how long have you been carrying them around? I mean, I know Thom and that assistant . . . But he . . . you . . . " She wasn't even sure what to say.

"Of course not!" Sasha said. "No! But this man offered to 'take

Thom out' like we were on *The Sopranos* or something. He insisted I take the pills. What was I going to do? Tell the mobbed-up maître d' that he'd made a mistake? What if he thought I'd go to the police?"

Claire laughed so hard, she forgot all about pregnant girls, movie stars, and dead husbands. "By the way, I had two movie stars." Claire said as she walked to the kitchen to retrieve the rest of the wine.

"What?" Sasha said. Claire handed her a new glass, with a generous pour.

"Yeah. Two new leopard species, two falling stars." Claire smiled mischievously, remembering how all of this had started.

"Did I miss something somewhere?"

"I accidentally slept with Brad Hess, the night I met Jack at the premiere." Claire said. "I may have had too much tequila and they were both wearing black."

"Oh my God!" Sasha shrieked. She clinked her glass to Claire's. "You've had quite a year." She smiled and shook her head. "Wait a minute—who's Brad Hess?"

42

THE TEXT CAME, THIS TIME FROM A FRONTIER EXPLORER:
Sorry I disappeared. A lot going on, long story. i'll be in ny next
week and want 2cu. William Clark

Claire replied, Okay. Sure.

When Jack Huxley was in town to promote a movie, the proto-
cols were elaborate, as if a movie publicity tour was actually the
G-7 Summit. Invitations were stamped and mailed, there were
secret phone numbers to call; there was a labyrinth of winding
curves to follow just to say, "Yes, I will be at the event." This time
around, there was a three-day Felliniesque production. There were
parties and cocktails and the movie screening, of course. It kicked
off at the house of Glenn and SallyAnn Roberts on Fifth Avenue
because Glenn had three billion dollars and a lot of expensive art.
It had crossed Claire's mind that she might run into Walter White.
This woman had arranged for Jack to come to her party in the
same way people procure ponies for children's parties. He was
high-grade entertainment; there was a premium. Charlie would be

appalled at this kind of circus, but he also wouldn't have missed it for the world. Charlie would either cause a scene or he'd steal it—he knew that to secure a shard of legend meant smashing up against other legends when the opportunity arose. Those who insist on being immortal know all about it. The writer who throws a punch is remembered long after the one who leaves early and goes home, regardless of anyone's talent. Claire regretted that these two particular men never had the chance to pair up.

Claire walked in alone, Ethan had bailed, and right away she saw him. It had only been weeks. It felt like years. He had his head down. He was leaning against a chair by the door, concentrating on something someone was saying (or keeping his head down so it would appear that way). The man speaking was close to Jack Huxley's ear; there was noise at the bar. There was a drink in Huxley's hand. He nodded, listened, nodded again, mimicking concentration, complete attention, pretending he'd shut everything out. Claire had seen this before.

He rolled his drink around abstractly, to move the ice. He made a gesture with his hand. He was someone film critics have described as both "fluid" and "animated." As Claire watched him, she saw that they were not saying this carelessly. Jack Huxley's entire body played into each moment. Not one of his parts ever wondered what to do. He moved as if he were choreographed.

There had been a mild scandal in the press recently, but, unlike the fake pregnancy, this was real. The room was buzzing with it. They wanted to be the first to hear it from his mouth. He would get to it when he's ready, they all knew he will, because SallyAnn and Glenn had three billion dollars. There was a brawl outside a club in Miami, the details were sketchy, but it was seedy. The club, the alley, a garbage Dumpster no less. There were reports that Jack

Huxley was not valiant but stumbling. Not polished and neat in his loosened tie and smooth suit, like tonight, but crumpled, his shirt pocked with bar spills. The story in the tabloids was that it was over a girl, and that the girl had to come out and help him back inside. People had to be summoned to help him leave through a side door.

On Fifth Avenue they were waiting for Huxley's version, the one where a dark brute insulted the maiden and Jack Huxley slew him in one blow. The version where he marched the cheering crowd back in and declared, "Drinks are on me!" The one where Jack Huxley had his driver take the brute to the hospital, got him patched up, and then paid the bill.

Claire had been nervous for him. The mainstream media had picked up the sad bits of the fight. For once he hadn't been spared. But tonight he was charming them silly, and the moneyed crowd on Fifth Avenue was transfixed. If he moved one way, they swayed; another way and they leaned.

Claire scolded herself for watching, yet she couldn't stop. One look up, away from his guest, and he would see her. If she walked across the room, to a table, the movement might catch his eye. If she stood too long where she was, she'd look curious. She was exposed. She didn't want to be caught like this, vulnerable and alone. There was another bar set up, opposite. It was the only possible out, to cross over and order a drink. Claire moved quickly.

"Double vodka, rocks," she said.

The hired bartender was young and close-shaved with short black hair, the kind of boyish man who played pickup football games in the park during the day and didn't worry about a career.

"Are you sure? I make a killer martini." He smiled and showed his perfect white teeth.

"Well, then, I want a martini."

"I don't recommend, though, a double."

She was feeling more comfortable now. "Okay, then. I want a double."

He laughed.

Claire's mind wandered as she watched him set the glass up, shake the liquor, scoop three olives with two fingers and thumb.

And then, like it was written in his script, Jack Huxley appeared at her side.

"You don't like martinis." His voice felt like a warm towel pressed against the back of her neck. She turned around slowly.

"Actually, it turns out I do."

There was a hand rested upon her elbow. Nudging a bit, then a bit more, like a boat starting away from the dock.

Claire smiled to herself. She could pull off a good first fifteen seconds. In the first fifteen seconds, she could be clever and confident and capture, if not his whole heart, at least his desire to sleep with her again.

"I wondered if you'd come," he said.

"I wouldn't miss it. This crowd, though. Ruthless." She wondered if the art was real.

"If I stay right next to you, will it help?"

"Are you kidding? It wouldn't be fair to everyone else."

"Two stories, then I'm out of here."

Claire was uncomfortable about the attention his standing near her brought. The Roberts had paid a lot of money for him.

"A perfect point seven?" Jack said. He put an arm casually across the back of a chair, to brace his body as he leaned in. She was surprised. *Misconstrued* had recently run her piece on Dr.

Singh. The piece she'd flown to Texas for, the day Charlie died. How had he come across it? It crossed Claire's mind: Was he keeping track of her?

"I have to say, I don't believe it. This ratio theory. The hip and the waist."

"I bet if you took the measurements of all the women you have known, you'd find they support it."

Claire had put her back against the wall because she felt unsteady. But this pose had the effect of making her look vulnerable. It was very different, she was aware, from the way other people in the room were moving around and interacting, and it had not gone unnoticed.

"There's also the theory that if you sample a third of your total number of viable romantic candidates—likely matches based on age, religion, etc.—and randomly propose to any one of them, it's mating jackpot."

"You're clever." Claire liked this part, when they sparred. "Are you debunking my hip-to-waist theory?"

"Just upping my odds."

There was a pause and Claire knew she had to head it off quickly because a pause is an opening, an invitation for "Why?"

In the movies you take chances. At well-appointed parties in New York, Claire knows, you don't.

"You're right, I don't like martinis. And yet I'm wondering when it will occur to you, your arm on the chair, watching me cradle an empty glass, to get me another."

"Olive?"

"Yes, please. Two."

Soon, then, the other guests closed in on him and for the next three hours, he didn't come out. A hard circle formed, and a complex migration, whereby people came and went. Spots were ceded, or not, wordlessly. Some moved away, obligingly, some didn't. There was no taking cuts. Claire saw, occasionally, hard looks exchanged. She watched them all watch the cues. You don't interrupt. These are his stories, and you don't take a part in them unless he asks you to.

Three hours later there was no sign of an end to the show, and she'd had too many olives and too much to drink. She'd made small talk with too many acquaintances she didn't care to see. Jack appeared to be on for the night. There were women stacked in layers and folds in front of Claire. Finally, tired and resigned, she moved slowly toward the door.

But he spotted her. The great hunter saw movement in the brush. "Claire!" he called from the head of the circle he was commanding. The entire room got quiet and turned. "Wait, don't go."

The entire room retained its gaze—equal parts curiosity and disdain. Who was this Claire who'd distracted their hero? He beckoned them back and then gave them one more story.

When Jack finally left—yes, with Claire—it was quick like a jailbreak. Coats went on fast. A few lucky ones got whisked along with them out the door like windblown leaves. People got into cabs. Claire and Jack got in a car, and then the doors shut and the tinted windows were there and then the worrying, curious, niggling eyes disappeared. He could relax.

"Oh my God, I'm tired. When did talking become bricklaying?" He was laughing, his legs crossed and his body pivoted toward her, he yanked at his tie; his movements were beautifully seamless.

An arm went up behind her. Here were his eyes. "I'm not kidding. Jesus . . . did you hear what SallyAnn-what's-her-face asked me? Did you hear how many times I had to tell that fucking story?"

For a moment, Claire felt sorry for him.

He was in character, though. He chuckled at these things. He'd be a pawn and find the laugh in it. So she laughed with him, they poked fun, their shoulders pushed together. It was like a warm bath in the dark black leather of the car, in the shadow of Jack's driver. This is how the womb must feel, Claire thought. Safe and warm, and lovely. Oh how natural his hand felt on her leg, as if they'd been measured and fitted—his hand to her leg. It felt as though it had been months since she'd seen him, and now there was so much to tell, she felt it all bubbling up, she felt like a jeroboam of champagne. So many anecdotes she'd saved up, so many gossipy items she knew he'd enjoy, so many soft little kisses for him to give her on her forehead, on her elbow, on her cheek. So what if he'd disappeared. Who cares about other girls? Claire was just beginning to think where to start when the car stopped short and Jack, with a hand on the door now, and the other still on her leg, was telling her good night. His movements were beautifully seamless.

"I have a hell of a press schedule tomorrow, starts at seven. I'll have to tell that same story four more times." He leaned past her and forward, toward the front of the car. "Sal, Claire needs to go downtown. Get her there safe, or I'll have to kill you." He asked for her number. *What? My number?*

Claire knew shtick when she heard it. Sal was probably mouthing the lines. Huxley kissed her softly but quickly and then he was gone. Claire was too bewildered to react. She had words but she couldn't get them out. Could not manage, even, a simple stammer. But . . . I thought . . . wait.

She looked around her in the car to confirm, she felt the spot where he'd been sitting, it was warm. It turned midnight and Jack Huxley disappeared like Cinderella. Claire Byrne's carriage made its slow way south through Broadway traffic, to her home.

43

C LAIRE ENTERED HER APARTMENT, TIRED. SHE WENT TO
her bedroom and began to undress. She held her breath and
turned on the light. No one was there.

She picked up the phone.

"Sweetie, where are you? It's after midnight," Sasha said.

"Crazy. I'm in crazy."

"And your movie star?"

Claire let out a long sigh.

"Gone. I saw him. It was nice. And then he left. We got in his
car together and then he left—got out at his hotel and told the
driver to take me home."

"Oh."

"He kissed me on the forehead and asked if I was in town for a
spell—he said 'spell,' he's cute that way—and I said, 'Yes I am, I live
here, remember?' He's doing a press thing or a promo thing or
some sort of stupid thing and he said, 'I'll call you.'"

Claire could hear the clinking of a glass on the other end, the shush as Sasha told Thom to go back to bed. It made Claire feel lonely. "What if he calls?" Sasha asked.

"He's not going to call. It would be insulting at this point to call."

"Why?"

"Because we start at the same place every time. Except I've gone back a step and now we start there. Now he doesn't even go home with me, he doesn't even invite me in. But wait, the next part's pathetic. He asked for my number. He's so damn good at this, he can ask for the number of a woman who could have sworn they'd recently been intimately involved without even batting an eye."

"He asked for your number . . ."

"Yes, and I gave it to him. And then he paused and said, 'Hey, that's a great number. Did you know the guy?' "

"Know what guy?"

"The phone guy, you know . . . did I know the phone guy to get such a good number."

"I don't get it."

"Yes, well. There's nothing to really get. The point is . . . the pathetic point is he already said that exact same line to me. The first time he ever asked for my number. The first time he asked, when it all seemed spontaneous, when I didn't know I was watching the first act of a play that I was never going to see the end of."

"I don't know what to say."

"Nothing to say. I'm merely illustrating a sad denouement. I have to go."

"When will I see you, sweetie?"

"Soon."

Claire hung up and climbed into bed.

*   *   *

HER CELL PHONE rang a few minutes later. "You're up late." Ethan's voice was reassuring.

"Why couldn't my husband just not be dead so I could be married and living happily ever after?"

He would not indulge her.

"I adored the man, honey, but stop romanticizing it. He wasn't your fairy tale, and this one isn't either."

Claire started to argue, then stopped.

"The curtain closed on your first act. You were just finding your second and this guy comes along. Huxley is exactly like Charlie. Wake up, Cinderella. Get a new pair of shoes."

"How come I paid Lowenstein and Spence two hundred dollars an hour apiece and they never noticed this? I'm scared of second acts," Claire said. The room felt hot. She punched her pillow. Turned onto her side.

"Of course you are, second acts are messy. There are obstacles, twists and turns, in a second act. You have to fix things that came up in act one." Ethan continued. "You'd rather avoid it. That's what you did with Charlie and then he suddenly died so you never had to. Then you pick another first act guy."

"I like first acts," Claire mumbled.

"Everyone does. All action, no accountability."

"I need to look for a second act."

"Yes, Clarabelle, you do."

AT THREE IN the morning, Claire committed a desperate third act. Three o'clock is the time when desperate acts occur. It took an hour to compose it. To write and then delete and then revise—is that too strong? Too flippant? Will he understand I'm being funny there?

Four hours later, at seven that morning, she turned on her television in time to see his legs crossed casually in front of Matt Lauer and his smile at full morning wattage. He was wearing the black Armani suit, a stark white shirt. Tan and fit, his jawbone lean, he looked like a well-behaved rogue. He looked like what heroin must have looked to Billie Holiday, like vodka to Liz Taylor. His gestures were fluid; his head bobbed playfully from side to side. At this exact same time, her e-mail to him was arriving on a gadget in his dressing room, in the room where he'd likely taken fifteen minutes to prepare and in that fifteen minutes had claimed the world as his again. The camera had almost certainly been invented with Jack Huxley in mind.

Claire had sent the e-mail; it was sent.

I wanted to call your room, but forgot your fake name.

I stayed at that party, suffering over all those sycophants so I could spend time with you afterward. I'm clumsy, though, and for a writer, still incapable of expressing myself next to you in a Suburban with Sal.

I thought we could be more, Jack. I was wrong . . . fairy tales are best left for the books.

My late husband was much better suited for writing your story than I am. Take care, Jack.

Claire

It was the end, for Claire, of actors.

44

RULE #18: "Never discourage anyone who continues to make progress, no matter how slow" (Plato).

"THAT'S INTERESTING." EVAN Spence was wearing a scarf around his neck and it was distracting to Claire. She had impulsively decided to see him again. She was impulsively deciding everything.

"What's interesting?"

"What you were saying."

Claire for an instant, and then two, stretching into three, was unable to reattach to a single thread of what she was saying. She was going on four and decided to move. "Can I sit over there?"

"I don't see why not."

"It's just, I'm distracted over here."

"Whatever you like."

"Okay. Now I remember." She was facing the window now, and couldn't see Evan Spence.

"Claire, excuse me."

"Yes?"

"Never mind, go on."

"Ummm. I was talking about people as punctuation, right?"

"Yes."

"So there are periods and commas and ellipses . . . and colons and semicolons, of course, all that. But I'm a parenthesis."

"And what do you mean by that?"

"I was Charlie's plus one, I was his parenthesis. My botanomanist, Eve, is a semicolon. Ethan's thoughtful, like a comma. Sasha's definitely an exclamation point. I go to events, I go to places, and no one quite remembers my name but they remember my face. I'm a parenthesis. Charlie was a period. And where does a parenthesis go after a period?"

"I'm not sure I follow."

"I'm just saying. I haven't enjoyed, really, being a widow."

"No one particularly enjoys it."

"No, I know, right. Not enjoy, but everyone knows there are perks. That's what I mean. You're a star, center stage for—well, you can stretch it out for a long damn time. I realize now why I don't enjoy it and why I liked Huxley."

"Because you're a parenthesis?"

"No, because I'm a period now."

Claire smiled at her reflection in the window.

45

T ROLLOPE WROTE THREE THOUSAND WORDS A DAY, BUT
Claire was not Trollope.

What He Wants: Jack Huxley and the Art of the Narcissist. The
book. The ghost of Charlie, she hoped, might revisit her for his
book. On the occasions when he haunted her, however, neither of
them brought it up.

"It's about tragedy," she said. She was in Richard's office. Her
eyes were fixed on his bookshelf. "It's a crisis of meaning."

Richard's eyes were closed, presumably to more deeply
absorb the essence of the subject at hand, Claire's work. That's
right: her work. The book she wanted to write. He was obligated, for a number of reasons, to humor her. They were both
aware of this.

"A crisis of meaning?" he said.

Claire walked to the side of Richard's desk, though she couldn't
get behind it. Outside, it was an ordinary day.

"Describe what you mean," he said.

"Crisis of meaning. Well, a person or a whole country can experience it. It could be happening right now."

Richard put his hands together beneath his chin; his eyes remained closed.

"It's like Bob Dylan before his motorcycle accident that may or may not have actually happened, and then Bob Dylan shortly after. He was an entirely different person. Before the accident, he was reckless and drifting. Then he crashed and disappeared and came back married and serious. He had a crisis of meaning. One day you know who you are and then you don't. Charlie was alive one morning, coming to see you, and then he was dead. I was married when I flew to Texas and then a widow before I got back home. I'm not the same person anymore, and it was sudden. A physical change— look at me, I don't even look the same—and then spiritual. It started on the plane, after you called me and I flew back from Austin—I ordered gin. I would never order gin. I let a man wear Charlie's robe, I opened up the expensive wine, I got a second-opinion shrink, I lost my virginity again. That's what the book should be about."

Richard nodded and cleared his throat.

Claire scowled at the bookshelf. "Richard, open your eyes please."

Richard opened them.

Claire put one hand on her hip and with the other one gestured behind Richard's head. "What is that?"

It was *Tête sur tige* (Head of a Man on a Rod), 1947. They both knew this very well. "It was a good investment, Claire. These things go in cycles."

"Is it real?" she asked. She knew very well that it was.

Richard, with his hands still folded beneath his chin, nodded.

"A fake Giacometti kills Charlie, and there's a rush on the real ones? How long have you had it? I don't want to know. How do you know it's not fake? It's ugly." Claire was furious; this didn't seem right. "If Charlie had been murdered with a gun, would you have rushed out to buy one? In homage?"

"Charlie wasn't murdered. It's comforting having it here."

"Charlie wouldn't agree with that. It's morbid, Richard."

"How many pages do you have?" he asked.

"A Giacometti was my crisis of meaning. Thirty-eight."

Richard's eyes popped open wide.

"I think we need a new play, Richard," Claire said. "I have an idea."

PART IV

The Widow Finds Meaning

46

A DIFFERENT YEAR, ANOTHER MONDAY IN NEW YORK, and on this one a woman found meaning. It was sunny. There was a breeze. Birds chirped in the suburbs, trains ran on time, the postmen made their rounds. It was the kind of day when art might fall from the sky, the kind of day a leading man might walk into an ordinary bookstore, the kind of day when the improbable makes sense. No one expects anything to happen, so it does. Blue skies can be misleading.

Nearly one year after Charlie's death, Claire began her stroll through lower Manhattan, along Prince Street toward Crosby, at approximately ten after nine in the morning. She wove her way through sun-dappled shade and baby oaks sprouting up from the sidewalk, traversing the concrete and crosswalks, dodging harried commuters beelining toward the subways. Jack Huxley was back in town.

He was filming *Moving Violations*. Although Claire had forgotten, by now, his secret phone number, although she'd stopped noticing his pictures on magazines at every newsstand, and his face on the billboards, she still kept track.

The day before, she'd gone to his hotel, the Mercer. Somehow, she'd known he'd have checked in under the name Larry Darrell—it was his favorite. She shivered a little with old feelings—maybe he'd been thinking of her, here in New York. She'd left a note for him, at the front desk, on pale blue stationery.

Meet me at McNally Jackson Books on Sunday at 11. If you're not there I'll know you would have wanted to be. Claire

Along her walk, she stopped for coffee, perused the paper. At 10:59 she crossed under the pale awning of the little bookstore and walked inside. The smell of paper and poetry and the comfort of words wedged into shelves and stacked up against walls gave her confidence. She was surrounded by everything that was ever worth saying.

And there he was. A man of average height, and from the back almost unnoticeable. Then he turned and there was the smile, and it wasn't just poetry but a reminder of where the line is drawn between those who are mortal—and those who are not.

He saw her and moved her way. "Hubbell Gardiner," he said, introducing himself. "Of course," she said in reply, sticking a hand out, "Katie Morosky." This was easy; he knew how to make it be. He had *The Great Gatsby* in his hand. "At the risk of you writing me off as some shallow Hollywood hack, I confess I've never read it start to end."

"Well, you know the highlights—love, sex, and death, not necessarily in that order. Somewhere between pages seventy and one hundred and forty, a crisis of confidence, a crippling one. Then a coupling, an entanglement—"

"—and it all comes undone, yes. There are broken dreams and a futile pursuit. Maybe I have read it." He looks at the ground. Kicks at it with the bottom of his shoe. "How are you, Claire?"

"I'm really good."

"You know—"

"Shh . . ." Claire put her finger to his lips. They felt lovely. She was writing the ending. She was bringing the characters back home. There was no more longing, just an overall sense of serenity.

"I didn't write the book," she said.

"I heard. Subject matter's dull. I'm not surprised."

So much had happened. "I couldn't write Charlie's book, it was crazy. I don't think even Charlie could. The world isn't ready to find out that Jack Huxley knows every word to 'MacArthur Park.' "

"Right," he said, and laughed.

She explained to him that Knopf had canceled the book but that Richard had worked his magic. He got them to agree to substitute an essay collection as well as an original project of hers, so that she could keep the advance.

She got a little shy, then, as writers often do with a work in progress, with a work that feels so delicate that to describe it out loud seems like it might change it, might send crystalline insights and subtle grace notes fleeing from the mind, never to be recaptured in magical combination again. Where to begin, she tells him, was the problem. It's all for naught without a knockout first line, she knows this from Charlie. Every story lives or dies on where you start.

Once upon a time and a very good time it was . . .

All this happened, more or less.

It was love at first sight.

It is a truth universally acknowledged . . .

It was a dark and stormy night.

Once upon a time there was a girl named Claire. She had a manageable sort of life and then her husband died and her life became unmanageable for a moment. She became smaller and quieter until it seemed there was nothing. But then . . .

"How about your film? How's it going?"

He was directing this time, from a script he'd adapted from a book. He gave her his aw-shucks grin, said behind the camera is harder than he remembered. A different sort of creativity. He hoped to do more of it. The film, he said, despite its action-packed plot—an accident, lovers, war zones, a hero in a wheelchair in the desert—is something of a fairy tale. He looked right into her eyes. "That's what drew me to the project," he said. "They're the only stories worth telling."

She congratulated him, and as they talked they wandered among the stacks of books, the shelves of biographies and memoirs, all those stories of heartbreak and futility. In the large section labeled FICTION, she allowed herself to imagine a slender novel by Claire Byrne on the shelf next to *Thinker's Hope*—her novel a perfect .7 ratio next to Charlie's tome—and the oddity of that pairing seemed no less momentous than the moon and the earth switching orbits, or love and sex sharing a home.

Jack referenced a girl, but then waved off her queries: no one special. He said he'd heard Claire was with someone, and she was surprised. She was pleased to think that he'd tried to keep track of her. She wasn't going to marry again. No. But she thought *he* should try it. They laughed at that, and the conversation flowed through other topics.

This is why she loved him, she thought. Publicly he's imperfect, but privately he tries. There are moments of sincerity. Those moments float away like bubbles but he takes the trouble to dip the wand in the soap and blow them through. Charlie, publicly, was a husband, an intellectual, a serious writer, but privately he screwed publicists and the wives of his friends and he couldn't address the incongruity of this with his own wife. Instead, he couched it in theory. There was the unhappy Sasha with her philandering husband; she'd rather get jewelry than face the truth about her life. Richard, and Bridget, who somehow knew intimately the particulars of Jake the hockey player's, um, dick. Ethan and Kevin might come closest of all of them to, well, something—maybe Ethan still had a chance.

"The Way We Were" came over the speaker in the store. Or was it just in Claire's head? Maybe she was just playing it back.

"I should be going," she said. Jack nodded. He seemed nervous. She tried to imagine all the reasons for this: that he didn't want her to go, that he realized they could have been so much more, that he knows they still can be but he's trapped—by a name, a face, a persona too big to escape.

Right. And then she laughed. He was nervous because he wanted to leave. The scene had run long and he was too polite to yell cut. Fairy tales, that's what sells. She reached up slowly and pushed a lock of hair off of his face, the way Barbra Streisand did to Robert Redford. It was one of the silliest things Claire had done in her thirty-three years. Ethan was going to love that little touch. Huxley, though, looked confused. Then he asked, "Would you mind if I kissed you?" Claire leaned toward him. He kissed her, right on the lips, and Claire realized the reason the store felt so quiet. All the players were off the set—the sales team, four of them,

47

CLAIRE PICKED UP THE TWO HUNDRED PAGES OF HER double-spaced manuscript—the first half of her book—from the printer down the block from her apartment and took a cab to Richard's office. She handed the stack to his assistant and walked out. She took another cab to Kennedy Airport and an airplane to San Francisco, where she rented a midsize passenger car and drove to a small town a short distance away. She parked in a driveway and entered a pretty white cottage, then waited.

She sent a text.

The sheets still smell like you.

He replied immediately.

I'm hurrying home.

THERE WAS A night before this, before this escape to a small town on the coast. There was more than one night, actually. I just didn't want to interrupt the story to tell you.

Claire had not only finished the first half of her book, she had also helped Ethan put the essays together. The book of essays was titled *Sex Matters.*

Charlie had left thousands of pages of unpublished work, and they had picked out the best of it. Claire went back and forth with Ethan—they were very careful. It was not her desire to see her late husband buffooned. She took very seriously this responsibility of letting Charlie have an eloquent postscript.

The essay collection turned out nicely; Richard had gotten a respectable sum for it, and every critic worth his salt gave the book a twirl.

The reviews were mixed, of course.

Which was fine. Claire knew in her heart it was good.

And then, *he* reviewed it and, surprisingly, he liked it.

This, unlike the dry tenor of much of the late Byrne's other work, has some stardust sprinkled in, is what he said. *An elegant flourish graces these essays. As if the author found divine inspiration from the grave. There's a playful element, even, that I found startlingly refreshing. It was a bittersweet pleasure to read them.*

She'd sent him a note.

He'd sent her one back.

He felt like an old friend. He felt comfortable. He felt warm and nice and funny.

Time had passed. (It does that.) Things had changed. (They often do.)

Then one dull night out with Sasha—one of those nights where one doesn't want to go out but, to satisfy someone else, does—one late, awful night as her head reeled from the noise and the same disjointed chatter about this or that or nothing, Claire, with no relief from any drink, found herself feeling a little bit low and dispirited. And then she spotted him. He was in profile to her, and she was rolling off her tongue the things she might say—*What are you doing? Hey, how've you been? Oh, how funny to see you here.* She saw him and a series of impulses set her in motion, propelled her to walk to him, to say hello. She'd gotten a sudden warm feeling, the kind of pleasant surprise you sometimes get on a terrible late night, in a place you don't want to be, with the music booming and an end nowhere in sight. Claire was becoming infused with that good feeling, leaning over to Sasha to say, "Wait here, I'll be right back." She was just looking forward to Hello, when another girl walked up, not her, and kissed his cheek and held his arm.

Figures, Claire thought. She changed direction and walked out of the club, but not before he had seen her. And he, a little drunk, and not knowing why but just reacting, unwound his arm from the girl's and followed Claire out.

"Hey!" he shouted to Claire. "Wait."

Claire turned around. "Hey," she said back. She waited for him and he caught up to her, and neither of them knew what to do so they giggled, then they laughed.

It felt good to laugh with him. Really good.

"I'm sorry," he said. "Hi. I want to say something, I'm a little drunk now, though. Share a cab with me, okay?"

"But the girl."

He smiled.

"The girl, yeah. She came with friends. I promise I'm not a jerk, Claire Byrne. She'll be fine."

"Okay, then let's walk," she said. "How far are you?"

He was on Seventy-Fourth Street, it was a mile or a little more, but it was a nice summer night in New York, one of the nicest nights. They started talking. Right in the middle of things. No past, no future. They just started right there on Fiftieth Street. Talking.

About the loud club, about New York at night, about Claire's favorite view from the twilight tourist cruise that left every evening from Pier 39. About a play he was trying to write, about his dwindling savings, the various enemies he'd made through the years, including—and they shared a fond laugh over this—Charlie.

"It wasn't that bad a book, *Thinker's Hope*," he said. "I am guilty. I have vanity and ego, too. He was an easy target. I won't pretend I didn't enjoy the notoriety of taking on a giant."

When they got to his apartment, it started to rain. "Thank you. This was really nice." She kissed him quickly. She said good-bye and walked away and caught a cab on the next block.

He watched her and then the spot where she had been. Long after her cab had turned the corner, long after her cab was out of sight.

ONE WEEK LATER, Claire woke early and showered and put on her flowered sundress. The one Beatrice had divined. It was time, she had decided, for Charlie to go.

Grace was not yet ready to part with her share of her son, so Claire alone took half of Charlie to what she supposed was the most fitting place. She held him, in her bag, close to her side, as an elevator whisked her to the 80th floor, where she caught another elevator to the 102nd, to the upper observation deck of the Empire State Building.

It seemed right for Charlie to reign in perpetuity over the city he loved.

The wind was low, the temperature mild, the sun lounged behind the clouds as Claire made her way to one end of the deck. Below her were Central Park, the Chrysler Building, and down on the Hudson the Circle Line boat was moving its way around the island.

A group of schoolchildren filed past her and started jockeying for the viewfinders. At the other end of the deck a Cirque du Soleil acrobat balanced herself on one leg atop a man's head. Security men in burgundy vests and matching police hats kept the tourists moving along. A pigeon sat precariously on a bit of ledge beyond the safety fence. The deck was a cacophony of dissidents. Claire and Charlie went unnoticed.

Claire walked close to the fence and took out the urn.

There was, when it came down to it, very little of him in it. The body is made mostly of water.

Claire unscrewed the top of the urn and tipped it so that the ashes were at the lip of the opening. Then she upended him. Out, over the barrier that separated them from the sidewalk 102 floors down.

A gust of wind, ill-timed, blew some of him back. Claire blinked the dust from her eyes. What was left swelled for a moment, directly in front of her, then the wind surged again and he was gone.

Claire remembered the priest from the morgue, the one who looked like Jimmy Cagney, and wondered if she should say a prayer.

"To hell with that," she said out loud. "You had a nice go of it while you were here. That's all you would have asked."

Then she put the top back on the urn and took her place in the growing line to catch the elevator back down.

CLAIRE FLEW TO San Francisco, in July then drove to the small town of Petaluma and to the cottage at the end of a long driveway, a small inheritance from his grandmother, which he playfully called the "Estate." He is the only one in the family who makes use of it. He has come out here to work on his play. And he's rented an office in the small town to keep up with ongoing assignments.

Claire was not doing anything, except finishing her book. This time her own book. She's promised to have the second half, a full final draft of it, in Richard's hands at the end of the month.

Ben is the one who gets up early. He makes the coffee, he kisses her forehead, and leaves at eight for his office in town. Claire gets up at nine, drinks the coffee, pads lightly through the wide doorways of the house, from room to room, then after a time pulls on clothes, a backpack, and walks the mile into town. There's a small coffee shop there, where they know her by name. She settles in, and works on chapter eight, which is faltering just now—her protagonist is in limbo.

Ben. This might surprise you, but it shouldn't. It is standard romantic comedy. The fix was in from the start: guy pans girl's husband's book; husband dies; there's a misunderstanding. Guy bumps into girl around town. There is a kiss in the rain. Love ensues.

It could only have been Ben Hawthorne. That's why he popped up along the way. Book critic of the *Atlantic.* Charlie-bashing, funeral-crashing, sweet guy Ben.

In the evenings, they have clever conversation and repartee. When they go out they get approving glances from strangers. Sometimes they take a ride along the river or go for a long walk. They're in act one but not the Charlie/Jack version of act one. Ben is eager for what's ahead. And, this time, so is Claire. Ben forgets to entertain nonstop, and Claire likes that. They talk about what's to come.

Over drinks one night in an old inn that has been converted to a pub, Ben says, "I think we might be onto something."

"You do?" Claire asked.

"Yes. I think we might warrant more than a seven-hundred-and-twenty-three-word review."

She smiles and falls against his arm, and then his arm pulls her close. They'd skipped stages. They'd skipped posturing and awkwardness and worrying who might call or when or what. They'd skipped false devotions and puffery. They hadn't skipped sex, but they'd also not rushed it. They had conversations that carried over, that picked up where they left off. They spoke every night if they were apart, they had passionate kisses, they touched each other as they slept.

He was charmed by her. He couldn't get enough of her smell, her hair, the softness of her cheek. "We have dinner tomorrow night with my parents, don't forget. With Mummy."

"Mummy?" Claire laughed.

"She likes 'Mummy,' " he said.

"Who else?"

"Oh, stuffy friends of the family. Old stuffy friends."

"I like stuffy."

"I have to warn you. Henry—Hank—is a scoundrel. He'll tell you dirty limericks when he thinks no one's listening."

"I love dirty limericks."

"You won't always. Four years from now, you'll dread dinner with Mummy. Hank will bore you rotten. You'll have heard all my jokes."

"I suppose so," she said. "But I'm looking forward to being bored by your jokes."

Ben looked at her eyes, first the left and then the right. He was looking for her, not for his next line. "You are almost exactly as I thought you'd be." Ben kissed her on her cheek.

"You thought about me?" Claire whispered in his ear.

Ben smiled sweetly.

What she loved—maybe, no need yet to pin it down—what she

might love is Ben Hawthorne. Book critic of the *Atlantic*, skewerer of *Thinker's Hope*, nemesis of the late Charlie Byrne, current companion to Claire.

RICHARD HAS LEFT Claire three messages in the past two hours; the editor at Knopf has been calling him. They want her book, they're eager to see it. They'd like to see pages by the end of the month.

RULE #19: Deprivation breeds appreciation.

Claire shelved the messages. She didn't have time to talk about the book; she was writing it. She looked up at the clock: it read 11:00 a.m. She had fifteen thousand more good words, but forty thousand or so average words that she needed to patch up.

In the past, when Claire lost faith in anything, she had picked up her notebook the way another person might rub a rabbit's foot. But she has faith enough to fill buckets now. She has it spilling out over Ferragamo shopping bags and out of suitcases and Birkins and from gutters out into the street. Faith was pouring out of Ben Hawthorne's whitewashed Estate, down the long driveway and out onto Elm and all the way down to the Qwikstop store on McDowell Boulevard, spilling off onto all the other tree-named streets crossing its path. Claire has found herself in the unusual position of having more faith than she can use, more faith than she might ever need, more faith than she has room to store.

She was writing a decent novel. Richard would take it and he'd be happy enough with it to pass it on to Knopf. Her *boyfriend* would bring home champagne when she sent off the book. Ben would twist the cork off in his hand and pour some into a glass and hand it to her. She wouldn't screw up her face at it. She was the sort of girl who liked to drink champagne.

HE CALLED, AS he did most nights before coming home, to see what she'd like for dinner. There was a grocery store on his way. "How about red snapper and arugula?" he asked. "And the chewy bread you love."

"Yes," Claire said. "That's perfect."

"Are you reading to me tonight?"

Most nights after dinner, over wine (Claire found she enjoyed wine with Ben), Claire read her work from the day and sometimes Ben read something back.

"Yes."

"How many words?"

"You'll never guess."

"A thousand?"

"No, come on. I'm on a tear. A tear's not a thousand!"

"Three thousand."

"More!"

"Wow! We'll skip dessert. We'll watch a long movie."

"What movie?"

"*Casablanca.*"

Casablanca. He was her imaginary future boyfriend. He was here.

"Oh darling, the Wilkinsons are having a dinner on Friday, but let's not go," she said. "Let's tell them we're away and just stay home."

"What? Who are the Wilkinsons?"

"No one, never mind," she told him. "It doesn't matter. Hurry home."

So here they were, dangerously close to undoing Charlie's great theory. They were dangerously close to pulling off both sex and love. They were dangerously close to a fairy tale.

Claire Byrne, formerly Mrs. Charlie Byrne, formerly Claire Jenks, formerly date and/or lover to Jack, Jake, Alex, and Steve, formerly mired, formerly lost, formerly stuck at chapter eight, has found a second act.

It was the beginning, for Claire, of critics.

Acknowledgments

Thank you . . . to the supremely talented team of Michael Carlisle, Lauren Smythe, and Richard Pine for finding a home for this book and for their unwavering belief in it. Barbara Jones, my editor at Holt, for shepherding *Widow's Guide* through the publishing processes with passion, wisdom, and good grace. Thank you to my publisher, Stephen Rubin, for whom I have great admiration. Thank you to Joanna Levine, Richard Pracher, Maggie Richards, Pat Eisemann, Gillian Blake, and the entire team at Holt, the most dynamic and clever publishing house an author could hope for. The support and sound advice of Alexis Hurley, Lyndsey Blessing, Kassie Evashevski, and Jason Richman continue to be invaluable. Special gratitude to Caitlin Alexander, whose editorial help came at the perfect time. To all the boys I didn't love, and some I did. And to my friends who make me laugh every day I am truly grateful. Lastly, lifelong thanks to Teresa DiFalco, my confidante and co-conspirator, whose storytelling instincts, friendship, and faith kept it all moving forward. You have all been a great gift.

ABOUT THE AUTHOR

CAROLE RADZIWILL earned a BA at Hunter College and a master's degree at New York University. She spent more than a decade at ABC News, where she reported on stories around the world and earned three Emmys. Her first book, *What Remains: A Memoir of Fate, Friendship and Love,* spent over twenty weeks on the *New York Times* Best Sellers List. She has written for numerous publications and is a frequent contributor to *Glamour* magazine.